In the dead center of ⬚⬚⬚⬚⬚⬚⬚⬚⬚⬚⬚⬚⬚⬚⬚⬚⬚ re she was standing a⬚ ⬚⬚⬚⬚⬚⬚⬚⬚⬚⬚⬚⬚⬚⬚⬚ the Wheel of Dismemberment, a cir⬚ ⬚⬚⬚⬚⬚⬚⬚⬚⬚⬚⬚⬚ the ground.

Shit shit shit and d⬚⬚⬚⬚⬚ ⬚⬚⬚⬚

It dawned on her far too late what was happening.

Entry of the Gladiators was blaring on the loudspeakers.

"Laaaadies aaaaand gentlemen," Mark Winters announced in his very best grand entrance voice against the music. "Let's all put together a very warm welcome for the king of the ring, the master of disaster, the number one killer in the 'Try Not to Die Barn.'"

The crowd was going apeshit. Every single one of them seemed to be wearing a Denney t-shirt, though Dawn knew that was impossible unless it had just happened in the last few seconds. Then she saw Winters's two dancing girls frantically firing their t-shirt guns to every corner of the crowd. It was turning into a sea of pink shirts, all plastered with the goonish-face of the greatest slasher who had ever lived.

"Weighing in at nearly 600 pounds and standing over seven and half feet tall, I present to you the most successful serial killer who ever lived. With four hundred and thirty-seven kills in the wild, eighty-seven of our finest guards, and forty-three contestants...and one visiting dignitary from the Soviet Union..."

The crowd chuckled. Denney's famous exploit of ripping apart the Politburo member who had asked to shake his hand was a staple of Try Not to Die clip shows and sizzle reels. Mark continued.

"...adding up to a lifetime total of five hundred and sixty-eight murders, I am very proud to present to you, on behalf of Farmer Brown's Old-Fashioned Moonshine, Hedare BeautyCompany, and the producers of Try Not to Die...please put your hands together for Denney the Killer Clown!"

SLASHVIVOR!

BY STEPHEN KOZENIEWSKI & STEVIE KOPAS

Stevie would like to dedicate this novel to the underdogs.
Stephen would like to dedicate this novel to his stupid sister.

OPENING SCROLL

In 1983, a Soviet military officer named Stanislav Petrov failed to ignore orders, and launched a nuclear attack based on what was later discovered to be a system error. The "mutually assured destruction" which followed proved to be a lot less mutual than anticipated. At every turn, it seemed that American counter-measures triggered too late, or failed to trigger at all, and Soviet attacks landed where they were not anticipated, or at unexpected times. The resulting exchange left the Soviet Union relatively intact, while the United States, as a functioning society, ceased to exist. It turned out nuclear war was not such a great idea.

Less than 1% of the U.S.'s former population of 234 million survived to eke out a hardscrabble existence in the irradiated desert. Those that did often suffered from mental and physical illness. Mutation was widespread, and crime ran rampant. An unusually high number of colorful and seemingly unstoppable serial killers, known as slashers, devastated what little remained of the populace, before a loose patchwork of warlords and gangsters managed to impose some form of law and order at the end of their gun barrels.

In the Geiger Lands, life is brutish, cheap, and short. Plagued by madness and the ravages of radiation, the survivors labor each day in the wasteland, hoping only for some clean water and a crust of bread. They live for only one thing: a welcome distraction from their grueling lives...

COLD OPEN

A silverfish-like creature with legs as long as spaghetti strands scurried up Rudy's wall. A well-aimed mud-encrusted boot flew through the air and smashed it into a lump.

"Fucking bugs," Rudy grumbled, settling back into his couch.

The old Rubin-brand TV set flickered, bathing the room in an eerie glow. A hairline crack deformed the lower right hand side of the screen, but for most shows it didn't bother him much. Right now, a bald, emaciated man in a cheap suit was shouting at the viewers.

"*Do you live in the Geiger Lands? Do you have trouble getting around? Do you find yourself picking your way, step by brutal step, across the ruins? Do you find yourself slip-sliding away on fields of glass?*"

The salesman wheeled his arms wildly and there was an obvious jump-cut to him sliding across a showroom floor. As he passed by compact, jury-built vehicles, he pointed them out while the stagehands continued to pull him along as though he were sliding.

"*Then come on down to Albino Al's Discount Surplus! We've got 4-wheelers! We've got ATVs! We've got choppers, hogs, crotch rockets, and even the occasional motorcycle!*"

The sliding conceit ended and Albino Al was suddenly standing again, wearing a bike helmet and a grin as wide as his face.

"*But if you're more security-minded and you've got the gold, then we've got the big guns!*"

The camera panned out and revealed Al was standing on top of an antique tank. It was stamped with the letters USA, and was obviously pre-war, but Al had gussied it up with more modern salvaged Soviet parts.

"*Come on down! It's not illegal. In the Geiger Lands, nothing is!*" At the bottom of the screen a chyron read "*Soviet and Cuban citizens should consult local laws before purchasing goods from Albino Al's Discount Surplus.*"

Rudy grunted.

"Fucking commercials."

The news came back on. Situated where he was in the panhandle, Rudy had the best of the best when it came to channel line-ups. Not only did he have access to the standard Russian stations, but he could also get both the Spanish-language stations from Cuban-occupied South Florida as well as the Geiger Lands ones that were typically no more than half-assed commercials and piss-poor renditions of pre-war soap operas. Rudy thought the Russian stuff had a little more polish, though.

A severe woman in an achingly drab, grey suit was rattling off headlines in her native language, while the words scrolled along the bottom of the screen bringing him up to speed.

"*President Baio attended state dinner in Moscow this evening to mark the twentieth anniversary of Soviet victory over the...*"

"Fucking news," Rudy grumbled, and flicked to the next channel.

Normally the station was just static. Not now, though. Now, a grinning skull and crossbones was staring back at Rudy. A jolly roger. A pirate flag.

The Soviets and the Cubans usually came down on pirate stations like a hammer, but there was one exception. One show that, every couple of months, everyone across the shattered nation was in unison about loving.

Rudy wrung his hands restlessly. *Was it that time already? Could it be?*

The pirate flag was replaced with a test pattern, and then a blank screen. An announcer spoke, of all languages, in English.

"*From the ruins of Vancouver to the Cuban Keys, from the Allied Texas Republic to the Irradiated Plains, welcome back, ladies and gents, to the most popular show on the continent!*"

Then, in unison, a pre-recorded chorus of two dozen kids all shouted: *"Try...Not...to...Die!"*

The chanting children were soon washed out as long-forgotten pop music faded in. The picture pixelated and the handsome face of the show's host filled the screen. The camera panned out revealing his fancy, white suit glittering under the spotlights. He hopped around, pumping his arms in the air, rousing the crowd while big-chested Latin women danced around him. Rudy grinned from ear to ear, excitement building in his chest. It had been months since an episode had aired, he could barely keep himself from sliding off the edge of his seat when the off-screen announcer's voice bellowed his next words.

"Ladies, Gentleman, and Miscreants of North America, here's your host, Mark Winters!"

The crowd went wild and the large audience jumped to their feet all around the arena. Four projectors powered on, breathing life into the enormous screens that allowed the spectators to feel as if they were standing right next to Mark and his two beautiful cohosts, Camila and Wendy. The trio, bedazzling in matching outfits, stood on a sparkling platform suspended from the ceiling of the arena, giving them a three-hundred-and-sixty-degree view. He smiled and raised his microphone to his lips.

"Geiger Lands! How we doing tonight?" His silky voice echoed in every ear and he received a loving response.

Spectators fought to climb over one another; some clawed and kicked while others pushed or punched, all trying to reach the front row. They'd do anything to get closer to the impending action. Fans of *Try Not to Die* weren't the sharpest tools in the shed, though, as no matter how many times the show had aired over the years, the members of the live audience never learned.

Rudy chuckled as he cracked open a beer.

"Dumb fucks!" he shouted at the half-broken television set.

The unlucky few that had fought so hard to make it to the front row were met with 15,000 milliamps of electricity upon reaching the security fence that surrounded the event floor. The animals in the crowd, ranging in age from eight to eighty, went into a frenzy as the lights in the building flashed and the smell of burning human flesh filled the air.

Mark raised a hand to get the swelling crowd's attention, he waited patiently for them to simmer down before bringing up the microphone again.

"Boy, have we got a show for you all tonight!" The crowd began to erupt, but he put his hand up, silencing them. "Before we get on with the main event, I'd like to welcome some very important people to the stage. Without these fabulous folks, none of this would be possible in the slightest! So, without further ado, allow me to introduce...The Producers!" Mark swung his arms up into the air, signaling to the crowd that it was time to go wild again.

In a spectacle just as absurd as the show itself, four figures emerged from the mist of a fog machine behind Mark, cloaked in red robes, their heads bowed. Music began to blare and fireworks exploded from the left and right as The Producers ripped the hoods from their heads and tossed their robes off the platform. The screaming crowd actually drowned out the music as the red robes floated down to the filthy arena floor.

The Producers smiled and waved to the crowd, dressed in designer fashion of the old world, unashamed to flaunt their illegal wealth. They were well aware that neither the Cubans nor the Russians would step foot in the Geiger Lands to seize what remained of their old American currency.

Mark introduced each of the four:

Marisol Martinez, clad in head to toe red with her billowing, regal robe, the Queen of The Allied Texas Republic; her husband beside her, Derron James, last living citizen of whatever remained of Arizona; Amy Green, the mysterious and deadly arms dealer; and finally, Jacob Graves, the only fat man on a continent facing an epic food crisis.

These were the people who made *Try Not to Die* possible. The wealthy few who kept what little remained of the North American people entertained and the maximum population levels in check when necessary.

The Producers took their seats after their elaborate introductions and Mark once more settled down the crowd, telling icebreaking anecdotes and finally leading into one of the most important parts of the evening.

Rudy pissed into his empty beer bottle, refusing to peel his eyes from the television set. He turned the volume up as Mark said the words that he, at home, along with the live audience, had been dying to hear since the start of the show.

"It's time to meet our participants!" Mark pointed to one of the gigantic screens as the crowd roared, and a countdown began from the number five.

The lights in the arena dimmed and the off-screen announcer's voice boomed.

"Tonight, on The Selection..."

The voices of the crowd dimmed to a dull roar. Scum they might be, and lunatic scum at that, but they still had some sense of the difference between the sacred and the profane. And for them, nothing was more sacred than this.

An old American flag, pocked with holes and tattered at the edges, flapped on a crooked flagpole outside a desert way station. For a moment, the wind caught the flag just so that it was out of view, and when it returned, it was replaced with the more familiar circle and three wedges of the Geiger Lands.

"Mommy, do you think we'll ever be selected?" a young child's voice asked, full of earnestness.

"I don't know, dear," the mother replied, "I just don't know. We can only hope."

A slideshow began, showing the hardy faces of a variety of generic Geiger Landers. A little girl walking her coyote. A postal carrier armed to the teeth. A butcher looking up from his rats. A doctor, sawing away at a particularly troublesome third limb on an uncooperative patient.

"Over half a million people still live in the Geiger Lands. Keeping an accurate census is sometimes described as the hardest, most expensive job in the world. But the Producers do it...and they do it for you."

Rudy looked down to see his hand was over his heart. He hadn't done that in years. An emotion was swelling in his breast, one he didn't feel very often anymore: pride.

He almost felt let down as the scene changed to The Producers, in full red cloaks and surrounded by an army of armed-to-the-teeth security personnel. They began walking toward a house that was decidedly not Rudy's own bunker. At the bottom of the screen, words scrolled by reading "recorded earlier." Of course it had been. Rudy would already be in Biloxi if he had been selected.

The house on the screen was part of a cul-de-sac of town-homes, most of which had been reduced to skeletons of scorched lumber. One of the townhouses, though, was in relatively good condition, its holes patched with sheets of scrap metal and a fence of concertina wire standing where the white picket one that had formerly occupied the space had been ripped out.

The security personnel surrounded the building, and a small team laid lumber bridges over the concertina wire to make their entrance. Shouting, "hup hup hup!" they pounded toward the door, and the leader of the team began pounding on it with the bottom of his fist.

After a few excruciating moments that found Rudy literally on the edge of his seat, the door opened wide enough to allow the barrel of a shotgun through.

"Who...who is it?"

The leader of the security goons pressed a button on the side of his helmet so that his voice, garbled as it was, would be audible.

"Congratulations, ma'am, you've been Selected. Please put the weapon down and you and anyone else inside come out unarmed with your hands up."

There was the sound of shuffling inside, and then the door opened all the way, prompting the guard team to step back and level their weapons at the doorjamb. A woman with her hair in curlers and a small, ripped day-gown stood in the doorway, tears in her eyes.

"Is this real? Can it be? You're not just marauders, are you?"

"Take a look over there, ma'am," the leader said, gesturing at The Producers who stood just outside the wire fence.

The woman began shrieking and flailing her arms.

"Is it just you inside, ma'am?"

"Oh, yes, yes," she replied, "I'm alone."

"Go on ahead, then, ma'am. Congratulations."

Flanked by severely armed and armored guards, the woman in curlers crossed the lumber bridge and stood before

The Producers, her face the perfect picture of joy.

"Congratulations on your Selection," Marisol Martinez spoke from under her large hood. "Out of five hundred thousand people, your name was one of a very special few chosen at random."

"This is a great honor," Marisol's husband, Derron chimed in. "We're pleased to have you, Dawn."

Suddenly the woman's smile turned to a rictus.

"Dawn? My name's not Dawn."

Rudy put his hand over his mouth. *What the fuck?*

The Producers stepped aside and huddled, only a few scant words audible from their heated exchange. Finally, Amy Green stuck her head up from the huddle.

"This isn't 221-B Baker Street?"

"No, I live at 221-A. You have to go around back for my neighbor's..."

The woman clapped her hand over her mouth.

"Oh no!" she screamed. "Oh, God no! You mean I wasn't chosen? I wasn't...no...you have to let me go! You can't do this to me! Please!"

A few of the goons wrapped their arms around the hysterical woman, who through some marvel of medical science burst out of the grasp of the giant men and went running towards The Producers, her mouth wide, screaming at the top of her lungs. Luckily, the other security guards were more adroit, and one of them managed to bash her temple in with the butt of his gun before she got within a yard of the Producers. Still too close, Rudy could see, from the outraged poses they struck. The guards dragged the unconscious woman off and returned a moment later.

"All right, take two. Let's see if we can get it right this time." Someone behind the camera said.

"No, wait, don't cut it out." Marisol Martinez said. "The fake out will make for good television."

Rudy nodded from his couch; he was captivated.

CHAPTER 1

A small-framed blonde with an arrogant stride whistled through a smirk as she headed for home. She wiped the endless sweat from her brow and readjusted the heavy bag on her back; she couldn't wait to rifle through today's score. An unsuspecting elderly man would soon be waking up from the nice knock to the back of the head she'd given him.

He's old, I need the stuff more than he does, Dawn thought, shrugging to herself and adding a little skip to her step.

She made a mental checklist of the loot she stuffed into her bristling backpack before fleeing his shack earlier that morning: cans upon cans of food; old, expensive looking jewelry; fresh dog jerky; a collection of knives. She knew she would be able to cash in on the knives and the jewelry for sure, food was her main concern, and she'd have enough to last her the rest of the month once she visited the trade tents tomorrow.

On any given day Dawn was lucky to see her neighbors out and about, but today was different. The row of townhomes up ahead seemed alive with activity. She squinted as she approached, straining her eyes and ears. The cul-de-sac was full of armored cars and armed men. That could only mean one thing: trouble.

Surely the old man she'd attacked and robbed hadn't alerted the authorities. And if he had, why would they give a rat's ass about some GL garbage anyway? Out in the Sands, where Dawn lived, well, nobody cared about the citizens out there. They might as well have been on the moon. She grew closer and discreetly reached for her trusty carving knife. It would be no match for the weapons those guards were toting, but it was better than nothing. As she approached the bustle of activity, the tension in her body gave way a bit when she realized nobody was paying attention to her in the slightest. They were more focused on her neighbor Marta's place.

My lucky day. Dawn smiled and headed straight for her apartment.

She threw her bag to the ground and threw her arms up, moving left and right, stretching her back and arms until they no longer ached. She gave the bag a kick.

"You better be worth it," she mumbled, fiddling with her keys until she found the right one.

As she slipped the key into the old lock on her front door, Marta's excited shrieks could be heard from just around the building. Her curiosity getting the best of her, Dawn left the keys dangling from the lock and crept to the edge of the wall, popping her head out just enough to see what all the fuss was about.

"Ah shit," she whispered, pulling her head back in and hoping she hadn't been spotted.

Marta's been Selected.

A shiver ran down the length of Dawn's spine, being in such close proximity to those monsters—The Producers—scared the holy Hell out of her. When you left with them, you never came back. The nut jobs in the GL worshipped these elitist assholes, but not Dawn, she knew better, she was raised right.

Dawn headed back for her front door, eager to get inside, but was once again interrupted by Marta screaming, only this time they were genuine shrieks of disappointment. Her neighbor's pleas were cut short with a violent thud and Dawn cringed, half of her begging to find out what happened while the other half, her instincts, told her to just get the hell out of there. She suddenly had a bad feeling, and as she had just decided, unfortunately a moment too late, to get herself inside, a man called out to her.

"Are you Dawn Churchill?"

She began to sweat, rubbing her palms on the front of her overalls.

"Ma'am, are you Dawn Churchill?"

She turned ever so slowly, just enough to get a good view of what she was up against: a shit-ton of armed guards and four assholes in red robes.

"We're going to ask you one final time." The goon's voice was stern. "Are you Dawn Churchill?"

Well, Dawn shook her head and turned back toward her front door, glaring at the backpack sitting there. *Guess this isn't my lucky day after all.*

Dawn took everyone by surprise and took off in a sprint. The goons started off after her, one taking a knee and raising his rifle, but Marisol Martinez ripped her hood from her head and brought her fingers up to her lips. A piercing whistle stopped the goons in their tracks and the one with the raised weapon turned to her.

"What are your orders, ma'am?"

"Take her alive." A smile spread across Marisol's lips. "*This* will make for even better television."

The crowd back in the arena screamed and rose to their feet. It had been ages since anyone had been so bold. The cowardice of running from a Selection typically meant execution, but The Producers had spoken; this episode of *Try Not to Die* would be that much more rewarding.

The crew rushed back to their vehicles, the camera jostling as they hopped inside. The Producers rode separately, their vehicle taking off like a bat out of hell, the crew car hot on their heels. The camera zoomed in on a figure in the distance, Dawn was fast, but she was not quite fast enough. A garbled order came through the radio. Marisol's voice barked at the armed goons in the truck behind the crew and shortly after, a roar sounded, followed by a massive utility vehicle appearing on-screen.

A hatch on the truck's roof popped open and a man appeared with an odd-looking weapon in hand. If the order hadn't already been given to take the girl alive, this would have signified she was about to be toast.

Half the audience's breath was caught in their throats. They'd never witnessed such a spectacle. Some covered their gaping mouths, others screamed and shouted, and some even climbed over one another, desperate to try and get a better look at the mysterious weapon on the screen. Hearts pounded in every chest as the goon brought the large object up and Marisol shouted, "Fire!"

A projectile erupted from the weapon and the crowd in the arena fell silent for the briefest of moments as the flying object opened up into what looked like a net and sparked once, then twice. The blonde contestant on the screen heard the obvious sound of electricity and made the mistake of looking back at what was coming for her.

She let out a scream as the electrified net encapsulated her and she collapsed to the dirt, unmoving. The crowd hooted and hollered, throwing their fists into the air, celebrating the extravaganza of Dawn's capture. It wasn't often that they got to see advanced Soviet tech in action.

Two goons hopped out of the utility truck and retrieved the unconscious girl.

Marisol's voice came back over the radio.

"Good work, men. Now let's head out, we've got a show to produce."

CHAPTER 2

Dawn struggled to open her eyes. Despite being electrocuted into unconsciousness and taken prisoner, the cool metal beneath her actually felt nice on her warm skin. She just wanted to sleep a little bit longer, but she knew that now was not the time for sleeping.

She willed herself to sit up and get familiar with her surroundings. She heard a thump and her body was thrown up. She came back down to the floor hard, wincing in pain, realizing she was in the back of a moving vehicle. She brought her hands up to her neck and felt a shock collar there. More Soviet tech. She seethed with anger. If she had only been able to run thirty more feet she would have made it to safety.

There were tunnels and interconnecting bunkers all over the GL that the powers that be didn't know about. Nine times out of ten that's how Dawn was able to get away with robbing people blind. Left over from the sewer systems of major cities and pre-war attempts to establish underground shelters that would be safe from the bombs, hardly anyone knew about the old tunnels these days. She cursed herself for not being fast enough, but at the same time, she was relieved to have not made it. It would have exposed the whole hidden catacombs, and if she could find some way to escape this she'd need somewhere to hide. She swallowed the lump in her throat and sucked up her fate. Surely she would figure a way out of this. She had to.

The window to the cab slid open and the passenger peered back at her. It was probably one of the goons that had captured her, but as they had all been wearing helmets it was impossible to be sure.

"She's awake," the goon said, his sentence punctuated by

the sounds of a radio handset clicking on and off.

A man replied. "About time. Come grab me. We're doing exterior shots. We'll just do it on the way. What took so long?" "I gave her the wakeup drug," the goon replied. "I can't control her body weight."

Dawn's eyes narrowed.

"What's wrong with my body weight?"

The masked goon glanced at her and wordlessly slid the glass closed. After a little while the truck came to a halt. The back door opened and a young boy struggled to climb into the cargo bed, encumbered by pounds and pounds of camera equipment. Once he was up, he helped pull up a man in a spangled suit who was carrying nothing heavier than a handheld microphone.

The man in the suit looked like the weight of the entire world was weighing him down. With a sigh, he took a long drink from a flask. He looked down at Dawn as though she were a bug. He made the "start rolling" signal with his hands to the cameraman.

"All right, let's get this over with."

Dawn was suddenly aware of how woozy and cottonmouthed the wakeup drugs had left her. She clutched at her shock collar, desperately thirsty. The last thing she wanted to deal with right now was an interview. The spangle-suited man obviously wasn't giving her concerns a moment's thought.

In an instant his eyes were sparkling almost as much as his over-wide smile, and with his television persona suddenly plastered on, she finally recognized him, whereas the broken-down husk who had just boarded the truck could've been almost anyone.

"Well, hey there, sleepyhead!" he said.

Dawn cleared her throat. She had no idea what to say.

"You're Mark Winters," she finally stated flatly.

"Why, yes, I am," Mark replied, turning to look at the camera with an even wider smile than usual, vamping for the audience. "I'm so pleased you recognize me, but, my dear girl, we don't know a thing about you!"

"How long have I been out?"

"That's not important. What's important is that you're on your way right now to the most fabulous place in the Geiger Lands!"

Mark turned and gestured toward the bright lights of the South Geiger Coast Coliseum, which was growing in size as they approached.

Dawn narrowed her eyes. "So, I've been out a day at least. What, you all kept me on ice like a slab of beef so I'd be as disoriented as possible when you just chuck me into the arena? Is that how you people do things?"

"Aw, come on now, that's not what everyone wants to hear about! Everyone wants to know everything about you. What's your favorite sport?"

Mark pointed his microphone at Dawn. She was picturing a crowd of open-mouthed yokels staring at her.

"Uh...I like tennis?"

Mark bounced the microphone back toward his own mouth. "To play or to watch?"

"I don't really play many sports these days," Dawn replied with an eyeroll.

"I have a suspicion you're not going to be much of a fan favorite with these kinds of answers! Liven it up a little, what do you like to do with your time?"

Dawn stared at the plastic man, unsure what to do. These shotgun interviews were always one of the highlights of *Try Not to Die*. The audience lapped it up, loving the combination of confusion, excitement, and stage fright that usually came with knowing everyone in the GL suddenly cared what you thought. Inevitably, the highlight reel spliced clips from these interviews together with particularly gory moments from the arena run, made all the better if the subject had made an inadvertent pun early on like "give me a break" or "cut me some slack" being juxtaposed with a shattered femur or a severed lifeline.

"I'm into fashion," Dawn finally answered. "Can't you tell?"

She gestured down at her hole-riddled t-shirt and denim overalls and flashed him a big fake smile. Mark chuckled, a noise he had obviously spent years perfecting and yet so divorced from any real human emotion that it grated on Dawn's ears like nails on a chalkboard.

"Well, maybe your fashion sense will catch on. Maybe they'll call that look 'the Dawn!'"

"Yeah, great," Dawn muttered, yanking at her collar again. "The neckwear might be a bit hard to come by."

Something distant and officious in Mark's eyes told Dawn he was pleased in a very animal sense. Dawn wasn't playing for the crowd, but the crowd, judging by Mark's expression, would be pleased. All was well in television land. "Well, there you have it folks, everything you wanted to know about Dawn Churchill, one of our latest selections, who you'll be meeting *live* in just a few hours. Best of luck to you, Dawn, and remember...try not to die!"

When the cameraman gave the thumbs up, Mark's smile disappeared without a trace. He glanced down at Dawn like she was some kind of alien organism.

"Not bad. I usually can't get them to shut up. You might have a career in television."

"For a few hours, anyway," Dawn spat.

Mark shrugged, taking another long swig of alcohol. "They're the only hours that matter."

The truck came skidding to a stop at a heavily reinforced loading dock outside the stadium. Without a word of parting, Mark and the cameraman clambered out of the truck, locking the door behind them.

Dawn hopped to her feet and balled up her fists. Next time someone opened that door, she'd be ready for a fight.

Her eyes scanned the dark cargo bed, desperate to find a weapon. She spotted the rusted rungs along the wall opposite her and assumed once upon a time they'd been used to chain past contestants of *Try Not to Die* during studio conveyance. Apparently Dawn's experience with a shock collar and a private cab had been an upgrade from the harsh tethers and cattle-like transport of years past. Dawn scurried across the floor, pulling with all her might on the rusting bar. As she worked it back and forth in an attempt to loosen it, she couldn't help but wonder how The Producers were smuggling all this Soviet tech into the Geiger Lands.

She heard someone fumbling with the lock and she dropped

to the floor, placing both feet on the wall for leverage. "Come...on...stupid...fucking...thing." She grunted the words with each pull and finally the rusted piece of metal broke free.

She slid across the truck floor and jumped up into a defensive stance, the bar raised in her left hand, prepared to lunge at whichever unfortunate goon had just opened that door. To her surprise, Marisol Martinez greeted her with a wide smile.

"Just as I expected." Marisol said with a snicker, and raised a small remote.

"Shit." Dawn managed to mutter before Marisol pressed a button and activated the shock collar.

The bar fell from Dawn's hands and her body seized momentarily before collapsing in a heap. She lay there twitching as Marisol pulled herself up and into the cab, her red heels clicking as she approached.

"I've never been so pleased with a contestant so early on," she said, beaming down at Dawn.

Dawn struggled to speak, her tongue thick and noncompliant.

"Shh, save your energy. See you soon!"

Marisol waved goodbye and pressed the button once more, rendering Dawn unconscious.

CHAPTER 3

Dawn groaned as her eyes fluttered open. Her hands shot to her head and she rubbed her temples. She was seriously sick of being knocked out and waking up in strange places. Her back ached and she realized she'd been sleeping on what someone thought was a good excuse for a bed. She sat up on the metal slab with the sleeping bag and brought her legs around, dropping her feet to the floor.

She was basically in a prison cell. A cracked toilet with a missing seat sat in a corner of the room, a lopsided table with something beige on it was directly across from her, and a metal door was to her left. She winced when she rose to her feet, the pain in her head excruciating, but suddenly she experienced the most wonderful thing she had in ages: the smell of roasted meat.

As her salivary glands activated, her headache receded to a dull thud. When was the last time she'd eaten? Her stomach growled at her, fueling her ferocious appetite. She rushed to the table and tossed the beige, plastic plate-cover off to the side. Her eyes fell upon a generous portion of meat smothered in a brown sauce. Dawn struggled to keep herself from drooling and tore into the meal with her bare hands. She didn't need to overthink it, she knew they wouldn't poison a contestant of *Try Not to Die*. It would kill their ratings.

She didn't care what kind of meat she could be ingesting either. She'd basically tried it all, though if you asked her, she'd deny ever having eaten that stew that one time. Dawn was no cannibal, just hungry.

She heard a loud *click* behind her and spun around, half empty plate in one hand, and a slab of meat in the other. Marisol entered the room, red robe trailing behind her.

"Leave us," she instructed the goon in the hall, and he obliged, shutting the door and locking it.

Dawn looked her up and down. She was unusually well put together for a denizen of the GL. She certainly carried herself like a queen. Dawn instantly felt self-conscious and put the food down on the table, discretely wiping her hands clean on her overalls and checking that no gravy was smeared on her face.

Marisol snickered, noticing the sudden flush in Dawn's cheeks.

"No need to be embarrassed. Continue eating, please, that's why it's there. I can only imagine how famished you must be." She motioned to the plate, but Dawn didn't move. A scowl replaced the smile on her face and she changed her tone of voice. "I said eat the fucking food. Are you deaf?"

Dawn grimaced but picked the plate back up to continue her meal.

Marisol smiled again and cocked her head. "Good girl. Can't have you going into the arena on an empty stomach, now can I?"

Dawn mustered up a fake smile and looked around awkwardly. She had never been a fan of people watching her while she ate.

"Is it good?" Marisol asked. "Jacob, one of my colleagues, you may have seen him before, procures only the best of the best in the GL for our contestants. Consider it a token of appreciation from The Producers. Your participation means everything to your...*broken* nation."

Marisol stared at Dawn expectantly, her eyebrows raised.

"Thank you?" Dawn said through a mouthful of food.

She stared at the Producer before her, decked out in her designer clothing with a smug expression to top it all off and felt the sudden urge to laugh. This really was the most absurd thing she'd ever experienced, and she grew up in the GL, so that was saying something.

"Is there something you'd like to say, Miss Churchill?" Marisol asked.

Dawn shook her head and finished off her meal, scooping the last few grains of rice into her mouth with her fingers.

"Oh, I see," Marisol looked down at the floor, her hands now clasped behind her back, and began to pace back and forth in front of Dawn like a predator, her heels clicking loudly. "It almost looked to me like you had something to say."

Dawn pursed her lips, and shook her head again. She tried avoiding the woman's eyes, she was starting to creep her out and she didn't like being in this small room.

Marisol stopped pacing and stepped up to Dawn, mere inches from her. Dawn could smell her sweet perfume mixed with the faintest hint of body odor, yet even that was alluring. She placed a delicate hand on Dawn's shoulder and gripped firmly, unnerving the blonde even more.

"I wanted to be the first to thank you for leading us to those pesky tunnels. So many criminals were using them to undermine—if you'll pardon the pun—the society we're trying to build here. But not to worry. They're being collapsed as we speak."

Dawn groaned. Now there'd be nowhere to hide when she got out of here.

"Suck it up. You've got wardrobe in five. And remember, Dawn, try not to die."

Mark Winters exhaled. It was one of those deep, existential breaths. The faces of all the contestants from the past several years were passing through his mind.

"It's just a job," he reminded himself.

But it wasn't, was it? At what point did one stop being a pawn in bigger people's games and start becoming complicit in them?

He wrapped his fingers around his glass of unadorned gin—bought with blood money, of course—and took a swallow. It seemed he was drinking more and more just to be able to take the stage. Used to be he could work up the gusto to do this work without a drop.

"You're getting old," he said to his reflection.

A loud banging came at his door.

"Thirty seconds, Mr. Winters!"

"Yeah, yeah, yeah," he muttered under his breath before cheerfully chirping "Coming!"

He staggered toward the door, and emotionally let his baggage drop away with every step. He shook himself like a dog getting out of a bath and then pulled the door open, his eyes twinkling and his famous smile broadcasting what a delight all this was.

He leaned against the door frame and glanced up at the last ten seconds of an anti-diarrheal commercial. In the old days, before the war and everything, he would have laughed about a sponsor like that, maybe even make a joke on stage. In the GL, though, that shit was deadly serious. Kids died of dysentery every day.

The commercial stopped, and Mark was lost deep in thought. A stagehand was frantically pantomiming to him.

Get it together, Mark.

The coliseum actually consisted of two domes. The outer dome enclosed the whole area from the weather, and radiation as best it could. The inner dome was much smaller, basically a latticework of electrified metal to keep the audience out of the arena floor. A few important offices, including Mark's dressing room, were actually located at the top of the outer dome, though most of the coliseum's functions went on underground. Mark stepped onto the mini-stage, which descended like a basket from the outer dome.

"Oh, hiiiii," he lilted, to much applause and laughter, "I didn't see you there. I thought everybody had already left."

He waved as he crossed the stage. Behind him was one of the huge screens, projecting whatever The Producers wanted the audience to be looking at. Right now, it was showing him. He looked up at his doppelganger, ten times his size, and now, like him, with its back to the camera.

"Oh, well, hey there, handsome. You come around here often?"

The crowd was eating it up. He stuck his fists on his hips.

"Can't even look at me when I'm talking to you, eh? Why, you stuck up..."

He turned around, dismissing his own image with a wave of his hand.

"Why, I'd rather spend my time with you folks anyway." He

cupped his mouth with his hand conspiratorially. "Although I wouldn't mind having a looker like him hanging off my arm."

He had been working with his dancers long enough that he could ad-lib like this and they'd still recognized their cue. After sliding down their individual poles onto the suspended stage, two spangly showgirls strutted out and each grabbed one of his arms. The one on the left was named Camila and the other was named Wendy, or maybe the one on the right was Camila and...

Ah, who gives a shit?

They weren't, as far as he knew, biological twins, but they had been selected because they were so similar in appearance that once they were covered in a coat of makeup, they were practically indistinguishable. And while there had been a time when Mark had been able to tell them apart, that had been a long time ago. He just didn't care anymore.

"Well, hello, ladies! I guess I have to settle for you two instead. Unless..."

He turned back, but now his image was turned back as well.

"Nah, forget him. He's not interested. What about you folks, though? Are you interested in what we've got going on tonight?"

The crowd cheered uproariously. Mark scanned the crowd, a flummoxed look on his face. He put his hand up to his ear, leaving the girl on his right to drop off his arm.

"Is there anybody here tonight? Anybody at all?"

The crowd roared again, not especially louder to Mark's ears, but it was all still part of the act. Part of getting them riled up. Not that they needed much riling.

"Now now, folks, it's time to talk seriously for a moment. Yes, yes, it is. I know no one watches TV to be reminded of real-world problems. But still, there is an elephant in the room that we can't ignore. And I'm not talking about Jacob Graves."

Mark's hand shot out towards the Producer's Box and one of the cameras zoomed in on the obese Producer, who, even at that very instant, was scarfing down chicken wings. Graves chortled as a spotlight fell on him. Mark always knew which buttons to push and which not to, and Graves's weight was always a winner. He didn't mind. He even held up his sauce-stained fingers and licked them gamely for the camera.

"Just kidding, of course. We love you, Jacob!" Mark blew him kisses. The crowd repeated the sentiment, seemingly genuinely, which went a long way towards ensuring it would be okay to make fun of Graves's weight again in the future.

"But, no, the *metaphorical* elephant I'm talking about is the plague of relentless, seemingly invincible serial killers who stalk our fellow citizens out there in the dangerous wastes of the GL. In a word: slashers."

The arena was so silent you could've heard a pin drop.

"When the phenomenon first started in the late '70s, there was a lot of pearl-clutching that it meant society was breaking down. Our very values were falling apart. And in the '80s, when it reached its heyday, particularly after the bombs fell, everyone seemed terrified that a slasher was waiting around every corner.

"But like every societal ill, all it took to cure was a clear vision. The vision of the four fine people sitting in the box right there. Yes, our Producers saw a society jumping at its own shadows and said: let's make lemon pie out of these lemons. And now instead of slashers hunting us on the streets...they're hunting for a slot in the *Try Not to Die* Barn!"

The spotlights shone down on a solid concrete building that had been built on as an addition to one of the arena access tunnels. It loomed ominously, covered in elaborate warnings, both in official signs and in graffiti. None of the guards ever worked the Barn very long. Either they were killed, quit, or were promoted in the space of days, or more rarely weeks. But solid work was always hard to come by in the Geiger Lands, so there was always grist for the mill.

"Now," Mark said, "you've all met our Selections for the night and we all wish them each a fun hunt and a painless death, but now it's time to meet their first of many exciting and dangerous opponents of the evening. Weighing in at 110 pounds soaking wet and standing a spritely five feet, two inches tall I give you a man—well, sort of a man—with a combined lifetime body count of eight."

The crowd was not particularly fired up, but why would

they be by the first slasher? You had to have something to ramp up to.

"Hey, they can't be all be heavyweights, folks. That is five innocents on the streets, two guards while in our care, and even one contestant on our last episode. Good for him! And now let's meet him, ladies and gentlemen, the Gimp Who's No Wimp, I give you the one, the only...Ziiiiiiiippermouth!"

The heavy barn door opened and two of the guards manhandled a heavy, thumping footlocker out onto the stadium floor. The footlocker was wrapped in chains secured with a heavy padlock.

The first guard pressed a key into the second's hand, who quickly pushed it back. They played hot potato for a solid ten seconds with the key, which made the crowd laugh, but Mark started making the "wrap it up" gesture. As soon as they saw him, they grimly began to shoot rock, paper, scissors.

The younger one, a slip of a kid who looked no older than seventeen, broke out in a sheen of sweat when he lost to a surprise rock. The older guard scrambled off, leaving the young one to drop the key no less than three times in his nervous state. This all made for some nice anticipation, but they did have a show to get to.

Finally, the young guard unlocked the padlock and started to skitter off, but it was already too late. Springing from the foot locker with staggering speed came a man—well, who could tell, really, in that get-up?—clad from head to foot in skintight latex. Zippers decorated every orifice of his body, ready for opening, but only the eyes were currently open. His wrists were handcuffed together, as were his ankles, but they didn't seem to slow him down any as he threw his arms over the young guard's head, and yanked back, choking the man with the chain of his handcuffs.

Zippermouth was almost tiny enough to ride the young guard, as he bucked and rocked and turned purple. Moans of glee sounded from the gimp's otherwise muted mouth as he delighted in taking a stranger's life. Finally, the kid stopped kicking, pain and terror flash-frozen across his rictus face.

"Make that nine kills!" Mark announced to wild whoops of approval.

Zippermouth began humping the dead body of the guard. Luckily, the camera quickly cut away.

"Whoa, come on now, Zippermouth, kids are watching at home," Mark said with a chuckle.

The audience laughed in unison as Zippermouth let out an exasperated grunt and climbed off the guard's corpse. He fished around in the young man's pockets and produced a key. He considered removing the cuffs from his wrists and ankles, but in true Gimp fashion, he left them on.

"Now, I know you're all chomping at the bit here, but there's just one more surprise for you all, and I know you're gonna love it." The audience quieted down once more. Their collective anticipation was so electric Mark felt chills run down his spine. "Without further ado, I give you...this year's course!"

Mark opened his arms wide and every light in the arena suddenly came to life, illuminating the enormous obstacle course fifty feet below him. A caged maze that resembled a pre-war neighborhood containing booby-traps, a few safe areas for commercial breaks, and kill rooms galore lit up like a Christmas Tree, and *oohs* and *aahs* erupted from the crowd. Even Zippermouth stood in awe at this year's course; it put the previous mazes from past episodes to shame.

"It's beautiful," Jacob whispered.

Mark turned and mustered a fake smile.

"Mr. Graves is correct folks," Mark said, turning back to the audience. "That is one beautiful death trap! Am I right?" The crowd cheered in agreement as Mark continued. "We present to you 45,000 square feet of mayhem, terror, and pure entertainment!"

The sound team ensured that Mark's voice echoed on his last two words as the giant projector screens displayed the maze up close in all its sadistic glory. Mark knew the maze wasn't designed for survival, it was just another ridiculous version of the obstacle courses of years past. The only thing that set this one apart were the rest areas; eight by ten foot rooms that auto-sealed during commercial break. After repeat incidents of contestants being killed off-camera during break time, The Producers gave the green light to create a whole new maze this year that contained small rooms for temporary reprieve while the sponsors soaked up their intermittent few moments in the spotlight. Mark wondered how this would play out this year.

The killers were given microchips that prevented them from entering the rest areas, but once the commercial breaks were over, the contestants had a mere sixty seconds to exit the rest areas before they were trapped in what amounted to over-sized ovens. The rooms were made up of metal walls and floors that super-heated to seven-hundred degrees in just one minute, serving up the ultimate punishment for non-participation. Mark thought it was almost better than letting one of those monsters get their hands on you.

As the cameras finished up their zoomed-in tour of the death course, Mark noticed Marisol signaling for him to *wrap it up*. He nodded and put his best face forward once more. He couldn't wait for the first commercial break. He needed a drink, badly.

"Geiger Lands!" He shouted, his voice echoing around the arena. The people knew it was almost time. They jumped to their feet, some screaming, some clapping, others weeping tears of joy. "Geiger Lands!" Mark shouted once more, eliciting another rowdy response from the crowd.

The Producers stepped up behind him and all raised their arms, egging the crowd on.

"What do we say?!" Mark screamed into the microphone.

A deafening roar of voices responded. "Try...Not...To...Die!"

As the lights in the arena dimmed and the roar began to dull, Jimmy, the off-screen announcer's voice could be heard, much to everyone's disappointment.

"But first, a word from our sponsors."

CHAPTER 4

The guy sitting next to Dawn was as bald as a plucked chicken. Not just on his head—his arms, and by the look of it his chest, were bare, and he had no eyebrows. It was a fairly common look in the Geiger Lands. Dawn didn't know if there was a scientific term for it, but she'd always just heard them called cue balls.

The cue ball was smiling from ear to ear, staring directly at her.

"Hi," he said, wringing his hands.

"Hi," Dawn replied.

"I'm excited."

"Yeah, I can tell."

A sob cut through the green room. Both Dawn and Cue Ball turned and looked at the twenty-something albino woman who was crouching in the corner, rocking back and forth. She'd been doing it the whole time they'd been sitting there, and had been unresponsive to any attempts to get her to speak or sit.

"She'll be fine when the time comes," Cue Ball said.

"If you say so," Dawn replied, turning away from the abortive conversation.

Except for being painted entirely green, the green room was more like a holding pen than a welcoming spot to gather one's thoughts before a performance. It consisted of metal walls lined with concrete and planks for benches. Two sturdy doors sat before the contestants, the sound of the crowd outside occasionally piercing them.

The other residents of the room were a grey-haired woman in her late sixties and a man who was about four feet tall with two small knobs growing from his skull that made it look like he had junior devil horns coming in. The older woman seemed to have been untouched by any of the common maladies of the Geiger Lands. Dawn didn't like to think of herself as superstitious, but somehow she felt a little relief at not being the only "normal" one.

The sounds of lock mechanisms turning brought Dawn and Cue Ball both to their feet in alarm. But they both sagged in relief when the inner door opened and a man in a bespoke seersucker suit walked in, clapping his hands at short intervals to get their attention.

"All right, people, people, people!" He glanced down at the sniveling albino. "And whatever you are. This is the last briefing you're going to receive."

"It's also the first," Dawn muttered, rolling her eyes.

He crouched down in front of Dawn and started knocking on her forehead.

"So pay attention!"

She swatted at his hand, her face red with anger, but before she could catch it the loudmouth had already stopped tapping.

"All right, Jimmy," he said to the man who was apparently monitoring them from within, "Let them hear the noise."

An annoying buzz filled the room. The loudmouth pulled a dagger he had made out of his hand across his neck.

"That is e-nough, Jimmy! Now, folks, when you hear that sound, that means any rest area you're in is no longer valid. For the next sixty seconds the temperature will gradually rise to seven hundred degrees Fahrenheit, and if you're still inside, the doors lock. So, to recap: when you feel the heat and hear the noise, get out!

"Now I'm going to tell you what's going to happen when those doors open. I'm going to give you some tips and tricks, and if you listen to me, you'll survive just long enough to put on a good show for everybody. And that's what everybody wants, right?"

Cue Ball nodded his head vigorously and leaned forward, concentrating on the man's face.

"Tip Number One: you must always, always, always..."

The loudmouth's next word faltered on his lips as the buzzing noise sounded again.

"Jimmy! I told you to cut the..."

Suddenly, the exit doors swung out wide. The loudmouth turned and first his lower lip quivered, then a stream of piss ran down his leg, ruining his seersucker suit. Surprised, Dawn and Cue Ball jumped up. Dawn already felt the heat. The temperature was rising in the little green room, the concrete keeping it baked in.

Grandma was out the door first, running faster than most women half her age. Much to Dawn's surprise, the albino jumped up and ran, too.

"Told you," Cue Ball said, nodding at Dawn.

She nodded in agreement. He had, indeed, predicted that the albino would rise to the occasion.

"Jimmy! Jimmy, you have to let me in! I'm still in here! Jimmy!"

The loudmouth's cries for mercy were met with indifference, and Dawn nearly swooned as the temperature really began to crank up. The dwarf stomped out of the green room, and when one of the slashers—apparently a gimp in all latex—came giggling and running towards them, Cue Ball beat feet, too.

That left just Dawn, with the loudmouth wildly pulling on the handle to the inner door. She dropped her hand on his shoulder.

"Come on, you idiot! They're not going to let you back in. We have to get out of here!"

A flurry of half-hearted slaps made her remove her hand from his shoulder.

"Jimmy! Jimmy, you son of a bitch!"

Dawn's eyes darted back and forth from the deluded son of a bitch to the gibbering, giggling maniac in the bondage gear who was fast approaching.

"Sorry, man," she said, "I tried."

She took off like a shot. Just in time, it seemed, as the doors slammed shut as soon as she dove through. She slid across the filthy floor and quickly hopped back to her feet. She looked around and though she could hear the roar of the crowd, the spotlights above were so bright that she was barely able to see anything beyond the latticework dome surrounding her.

Instinctively, she looked for a weak point, some way to escape the oversized cage, but she was no fool. No one ever escaped *Try Not to Die.*

She felt a sudden chill as she adjusted to her surroundings. Compared to the oven-like green room, the arena itself was downright cool. Screams for an uncaring Jimmy mingled with calls for an even more uncaring God snapped her back to reality. She spun on her heels, facing the green room. Existential shrieks of pain soon penetrated the heavy doors. The smell of broiling flesh hit Dawn like a punch in the gut and she stared ahead, stunned. Everything was already happening so fast, but there was no time to linger over the loudmouth's unpleasant demise. She turned away from the sealed doors and saw the gimp loping toward her. If she didn't move, he'd be on top of her in no time.

She had three options: run left, head down an enclosed hallway to her right, or face the slasher with no weapon and hope she could somehow make it past him. The gimp's laughter floated to her ears as he galloped nearer, his chains clanging loudly, and she sprinted to the right. She'd seen the older woman and the albino head this way. Perhaps there was safety in numbers. As she ran, she heard the gimp plow into one of the walls behind her and swiftly recover, his pounding footsteps alerting her that he was already in the hall and hot on her heels.

She made another right turn and then a quick left, there was a fork ahead of her and she was soon faced with having to choose directions again. She had a feeling the night ahead would be full of dreadful choices like this. As she grew closer to the fork she noticed the left path was enclosed and bathed in red light. She hoped like hell that it was one of the rest areas as she pumped her arms and picked up speed, the crazed slasher gaining on her.

"Damn it!" Dawn hollered when she saw that the other end of the red-lit hallway wasn't a safe room after all. It was wide open.

There was no time to be discouraged, though, and she raced for the end of the hall. The gimp shrieked with glee and the noise echoed all around her. Without the blaring sound of the crowd in here, the slasher's cries of joy sent shivers down her spine. She was just about to leap through the exit when a loud buzzer sounded and the red lights began to flash. A heavy metal door slid shut, trapping her. She slammed face-first into the door and bounced backward, falling onto her ass and, for a moment, seeing stars.

"No!" she cried out, jumping to her feet and pounding on the door. She turned back just in time to see another door sliding shut at the other end of the hall.

She cried out in frustration and placed her back to the heavy door, watching as the gimp slowed down to a stop. Mark Winters's voice suddenly invaded the hall, causing her to jump.

"I didn't think we'd get so lucky so early! But it looks like one of our contestants has just found herself in...*Sudden Death!* What advice would you give her, folks?"

The crowd responded with "Try Not to Die!"

"Our contestant and slasher have just sixty seconds to try and kill the other or they'll both be terminated immediately! And we all know how dull our auto-executions are."

The crowd booed in response and Dawn cringed, cursing herself for choosing the wrong path.

"Don't worry folks, round two has plenty of action and a whole new slasher in store! But something tells me Zippermouth will walk out of that room in tip-top shape!"

The gimp giggled and took a step forward, only to immediately jump back as a blast of fire shot out of the wall. He clapped his hands together as fire shot out once more, just two feet in front of Dawn. She shielded her face from the blast and when she looked again, fire was shooting out from the walls every five seconds on both ends of the hall.

"Shit, shit, shit," Dawn whispered under her breath as the gimp dove past the first stream of fire and dodged the second, pressing his back up against the wall.

She racked her brain for a way to defeat the psychopath with no weapon. She probably had ten pounds on Zippermouth, but she didn't think she'd be able to take him on in hand-to-hand combat. She had no intention of going down without a fight, though. She tucked her head down and moved forward, safely avoiding the fire trap. The gimp moved forward once more and barely stopped in time as an enormous blade swung out from a slot in the wall to his left. He sidestepped the blade as it disappeared into the opposite wall momentarily before swinging back down again.

"Oh, boy! That was close!" Mark shouted and the crowd cheered.

Dawn's heart pounded and she grimaced, watching the heavy pendulum of death. It almost seemed to be picking up speed. The gimp was getting closer, dodging fire blasts and avoiding yet another pendulum when it swung out faster than the first. The psycho shrieked in excitement, jumping up and down, his chains clanging together. He pointed at Dawn and clapped, doing a couple of bunny hops. Only two obstacles stood between them, and he had every intention of murdering her in this hallway. He made a big show of hopping and gyrating his way past the next blast of fire, his erection obvious through the skin-tight latex. Dawn balled her fists up and planted her feet, ready to fight.

As her attacker dove past the final obstacle, Dawn raised her fists and threw a punch, her left fist connecting with Zippermouth's cheek. He barely stumbled, clearly unfazed by the blow to his face. He let out a wail, more of pleasure than pain, and charged at Dawn again, wrapping his arms around her waist and lifting her off the ground. Before she knew it, her back was slammed against the heavy door behind her, the wind knocked from her lungs. Fire blazed from the walls in front of her and she realized she couldn't breathe. Her arms flew up and she clawed at the gimp's hands around her neck. The freak was screaming with excitement, rubbing himself against her as he attempted to choke the life from her. Dawn thought fast and stuffed her thumbs into the open zipper holes where his eyes were until he let out a shriek of real pain, losing his hold on Dawn and stumbling backward, almost tripping over his chains. Her eyes flicked down to the tethers on his ankles and she got an idea.

As the gimp rubbed his aching eyes, Dawn delivered a swift kick to his nethers and he doubled over in pain, gasping for air. All the while Mark Winters shouted witty commentary and narrated the bizarre scene in the hallway since it was hidden from view, although she was sure hidden cameras were broadcasting it on the big screen for the benefit of the crowd and the home audience. She ducked under the fiery blast and almost didn't make it to the pendulum before another stream of fire shot out. The end of her pony tail didn't make it as the smell of burnt hair met her nostrils.

The gimp roared in anger behind her and charged. Dawn prayed to the Old Gods she knew didn't exist that her plan would work and she took a few quick steps backward, so close to the pendulum that she could feel the air shift as it whooshed past. The gimp ran toward her at top speed and she sidestepped just in time, spinning around behind the slasher and dropping to her knees. With both hands she snatched up the trailing chain and pulled with all her might. Zippermouth's feet were pulled out from under him and he fell face-forward. The swinging blade sliced clean through the center of his torso and Dawn was bathed in her attacker's blood.

She cringed and slammed her eyes shut, spitting the blood from her mouth, trying, and then failing, to hold back a stream of vomit. She heard over the sounds of her retching both the crowd and Mark Winters cheering through the speakers when suddenly they were cut off. She was left only with the sounds of the gimp sputtering and slowly dying a few feet from her. She opened her eyes again when the metal doors on either end of the hall slid open. The lights no longer flashed and the booby-traps had stopped. She'd made it through her first, and what she desperately hoped was her last, round of *Sudden Death*.

She rushed out of the hall and stopped dead in her tracks in the next room.

"Hi." Cue Ball said, sitting on a bench in the far corner of the rest area.

"You've got to be shitting me."

Dawn laughed as the door behind her slid shut and *Try Not to Die* cut to their first official commercial break.

CHAPTER 5

Slapping away the desperate ministrations of his makeup people, Mark slouched down into the director's chair just offstage. Now that things were really up and running, he wouldn't have the time to run back and forth to the dressing room. He held up his hand and saw a tiny tremor run through it. Luckily, he was never so unprepared as to show his ass by walking onstage with the DTs. He reached into his pocket and unscrewed the cap on his flask.

"*Señor* Winters," a sultry voice said in his ear, shocking him and making him spill his flask all over himself as he desperately tried to screw the cap back on.

He hoped his smile didn't seem too plastered on as he turned to face Marisol Martinez.

"Marisol," he said, reaching up to kiss her on either cheek, much to the chagrin of the armed men flanking her.

Marisol paused. The look on her face was funny. He hoped she wasn't smelling the alcohol he'd spilled, then hoped it wasn't leaking through his suit pocket. If she had noticed, she said nothing. Either way, she took his hand and sandwiched it between her own.

"Markus, my darling. It really is a shame about what happened to that poor slasher."

"It is," he agreed. "It really is. It's just…it's a damned shame. I just wish sometimes that we could control all of the moving pieces, but you know, contestants are unpredictable and—"

"Maybe the issue is that you're going easy on them. Maybe that silly gimp was less of a challenge and more of a…sideshow act."

Mark swallowed a lump which had suddenly, but not so

mysteriously, appeared in his throat.

"Step up the challenge is what you're saying?"

She took both of his cheeks in her hands and planted a kiss on his forehead.

"You understand perfectly, Markus."

Marisol and her goons disappeared, back to their opulent box. Panicking, Mark wiped the sweat away from his forehead. This time there were no mistakes as he pulled out his flask, drank half of it, and put it back. He was disappointed to discover that his leak had seeped through his pocket, so he took his jacket off and hung it on his chair.

"Come on, Mark," one of the dancers said, grabbing his shoulder.

"Give me a minute!" he fairly shrieked.

"We don't have a minute. The show's starting now."

Hoping the vein in his temple wasn't throbbing visibly enough for the entire viewing audience to see, Mark took the stage as it descended back into view. He smiled, bathed in the applause, waved to a few different corners of the stadium, and pointed toward a specific area in the audience, signaling for the cameras to zoom in and say a special hello to a little baby someone had brought with them. The mother was holding a sign that said, "My First *Try Not to Die*."

Remembering he had left behind his jacket, Mark reached up and loosened his bowtie, to complete the disheveled effect.

"Is it getting hot in here?" he asked.

The crowd roared in appreciation.

"Well, our contestants have had their first little break. They've even managed to turn the tables on one of our slashers. But I can guarantee you that won't be happening for the next one. You all came out to see a little blood tonight, didn't you?"

Never before had the crowd seemed to be so composed of inbred hicks and mutants. They were practically frothing at the mouths at the thought of more people dying. Mark thought he might be sick.

"So, let's meet our next slasher!"

The screen behind him lit up with an image of a bald mutant wearing sunglasses and holding a battle axe. His kill count was seventeen. He looked to Marisol in the Producer's Box. She gave him a tiny, almost imperceptible shake of her head.

"Oh, *that* is an unpleasant looking customer, isn't it? But I think we can do better, don't you? Jimmy, what do you say we kick things up a notch?"

Mark stood with a smile frozen on his face for what seemed like an eternity before the image changed. The next contestant had a body count of nearly forty. She wore a burlap sack over her face but was otherwise stark naked, with gray skin spattered with blood. In each of her hands she held two dangerous, gore-coated corkscrews.

He glanced at the Producers box and yet again, Marisol denied him.

"You know what? Let's let the crowd decide. Do you all like The Connoisseur? Sounds like kind of a French name, don't you think?"

The crowd seemed kind of confused for a minute.

"Thirty-eight kills? I mean, that's pretty good," he said, deliberately elongating the word pretty. "I mean, if you don't think we can do any better…"

The crowd finally got the gist, and Mark felt a surge of relief as though someone was unclenching his heart as the masses began to boo.

"Let's try again, Jimmy."

A new face appeared on the screen. It was, in fact, the beloved face of an American icon. In a stovepipe top hat, with long bushy eyebrows and a long beard, Abraham Lincoln—or, rather, a wax facsimile of the old president—stared out beatifically at the crowd. Marisol was smiling and nodding in her box, and the rest of The Producers began clapping.

"Now, here's a challenge. Hailing from Orlando, from the Republic of Cuba, with a total kill count of four score and seven, you may know him as The Girl Splitter. You may also know him as The Great Eviscerator. He has almost as many nicknames as victims. Ladies and germs, I give you: Evil Animatronic Abraham Lincoln!"

Mark gestured toward the Barn. The doors opened and four goons, each holding a huge magnet pressed against the robot, struggled to manhandle the 16th President into the fighting arena. The Girl Splitter's head did a full 360 on its neck, and Mark halfway expected steam to spit out of its ears.

Mark hated the robots. The animatronic killers that the Cubans donated to the show didn't give the contestants a chance in hell, and worst of all, they had been built in the 70s. The crowd roared once more when The Girl Splitter whipped both weapons out and spun them in his hands, he raised each pistol in the air and mimicked shooting while he hollered "BOOM BOOM BOOM" in the worst human-simulated voice Mark had ever heard. The crowd ate it up though, and The Producers were satisfied, so Mark clapped along with the morons in the audience and danced alongside his sparkling cohosts, all the while just hoping this round would be over soon.

CHAPTER 6

Dawn collapsed onto the bench beside Cue Ball and exhaled with a whoosh.

"You did good," he said with a smile and pointed up to a tiny screen in the corner.

She had to squint to make out anything on the barely-functioning TV set mounted to the wall, but once her eyes adjusted she could make out that it was the hallway of hell she'd just escaped.

"Thanks," she mumbled, leaning forward and placing her head in her hands. "Where are the others?"

"Dunno. Just me and you in here. I didn't see anyone else."

She looked up at him and couldn't help but smile. She envied him. She didn't think being a contestant on this nightmarish show frightened him in the least. She thought back to the wailing albino curled up on the floor; now *that* she could relate to. While Dawn might have seemed cool and collected on the outside, she was definitely that fragile, terrified girl on the inside.

"Should we stick together?" he asked her, his smile everpresent and his wide eyes sparkling. "We should be friends."

Dawn nodded. His smile was contagious. "I'd like that."

She wasn't sure how much longer either of them would be alive, but at least neither would die alone.

An awful yet familiar buzz filled the room and the exit door popped open, signaling that break time was over. Dawn looked to her new friend and he nodded, and together they entered what she was sure was going to be an even more difficult Round 2.

She could hear Mark Winters's voice all around her as they walked, the roar of the crowd echoing in kind; they were cycling through the serial killers for some reason.

Perhaps Queen Marisol wasn't too pleased with my performance, Dawn thought, turning a corner with Cue Ball at her side.

"Look," he pointed up.

Through the latticework dome she could see the corner of one of the huge projection screens.

"Come on, this way." Dawn instructed, leading them to a better vantage point.

They were almost directly under it now. While it might not have been her or Cue Ball on that projection screen, she was sure the heathens seated in this area of the audience were looking directly at them.

A loud bang startled her and she tried to make out what had been thrown at the cage. What appeared to be somebody's disgusting leftovers oozed down between the latticework: greasy brown gravy and bits of meat and potatoes. Another bang sounded, followed by another. She couldn't hear them over the collective audience, but the mere sight of two contestants in such close proximity was sure riling them up.

"Animals!" She shouted and raised both hands, flipping them double birds before returning her attention to the large screen.

She could barely believe her eyes as an Animatronic Abraham Lincoln, reprogrammed as a death machine, put on a brief show for the crowd.

Cue Ball clapped his hands together and hopped up and down. "I love robots!"

Dawn cringed. "Not this kind you don't."

Lights flashed, music blared, and Mark Winters's handsome face filled the screen once again.

"Geiger Lands!" he shouted and the audience responded with their expected chant.

"Try not to die!"

Dawn and Cue Ball exchanged glances and nods, sprinting forward. They navigated the maze with caution. Dawn hoped to avoid another *Sudden Death* round, especially when her opponent was a seven-foot-tall robot wielding dual pistols, but much to her dismay a wrong turn had taken them exactly where she didn't want to be. Not into another booby-trapped hallway, but more than likely, and quite literally, into what was sure to be sudden death.

"Down!" Dawn shouted and shoved Cue Ball out of the way as the Animatronic Abe Lincoln fired two shots from the hip.

She felt a bullet graze her left leg as she flew to the ground, but ignored it as she scurried to her feet alongside her new companion. Glancing down, she saw that it was nothing more than a flesh wound, and she was so jacked up on adrenaline she barely felt any pain. Lady Luck, for once, had given her a break.

They raced forward, Abe Lincoln's heavy metal steps pounding behind them and bullets flying past their heads. No matter which path in the course she chose, they seemed to reenter the main room and Dawn was sure they were done for when she spun on her heels and found herself face-to-face with the dangerous end of a gun.

"Boom," the robot said, pulling the trigger, but Cue Ball had already knocked Dawn off her feet and out of harm's way.

Dawn's heart was caught in her throat and a sudden wave of nausea came over her. This was far more overwhelming than her bout with the gimp. All the lights of the arena combined with a hellish mixture of pop music and screaming people made her feel faint, not to mention the fact that a murderous robot had just nearly blown her face off.

Get it together, Dawn! she screamed internally.

Someone let out a furious cry and the robot spun in that direction, firing both weapons, but they met no human body as the robot had fired too high.

The man with the knots on his head from the green room charged Abe Lincoln, screaming obscenities. The four-foot-man leaped from the ground and climbed the robot like a spider, finally coming to rest on its shoulders. He punched and pulled at the robot's head, trying desperately to rip it from its hinges and render it useless. But with ease, Animatronic Abe Lincoln holstered his pistols and reached up with both gangly arms, plucking the small man from its body and tossing him away like a rag doll. He landed ten feet ahead and slid another ten before rolling to a stop.

"This is our chance! We need to go!" Dawn shouted above the noise, and without hesitation, Cue Ball took off across the main room floor while the robot was distracted.

Dawn hoped they'd have better luck getting as far away from the main room as possible by entering the other side of the maze. As she ran behind Cue Ball, curiosity got the best of her and she peered over her shoulder in time to see Abe Lincoln with hands on hips, a poorly simulated laugh escaping its mouth. The small man on the ground got to his feet and let out another wail. He was fierce, full of rage and determination, and he charged the robot one more time.

Dawn reached the other side safely with Cue Ball and they tore off into the maze. As they ran, she couldn't tear her eyes from the projection screen on this side of the arena, but wished like hell that she had.

As the small man made his second attempt at charging the large robot, the Animatronic Abe Lincoln pulled a mounted shotgun from its back and blew a hole the size of Dawn's fist into the center of the charging man's torso. The impact sent the small man flying back from where he'd first landed, but this time he stayed down, a pool of deep crimson forming around him.

The grinding of gears and metal-on-metal sounded as Lincoln opened its mouth. A speaker blared its words, but they didn't match at all with the movement of its lips.

"Nearly all men can stand adversity," the fake president stated with a strange grace, "but if you want to test a man's character, give him..."

The robot's eyes flashed red, its darker programming over-powering its folksy wisdom.

"...*a shotgun in the belly! BOOM!*" Abe Lincoln shouted and the crowd went into hysterics.

The robot looked around in an attempt to locate Dawn and Cue Ball, but they were nowhere to be found. The crowd collectively screamed and pointed toward the opposite end of the arena.

The halls in which Dawn and Cue Ball ran suddenly lit up like a Christmas tree and piercing alarms blared. Dawn's hands instinctively covered her ears and she looked around, terrified.

"We found them for you, Honest Abe!" Mark shouted into the mic.

The robot took off in that direction, running faster than anyone had anticipated, and Dawn knew it was only a matter of time before the thing hunted them down and finished them both off.

Dawn took one more step and heard a sickening mechanical click. She threw herself backwards just in time as a huge, razor-sharp piece of sheet metal dropped from the ceiling, blocking the entire passage. Cue Ball had been just an instant too slow, and had lost the fingertips on his right hand.

"Ah!" he shouted in pain.

Dawn turned and put her back to the wall-sized guillotine. She pushed and pushed but the sheaf of metal had locked solidly in place. It had been intended both as a death trap and a new barrier. She was now surrounded on all sides by inflexible metal, and only a few hundred feet away was the silhouette of The Great Eviscerator.

"Well, I guess this is it," Cue Ball said, attempting to smile through the pain in his hand.

Dawn couldn't help but smile, too. She reached down and ripped a strip off her stained, white shirt.

"Come here," she said, taking his blood-spurting hand and wrapping it.

The whirr and buzz of pneumatics and gears filled the death trap hallway. No longer running to make the catch, Evil Abe was now savoring the kill. It was slowly clanking forward, and its mouth opened to intone some words that did not at all match the flapping of its jaws. Each time it mangled the quote, its eyes glowed red.

"You can *kill* some of the people some of the time..."

"You should run for it," Cue Ball said, "Maybe he'll be distracted with me."

Dawn shook her head.

"I don't see getting past *that*."

"...and you can *kill* all of the people some of the time..."

"Maybe, though," she mused, "I could run into him and

distract him for long enough for you to get away."

"Don't," he said, "I'm a goner with this hand anyway."

"...but you can't *kill* all of the people all of the time," Lincoln concluded with stately diction, now standing only a few feet away.

"What's your name?" Cue Ball asked.

"Dawn. What's yours?"

"Tim," he replied.

"*Unless you're me,*" the robot added, mangling the quote beyond all recognition.

Lincoln leveled the shotgun, ready to blow them both away.

CHAPTER 7

A heavy rock struck Lincoln, sending its head spinning 180 degrees. Dawn was now looking up at the back of its head and the front of its body. She peered farther down the hallway. The albino from the green room was standing there, clutching a second rock in her other hand, a look of shock on her face.

"Go go go!" Dawn shouted, pushing Tim forward.

Animatronic Lincoln roared angrily and the shotgun went off, but with its eyes pointing in the opposite direction, the discharge went wild. Dawn still felt the sting of some shot, and hissed in pain, but by and large the blast had missed her.

"Hold my hand," Tim said.

"Tim, that's not—"

"Just trust me," he said, grabbing her hand in what must have been great pain with his recently bandaged one, "and go low."

As they ran past the robot, Dawn suddenly understood his intention. They passed by on either side of Lincoln and dipped their arms low, below his kneecaps, effectively clotheslining him. But since the automaton was a half-ton of metal, the only spot on his body where a clothesline would have been effective was his skinny legs, beneath the knees.

The robot went toppling over and they raced past the albino, releasing hands in time for Dawn to grab the albino by the shoulder and yank her out of her stupor.

"You did good," Dawn said, slapping the albino on her back.

"Thanks," she replied, a twisted smile briefly crossing her face.

They halted just in time to avoid falling into a pit of spikes that opened up in front of them.

"What's the plan now?" Tim asked.

"Get to a rest area, wait for the next commercial. After that, I don't know," Dawn said.

"No," the albino said, "we need to catch back up with Granny. She's a tough old girl."

"Where is she?" Dawn asked, "I haven't seen her since we left the green room."

"Come on," the albino said, "I'll show you."

They ducked and weaved as the pale girl led them along a route she already seemed to know. And then she turned a corner and stopped dead in her tracks.

Robotic Lincoln stood there, its head still facing backwards. The robot had simply adjusted its paradigm so that its back was now its front. It discharged the shotgun, cutting the legs out from under the albino. She let out a blood-curdling scream as she collapsed to the earth; Dawn and Tim scattered off in opposite directions, but Lincoln didn't give immediate pursuit.

Instead, it approached the albino writhing on the ground in pain, and reached out.

"A *ho* divided against *herself* cannot stand," it pronounced loudly.

"No!" the albino screeched, but the robot had no intentions of stopping.

With that, it ripped each of her arms out of their sockets, sending blood spurting in opposite directions. The albino, or rather, what was left of her, quickly succumbed to her wounds. Her screams finally subsided as she bled out almost immediately and she finally was still before the robot which had so brutally ended her life.

Dawn's hands shook as she covered her mouth, disgusted by the obscene way in which she'd watched the albino meet her demise. Doubtless that was the origin of the perverse epithet Mark had called it earlier: Girl Splitter.

Gotta keep moving.

She willed herself on, giving Tim a nudge and tearing off past Evil Abe with mere seconds to spare before the robot could grab either of them.

The albino might have known exactly where she was going,

but Dawn had no idea. Getting to the rest area was her top priority. Granny could wait. Dawn and Tim zig-zagged through labyrinths and avoided booby-traps, all the while the crowd chanted and the Girl Splitter gained on them. Several paths had been blocked off by the metal sheets while others reopened, but it was only a matter of time before Dawn realized they were getting nowhere.

"We're running in circles!" she shouted at Tim as they sprinted by the albino's body.

"They're trying to tire us out," Tim yelped through gulps of air.

The robot turned the corner behind them and began its preprogrammed speech again, filling Dawn with rage.

"I'm getting real sick of this thing, real fast," she said to Tim, and in poor taste, grabbed one of the albino's dismembered limbs.

Tim cringed. "What are you—"

"Follow me!"

Dawn reared her arm back as she ran at Evil Abe and launched the severed limb like a spear at the robot's head. Lincoln's head spun back the other way and once more the robot was disoriented, firing shots blindly.

"That should buy us some time!" Dawn and Tim sprinted past The Girl Splitter and left it to readjust itself back to its original, front-facing form.

The audience booed, growing tired of the seemingly endless charade. The contestants were clearly outsmarting the Animatronic Killer and they hadn't paid to only watch a robot chase a woman and a cue ball around all night.

"Markus."

Up on the platform, Mark shivered at the icy voice in his earpiece. He dreaded turning around, but knew he had to. He kept his million-dollar smile in place, but knew he would not get a smile from the Producers' box in return.

"This was not what I meant by *step up the challenge.*" Marisol glared at him.

Mark laughed nervously and peeked at the other Producers

behind the frightening woman. Even Jacob Graves, who seemed distracted trying to open a packet of peanuts, looked displeased.

Marisol touched the earpiece in her right ear, never taking her eyes off Mark's.

"Jimmy," she said. "Change of plans. We're going to move into a *Let's Play* segment. Get these idiots into a safe room, stat." She gave Mark a look that said *you know what to do* before retaking her seat beside her husband.

Mark inhaled deeply and spun around as a pathway in the course below him lit up green.

"Oh? Whatever could this be?" Mark feigned surprise as he watched the two contestants stop dead in their tracks and turn their attention toward the green-lit path.

"I can't believe it! Could it be?" Mark squinted, his hands on his hips, and he cocked his head left and right as if trying to figure out what the pathway led to with the audience.

Come on, you dumb shits, move! Mark thought, as the projection screens began to display a countdown from ten. With each number the green lights began to dim and a metal door slowly began to lower.

"Oh boy," he shouted into the mic with a laugh. "I wonder if our contestants are fast enough! What do you guys think?" He asked the audience and they laughed, shouting insults at Dawn and Tim.

Mark sighed internally as the contestants finally took the bait and charged the lowering door. They both slid in on their sides as the countdown reached "one" and the metal door dropped the last few feet, obviously intended to crush whatever—or whoever—might have been unlucky enough to be in its way.

Mark let out a high-pitched laugh. "A safe room? Whaaat?"

The audience seemed confused for the briefest of moments before random red spotlights began to appear over audience members throughout the arena. Suddenly the crowd buzzed with excitement as they realized what was happening.

"That's right folks!" Mark cheered. "It's time for...*Let's Play!*"

CHAPTER 8

At the top of the dome of rebar that separated the audience from the arena, a tiny hole suddenly opened up. At the same time, the thrum of the generator and the static field that had set hair on end in the audience suddenly stopped. The cage was no longer electrified, and the crowd knew it. Given time, rabid audience members might have been able to scrabble their way to the top and slip in the hole, so the Producers' goons were walking around liberally spraying the metal dome with oil to discourage the few who tried anyway. Most of them simply slipped backwards onto their asses.

The spotlights suddenly shone on an enormous and mysterious piece of machinery that had previously been shrouded in darkness. Dramatic music blared as every spotlight in the arena found its way to the giant machine and it roared to life. The crane, an old-world piece of construction equipment, had been rigged for remote operation and decorated in sparkling lights, as gaudy as everything else on the *Try Not to Die* set. A giant claw had been attached to the end; it deliberately and precisely resembled its antecedents that Mark remembered using to fish cheap stuffed animals and harmonicas out of prize machines in pre-war video arcades as a child.

"Isn't she a beauty?" Mark asked the crowd, motioning at the looming piece of equipment. "Now, we've already lost two contestants, and what fun would *Try Not to Die* be without, you know, people trying not to die? So we're going to pump up our numbers a bit! That's why each of the Producers is going to select an audience member to enter the arena!"

The crowd was going crazy, but not over his words. One Mohawked young girl, against all odds, had managed to scrabble up the oil-soaked latticework of the dome nearly to the top. The crowd was, apparently, distracted by her moxie. But then she finally lost her footing and slid all the way back down, striking her chin on each length of rebar as she slid. The first such strike severed her tongue and sent it fluttering down into the arena. By the time she slid back into the crowd she had lain still, more than likely dead.

Mark forced himself to chuckle.

"And *that*, folks, is why you want to enter the arena *the right way*. And it could happen! But, a word of caution for those of you who do get Selected. There will be a parachute waiting for you. Make sure to put it on, but don't pull the cord until you're inside the dome. Now let's catch up with our Producers."

A catwalk extended from the hanging stage to the Producers' box. Mark approached, but didn't dare climb in himself.

"Let's start with you, Amy," he said, gesturing at the arms dealer.

"I'd be honored," she replied, taking what looked like a video game joystick off of a platter that one of her goons was holding.

Green pushed a button and the crane was now under her control. The crane groaned as it swung toward the crowd. Amy didn't seem to be able stop it in time and Mark glued his eyes shut, expecting the entire back wall of the arena to crumble, but much to his surprise, he heard Amy snicker. He popped one eye open first to have a look, and breathed a sigh of relief as the crane swung back out, away from the wall, and she started lowering it towards the reaching hands of crazed audience members.

When the crane was about as close as it could safely get to the crowd, metal on metal screeched as the four-fingered claw opened wide. The claw dipped down, and after some bobbing and weaving, all with Amy's tongue sticking out of the side of her mouth, it finally closed around the shoulders of a heavyset, middle-aged man.

Well, not much of a challenge for Animatronic Evil Abe there, is it? Mark reflected.

The crowd practically ripped the man's clothes to shreds in

their jealousy, but it wasn't long before the crane bore him aloft. He snatched at the parachute waiting on a hook above him and struggled to pull it on from his awkwardly held position. Amy had a little more trouble getting the claw just above the hole in the dome, but when she finally did, she slipped it in perfectly.

The claw let go of the middle-aged man, who screamed for just a moment, but then pulled the rip cord and his descent slowed considerably.

Derron James grabbed the joystick next. In his eagerness, he had brought the claw's fingers right down on the skull of a teenaged girl in a tube top. Her head exploded like a pimple, sending brains splattering everywhere.

"Ooh!" Mark winced along with the crowd. "Maybe we should add you to the Barn, Derron. Kill count 1!"

"It was an accident!" Derron protested, more than a bit flustered, "Lemme go again. Can I go again?"

"You need to drop the claw where they're going to be, not where they are," Amy said sagely.

"I know, I know." Derron said, as if trying to convince himself.

Derron's second attempt went smoother, though not exactly *smoothly*, and a farm boy in overalls joined the dull looking, middle-aged man in the dome in scrambling to escape the attention of Evil Abe.

Marisol snatched the joystick from Derron's hands.

"Watch and learn," she said pointedly to her husband.

With a precision that almost made it boring to watch, Marisol brought the claw perfectly into position, dropping it over a gaunt, thirtyish woman who was probably suffering from radiation sickness. She was plucked from the audience and Marisol dropped her elegantly into the hole on the first try. The skinny woman parachuted safely to the ground and Marisol passed a smug look around to the other three.

"And, of course, we always save the best for last, don't we Jacob." Mark smiled.

Grumbling and wiping chicken grease from his fingers onto his clothes, Graves took hold of the joystick and absent-mindedly picked a member of the crowd whose face was scored with ulcers. Jerkily, he positioned the man over the hole in the dome and after a few false starts, managed to insert him into the arena.

Graves leaned back, a look of deep self-pleasure on his face. "There, see? Nothing to it."

He slapped the release button and the disfigured man went plummeting to the ground, having forgotten the parachute on the hook. Graves's face turned to one of shock as the player smashed against the ground, exploding like a sack of chunky soup.

"Hey, now!" Graves grumbled, "That's not my fault if he didn't pull his ripcord."

"Not so easy after all, is it, Jacob?" Derron asked smugly.

"Watch it, you skinny prick," Graves shot him a glare and Derron, not one for confrontation, quickly looked away, pretending to be distracted by something in the audience.

"All right, you two," Mark said, wagging his finger as though admonishing two silly kids, "What do you say, folks? Should we give Mr. Graves another shot?"

The crowd seemed to go wild, shouting, "Me! Pick me!"

"Okay, one more time then. And make sure to grab your chute!"

Muttering under his breath, Graves took an over-cautious run, finally snatching a modestly-dressed woman who might have been a teacher out of the crowd and successfully dropping her into the dome. She made a big show of grabbing her parachute before Graves would let her go, and she floated to the ground, where the Abe Lincoln robot blasted her to pieces with his shotgun before she managed to crawl out from under the parachute. She ended up looking like a child's conception of a ghost costume, a figure covered in a sheet, with a bloody mess down the center.

"Ooh, too bad!" Mark winced. "She didn't even get a chance to play!"

He turned his attention to the other three selected audience members as they pranced around the main room like newborn foals and had to keep himself from face-palming. He wasn't sure how much time Marisol was hoping to buy, but watching as the farm boy's face disappeared in a red mist as Evil Abe's shotgun fired, he figured they only had about another sixty seconds of this nonsense before round three began.

Marisol stepped up beside Mark once more and signaled for him to cut his mic off while the other Producers whooped and hollered along with the audience; they were encouraging Evil Abe, who'd finally got his hands on the sad-looking skinny woman, to perform another Girl Splitter routine.

"Let's give The Great Eviscerator a friend." Marisol whispered into Mark's ear, leaning in so closely he could smell her sweet breath as her lips grazed his earlobe.

It sent a shiver down his spine. His eyes met Marisol's briefly before he looked away again, intimidated, wishing desperately that he could take a long swig from his flask.

"Two killers in the maze at once?" he asked, shocked. They'd never set the psychopaths loose more than one at a time; the repercussions could be disastrous. "I don't know that that's such a—"

"Markus, are you questioning me?" Marisol stared at him, triggering a look of remorse on his face. She blinked rapidly and awaited his response, but Mark kept his mouth shut. She laughed and pretended to fan herself with her hands. "Okay, good, for a minute there I thought you were questioning me."

Mark's mouth opened and closed, but again his words found themselves lost and he mustered up his signature fake smile as Marisol gave him a wink.

"Tell Jimmy to throw out the *special* one." She waved at the crowd before falling back beside the other Producers.

Mark's smile didn't waver as he turned back to the audience who were expressing their approval with wild gestures as Animatronic Abe dismembered the unfortunate skinny woman in the arena. The robot set his sights on the final randomly selected *Let's Play* contestant and made a big show of unholstering his two pistols. He spun them in each hand, firing shots as he cowboy-walked towards the dull-looking man who was pissing his pants as bullets found their way into his frame; Mark couldn't believe the poor guy was still standing.

The man finally dropped to his knees. He clutched his

bleeding stomach and coughed hard, blood spewing from his mouth. The Great Eviscerator raised both weapons and fired at once, punching two enormous holes into his victim's skull, finally putting him out of his misery.

The crowd went wild as the off-screen announcer informed them of their incoming commercial break.

"We'll be right back after these messages," Mark said with a grin.

CHAPTER 9

A tractor ran up and down a scraggly, irradiated field, leaving perfectly parallel lines. Slowly, the tractor came to a halt, sending a cloud of toxic dust into the air around it. A grizzled old farmer leaned forward, folding his arms over the steering wheel.

"You know, some folks like to wet their whistles with vodka. And I'd never say nothing about someone who did. Others prefer a little rum after a hard day's work. Well, different strokes for different folks, I say."

The farmer reached up and adjusted his ball cap.

"But if you're like me and you live in the Geiger Lands, well, something just don't sit right about foreign drinks. We don't need nothing fancy to get along here. After I'm done ploughing the fields all day, I like nothing better than to sit back with old Maurice here and have us a drink of Farmer Brown's Country Fresh Moonshine."

A deeply mutated farmhand extended a purple tentacle-like arm towards the salt-of-the-earth farmer. It was clutching a Mason jar full of clear fluid.

"Thanks, Maurice." The farmer tipped his hat at the man before turning back toward the camera.

"Sure, the water's a little irradiated. The corn sometimes comes with eyeballs. But we don't need nothing fancy in the GL. Just good old Farmer Brown's Moonshine. Oh, and, in case you didn't realize it…" he smiled wide, *"…I'm Farmer Brown."*

CHAPTER 10

Dawn and Tim watched on the small, corner-mounted television screen as the robot destroyed the audience members one by one. They were merely puppets, taught to be excited about being murdered on live television. Dawn wondered if perhaps it was the only thing these poor excuses for human beings had left to live for these days. Perhaps it was fitting they die in such a manner. The whole farce disgusted her. *Try Not to Die* was disgusting enough, but this new segment she was witnessing gave a whole new level of depravity to the show.

Was there even a point in trying not to die? It seemed that all she and her new comrade Tim were doing was delaying the inevitable. She balled up her fists as some stupid moonshine commercial filled the screen and turned away, her face flushed with anger. It wasn't that she would die some random, savage death in that arena that was making her so freaking angry. No. It was the fact that it had become socially acceptable to maim and torture the citizens of the GL. It was mainstream excitement, accepted by seemingly everyone as a normal way to "control the population." The Geiger Lands didn't need population control, the radiation and ultimate lawlessness and anarchy did that just fine. If the Selection process was truly so random, why had there never been a contestant who *wasn't* living in some shanty town on the outskirts of a radiation hot zone? Why were the upper echelon citizens never so...*lucky*?

Dawn was pulled from her thoughts by the pain of her nails digging into her palms. She had been clenching them like a maniac.

I wonder how long Marisol Martinez and her posse of Producers would last in their own maze...probably longer than that idiot, Mark Winters, or one of his bimbos.

She didn't know any of them personally, but she didn't think she needed to. They were all the same to her. She hated them each equally for this.

"The commercial's almost over," Tim said, inspecting the wound on his hand.

She looked at him and frowned. "How're the fingers?"

"I'll live." He shrugged. "Don't know for how much longer, but I doubt it'll be this that kills me." He waved his mangled hand at her and gave her that goofy grin.

She couldn't help but smile again, but soon enough that smile faded from her lips. Tim was yet another reason to hate The Producers and everyone else associated with this show. He was so innocent and had already lived a life so marred by the bombs. And yet here he was, forced to endure this blatant and meaningless savagery for the entertainment of others.

"It's not fair," Dawn whispered.

"What?" Tim cocked his head.

She hadn't realized she'd said the words aloud, but the alarm sounded and Mark announced that Round 3 was beginning before she could respond.

"Come on," she motioned for Tim to follow, "let's get out of here before we cook like turkeys."

The fog machines were set to full blast, and music of the old days pumped into the arena at max volume. Marisol had insisted. The light show impressed some audience members while piquing the interest of others. Mark's dancers finished their short yet eye-catching routine and he brought the mic up to his mouth.

"Ladies, gentlemen, and mutants alike, I've gotta tell ya... you are in for a once in a lifetime experience this evening."

The giant projector screens were filled with the image of two metal doors opening in the arena floor and a mysterious silhouette standing in the center of a rising platform. A hush came over the crowd as the slim figure stepped off the platform and it disappeared back into the depths of the arena. Strobe lights kicked on, making it even more impossible to decipher who this mystery character in the fog was that now wielded two swords in a graceful and acrobatic display of expertise.

"Geiger Lands!" Mark hollered as the lights began their slow return to normal and the fog began to dissipate, revealing a striking, raven-haired woman clad in all black.

"With a portfolio boasting a whopping seventy-three kills... that's right! I said seventy-three! I present to you, The Great Eviscerator's new best friend, the lady in black from across the Pacific, and deadlier than the poison she uses on the tips of her trusty blades...it's the assassin herself, Dahlia!"

The crowd went mad with a new kind of fervor, the kind you might expect at a sold-out rock concert. Until now, Dahlia had simply been legend, a mysterious myth from across the sea, and her reputation had eclipsed even far more accomplished killers. Her supermodel-good looks probably had more than a little to do with it. But now there she stood, in all her glory, in the *Try Not to Die* arena.

Something tumbled out of the stands and landed at Dahlia's feet. Mark jumped up, worried.

A grenade? He glanced over at the Producers, who he saw were riveted in their chairs.

But Dahlia dropped the tip of one of her swords to the ground and brought up a camera by the neck strap.

"Please," a young boy with earnest, shining eyes managed to shout over the rest, the owner of the camera presumably, "it's all I've ever wanted!"

A cryptic Mona Lisa smile crossed Dahlia's face. With a barely-there gesture she indicated for the crowd to give the little boy some space for him to come forward. Eyes wide like a Keane painting, the boy came as close as the metal cage would allow.

"Turn off the power," she said, as though ordering a cup of coffee.

A moment later, Jimmy acquiesced, and the electrified cage turned to just a cage. Gleefully, the boy thrust his face through the latticework. Dahlia adjusted the angle of the camera and pointed it at herself and tried to catch the boy as well. Mark shook his head. *How vain did you have to be to take a picture of yourself?* Well, someone as famous as Dahlia could get away with it, he supposed.

The flash went off and the boy got his wish. Mark hoped he didn't cream his pants. Dahlia held the camera out for the boy to take and his profuse, teary-eyed thanks were cut short by a blade sliding up through his chin and out the top of his skull. The crowd roared in delight as the boy toppled backwards, camera still clutched in his rictus hand. Dahlia flicked her wrist and rid her precious blade of excess blood as the electric field crackled back to life.

Mark swallowed a lump in his throat and forced himself to chuckle.

"Well, they do say be careful about what you wish for! Now, let's get this show on the road!"

Dahlia strutted forward, her long legs eating up the distance between her and the evil robot like it was only a few feet. The two killers circled each other warily, like apex predators meeting in the wild, Abe's programming obviously going into overdrive and Dahlia considering whether she had the expertise to kill a robot. They came to a silent détente and a buzzing sound indicated that their prey was on the loose again.

CHAPTER 11

Dawn and Tim were in an entirely new area of the maze now. It was darker, more difficult to navigate, and proved to be even more dangerous. With every corner they scrambled around there seemed to be some trap awaiting them: a swinging blade here, a pit of razor wire there, and almost everything seemed to be as electrified as the dome above them.

The sound of the frenzied crowd combined with Mark Winters's distasteful commentary made it nearly impossible to concentrate. To make matters worse, there were now two bloodthirsty psychopaths on the loose. One may have been a mindless machine that Dawn and Tim had managed to outwit in the previous round, but Dahlia was a trained, world-class assassin. Dawn had a feeling there would be no surviving this time.

They sprinted along and came to what was starting to become one of Dawn's least favorite things: a fork in the path.

"Which way?" she asked Tim.

He looked at her with a smirk. "Come on, does it really matter?"

They exchanged amused looks and decided on the better-lit corridor over the pitch black one, only to soon discover that sometimes the darker of the two paths, while shrouded in the unknown, is the better choice.

They weren't even halfway down the corridor when the walls began to close in around them.

"Get your ass moving, Tim!" Dawn shouted as she pumped her arms and picked up the pace.

She could hear the unmistakable sound of loud, pre-war hydraulics and knew Evil Abe waited for them up ahead, but she would rather take her chances with The Great Eviscerator than be remembered, as what she could only imagine Mark Winters would refer to as a Dawn Sandwich.

Tim was surprisingly fast, shoving Dawn along the quickly narrowing path. The moving walls screeched on both sides of them, reminding them death was imminent with every passing millisecond.

"Get *your* ass moving, Dawn!" Tim cried out, the walls now brushing his shoulders.

A menacing shadow was cast just beyond their exit and the mechanical laughter came within earshot. Dawn grimaced, both in response to the robot's presence and because the walls were now too close for comfort. If Tim hadn't been behind her, pushing her along, she wasn't sure that she'd have made it out alive.

She tumbled out of the deathtrap and landed on her back, grasping Tim's hand just in time. She braced both feet on the closing walls before her and pulled him forward with all her might. Tim flew from the closing pathway like a cork from a champagne bottle, tumbling past Dawn and nearly ripping her shoulder from its socket. Their knuckles white; they refused to let go of each other's hands until the ordeal was finally over.

They laid on the filthy ground panting, barely able to wrap their minds around having just escaped yet another booby-trap, but there was no time to catch their breaths. This was no rest area after all.

A shot rang out and Tim screamed in agony as a bullet tore through his arm, causing him to finally let go of Dawn's hand. He rolled on the ground out of harm's way as the robot fired again, this time missing.

"Hey!" Dawn yelled, trying to get the robot's attention, but he ignored her, his focus still on Tim.

She searched her surroundings for something that could be used as a weapon, but her heart sank when she realized there was nothing to be found. She took a deep breath and hopped to her feet, ready to charge The Great Eviscerator and buy Tim some time when an obnoxious sound filled her ears.

"Take that! Ya filthy son of a bitch!"

The sixty-something-year old woman leapt from the ground with grace and strength that Dawn had never seen in a woman her age before. In one swift motion, Granny had mounted the robot and begun pouring a foul-smelling liquid over its head.

"Yee-ha!" the old woman shouted as the robot bucked and seized, sparks flying.

"Four score...*boom*...*boom*...seven years...*boom*..." Evil Abe stuttered as its arms flew about and its legs gave out.

Granny somersaulted with ease from the robot's shoulders as The Great Eviscerator's head sparked one last time before bursting into flames and then finally exploding.

"Holy shit...I mean...would you look at that!" Mark Winters cried from the suspended platform above. "Looks like the only thing Honest Abe will be splitting from now on is his head!"

Dawn made a face and brought her hand up, covering her nose and mouth.

"What is that?" she asked, pointing to the now-empty cup lying beside the dead robot.

"It's my piss, what else you think?" She croaked out in a heavy smoker's voice, one quite common in the GL, and made her way to the smoking metal heap.

She wasted no time in collecting the robot's guns, handing a pistol to Dawn and helping Tim to his feet. Dawn halfway wanted to ask where the old woman had found a cup in the arena, or for that matter how she had found a spot to pee in front of this crowd of gaping morons, but decided ultimately it was best not to look a gift horse in the mouth.

"Come on', darlin', time to get movin'," she instructed Tim.

He winced and cried out in pain, and Dawn rushed to his side. She checked for an exit wound and sighed in relief.

"Let's keep moving, buddy. You're going to be fine." She placed a hand on his shoulder and gave him an encouraging smile before turning back to Granny. "Thanks."

"For what?" Granny asked, lighting a cigarette and leading the way.

"Uh...for saving our lives?"

Granny laughed, which caused her to hack. She spit out a mixture of phlegm and blood before replying.

"Oh, honey, I was just sick of that got'damn robot, just consider yourselves in the right place at the right time."

CHAPTER 12

Marisol's blood was boiling and her face was as scarlet as the cloak she wore. She extended the catwalk and marched up to Mark just as he finished his bit about the dead robot. She grabbed the mic from his hand, causing momentary feedback before she was able to switch it off.

"Dance!" she screamed at the bimbos on either side of him and they quickly obliged.

Mark's face was white as a sheet as he spun to meet her fiery eyes.

"Urine, Markus? Urine? Really? *That's* what destroys 'The Great Eviscerator'?" She made exaggerated air quotes and had to stop herself from slapping him across the face.

"I- I don't really know...I don't know what you'd like me to do. How was I supposed to know the old bat was saving up her piss?"

Marisol cradled her head in her hands and tried not to pace, she pinched the bridge of her nose and looked back at her fellow Producers; she could tell by the looks on their faces that they weren't anywhere near as enraged as she was, but Amy was motioning for her to come hither.

Mark watched as the vicious women exchanged words and cringed as Marisol nodded and then marched back up to him. She placed a delicate hand on his shoulder and leaned in close.

"We're going to let Charles out of his cage."

"Charles? What? But we just let out Dahlia!" Mark stammered.

Marisol gave him a look, one that warned him not to question her decisions again.

His face turned a light shade of pink.

"Um… of course, I mean, really? Charles?" He let out a nervous chuckle. "When?"

"Immediately."

"I mean, shouldn't I at least do my practiced introduction?"

Marisol had already begun to walk away, but she stopped and turned back to him, a smirk on her full, red lips.

"Charming Charlie doesn't need an introduction."

Tim was turning white. Dawn glance down at his wounded hand to see that the bandage was dripping blood, leaving behind a tiny crimson trail of breadcrumbs behind him. She took his hand and gently placed it in his pocket. He looked, first into her eyes, then back behind her, and understood. No sense in giving Dahlia an unfair advantage. She checked the bullet wound in his arm as well. That wasn't dripping behind him, but his shirt was soaked through.

"I keep trying to staunch the wounds, but…"

"You're a hemophiliac, aren't you?" Dawn asked him, narrowing her eyes.

"Does that mean I don't stop bleeding?"

She smiled and hoped he didn't take it as patronizing.

"Yes."

"Then yes. I'm a hemophiliac."

She pounded him on the back, she hoped not too hard, although considering how exhausted she felt, she doubted she could have hurt him if she tried.

"Well, my new pal," she said, "I have a feeling things are finally turning around for us. Somebody who knows what they're doing is finally in charge."

She stuck her nose in the direction of Granny, who sucked on a cigarette, leaving behind a trail of smoke. In retrospect, Tim's trail of blood was probably not what would tip the killers off to their location while a cloud of smoke constantly surrounded their savior.

"I don't think she knows what she's doing," Tim whispered, "I just think she's batshit. Then again, in a batshit world…"

"Truer words."

A gout of flame erupted from the floor at Granny's feet.

"Son of a bitch!" she cried out, dropping her cigarette. "Now, see what you made me do? Eyes open, you two!"

"We see it!" Tim replied.

"Here, now, be a gentleman, Mr. Flame Spouty Machine."

With nimble fingers, Granny snatched another cigarette from the pack rolled up in her shirtsleeve and triggered the fire fountain again, this time deliberately. With her head just out of range, a few of her gray hairs got singed, but the cigarette sparked up as well.

"See?" she said, turning back to Dawn and Tim, "You've just got to make the most of what you've got."

Granny started stomping off again, and Tim began to follow, but Dawn found herself rooted to the spot. Her mind was racing. She felt the way she had back in elementary school when she felt like she'd dawdled in the halls far too long and had missed the bus and it made her want to pee her pants. She couldn't stand here. The killers would be on them momentarily, but something was tickling the back of her head.

"What is it?" Tim asked, his voice gentle and childlike.

It struck her all at once, a bolt of lightning, a proverbial lightbulb dinging above her head. She reached down and grabbed a half-crushed can of beans out of the dirt of the arena floor. It had no doubt landed there earlier when the crowd had been pelting them with food.

"Make the most of what you've got!" she said, wagging her finger at him.

"Hey, hold up!" she called to the old woman, "Hang on just a minute!"

She grabbed Tim's hand out of his pocket, unwrapped it, and dragged him towards the fire spout. She knelt down with him.

"Okay, this is going to hurt. A lot. But then you'll stop bleeding. And if you don't you'll die."

Tim made a face, reluctant to thrust his hand into the open flame. "I know."

"You ready?"

Tim sucked on his lower lip, but he slowly nodded. Dawn shoved his hand forward and flinched as he screamed. Even she had to look away from what she was doing, but not for too long. When she looked back she saw the wound was cauterized. Tim was breathing heavily. She slapped him hard across the cheek.

"Don't go into shock. I know it hurts. You can't pass out here. I can't carry you."

"Okay!" He shouted. "I'm okay."

With another gout from the flamethrower she heated the can until the far end was practically glowing, and she could barely hold the near end. She remembered in the movies she watched as a child that it had always seemed to take forever for metal to glow like that. It was a testament to the heat of the flame, she supposed.

"Hold still," she said.

Tim nodded, pinching his eyes closed as she pressed the can to the entrance wound first and then the exit wound, searing the flesh of each side of his arm in turn. With the not-so-exact operation complete, she tossed the can off into the distance.

A shadow fell over them.

"Thanks for waiting, Granny," Dawn said. "Jeez, I'm sorry. What's your name? We really shouldn't keep calling you…"

But it was too late to ever find out. Dawn looked up to see Dahlia, elegantly balancing Granny's now severed head, a still-smoking cigarette clenched in her teeth, on the flat of one of her blades. She eyed up Tim and Dawn as though they were bugs.

With a single sharp snap of her wrist she sent Granny's head flying off into the distance. It passed through the cage with a zap and landed amongst the crowd, one of whom jumped up, yelling in joy to receive such a memento. The rest of the crowd booed at him, and he was confused as to why, until he saw the four-year-old girl standing next to him who had also been try-ing to catch the foul head. Reluctantly, but since he wasn't a bas-tard, the grown man flipped the head to the kid, which elicited a pleasant murmur of applause.

Dahlia lowered her blades towards Dawn and Tim. Dawn fumbled in her pocket and managed to pull out the pistol Granny had snagged from the dead automaton, but before she could even level it, Dahlia had swept it out of her hand with a flourish, her blade never touching anything but the steel of the gun.

Now with her victims disarmed, Dahlia decided to put on a show for the crowd. She turned to Tim.

"Bald's not usually my type, but you're kind of cute."

"Thanks?"

"Yeah. I could have some fun with you. So..." she glanced at Dawn and cocked her head. "I think I'll kill you first."

She rounded on Dawn and lifted both of her swords over her head, a pose that made her look like a heron with its wings up, or a scorpion about to strike. Then, suddenly, Dahlia went as limp as a ragdoll, her swords clattering to the ground.

A syringe had sprouted from her neck, full, no doubt, of some kind of fast-acting sedative. And the thumb on the trigger belonged to the man who was now resting his chin on the unconscious woman's shoulder.

"Now now now," the legendary "Charming" Charlie Whitmore said, clucking his tongue, "We mustn't be overzealous in performing our appointed rounds."

After one final shudder of defiance, Dahlia collapsed into his waiting embrace. He lowered her gently to the ground, and snagged one of her swords by the blade. Without even looking, he swung the sword in a perfect arc, the hilt cracking into Tim's skull and sending him tumbling, unconscious, to the ground.

He began to advance on Dawn, who found herself unable to find her feet, and began to scrabble away from him in an improvised sort of crabwalk. He took a hard step and slammed the sole of his loafer down on her toe, arresting her backward progress.

He knelt down, straddling her and clenching her arms to her sides. She rocked and flailed wildly, but despite his demure academic demeanor, Charming Charlie was frighteningly strong. Without seeming to take much notice of her struggles, he carefully prepared a second dose of the knockout liquid, and once he had squirted the first few drops from the tip to evacuate the air bubble, he snatched her chin with his free hand and turned it to the side while driving the needle deep into her jugular.

The last thing she felt before blackness took her was his tongue running the length of her face. And the last thing she heard was him whispering in her ear.

"No, we mustn't be overzealous. Ladies of such impeccable breeding as yourself are made to be savored after all."

Charles gently lifted the unconscious women from the ground, one in each arm, and hoisted them over his shoulders, their lithe frames draped like silk scarves. As he marched back to the center of the arena from whence he came, he glanced up at the platform that hung stories above his head. He could see, even from where he was, the look of shock on Marisol Martinez's face. He smiled wide and waved an elegant hand. Several women in the crowd, and some men, proclaimed their love for him and begged him to desecrate their bodies. They didn't call him Charming Charlie for nothing.

Charles knew the cameras were on him. It was odd to find himself plastered on the giant screens like that. He was looking forward to a more intimate setting with his new friends.

He looked up at Marisol once more as the loading platform he now stood on began to descend beneath the arena.

"You do know I hate to disappoint, my dear queen." Charles said to her, and he heard his mic'd voice echo around the arena. "Care to join us in my chambers?"

Satisfied by the infuriated look on her face, his smile widened and he gave one last wave to the crowd who loved him, before disappearing from sight.

"And now, a few words from our sponsors."

CHAPTER 13

Marisol gave Amy a hard slap across the face.

"What the hell was that for?" Amy protested, rubbing her cheek.

"For your bright idea! You see how well that worked out!" Marisol sighed, looking back and forth between The Producers. "This is why it's up to *me* to do *everything*."

"Sorry, dear." Derron apologized and looked down at his lap like a child.

"Up to you?" Jacob laughed. "Who the hell do you think bagged Dahlia? Do you even know how much I paid for that bitch? I had all sorts of fun planned for us after the show."

Jacob licked his lips and rubbed his greasy palms together and Amy took a step away from him.

"Well, you can thank Miss Green for this disaster."

Jacob turned toward Amy and winked. "Maybe you can swing by my place after." He reached out a plump finger, attempting to caress a lock of her dark hair but Amy pulled away. "You can wear all black, pretend to be Dahlia for me. You'd like that, wouldn't you?"

Amy quickly switched seats with Derron.

"Morons, all of you." Marisol threw her arms up and spun on her heels.

I need to hold things together, the queen thought, pacing, *I need to figure out how to spin this disaster into gold.*

The idea came to her suddenly and, with a smirk on her lips, she marched off into the wings, pressing her earpiece.

"Jimmy," she said. "We need cameras in the cages stat!"

"B-but ma'am—"

"Don't *but ma'am* me! We don't have a show if we don't get

down there! This was a snafu and I'm dealing with it. Now get someone with a camera into the goddamn cages or I'll send *you!"*

Mark was slumping in the chair in his dressing room, trying to figure out what the hell he was going to do when the commercial break was over, when he felt two hands drop onto his shoulders, startling him and causing him to spill his drink once more.

"Markus," Marisol sighed. "Give me a drink."

He spun his chair around and made a face. "What?"

"You heard me." she held her hand out. "Give me a drink."

Mark looked at his flask with sad eyes, there was barely enough to get him through the rest of the show and now he had to share with the queen.

Why doesn't she have her own damn liquor? he wondered, reluctantly passing her the flask.

To his dismay, Marisol knocked the flask back and finished off its contents. She discreetly wiped her mouth and closed her eyes for a moment, relishing the warmth of the liquor as it hit her stomach. She snapped her fingers and signaled for someone to fix her lipstick.

Mark snatched the flask back from her and turned it upside down, shaking it lightly, wishing that there was still something left inside. With a groan, he leaned back in his chair and spun around, once, twice, then a third time, finally stopping when the stagehand was finished reapplying Marisol's lipstick.

"This night..." Marisol shook her head. "This night is an absolute disaster."

Mark said nothing. He was secretly grateful.

All of the Selectees were dead. Charming Charlie had taken down a fellow killer, and one of the most dangerous ones at that. Never on the history of *Try Not to Die* had this happened, but he was thankful that it had.

One more round, he told himself. *One more round and you can go home, preferably with Camila or Wendy, or hell, maybe both, and this will all be behind you.*

Mark had every intention of retiring after tonight. It was

getting to be too much. He didn't think he could handle another episode.

Marisol clapped her hands together, snapping Mark from his thoughts.

"Alright, Markus, I need you at your best. Put your jacket back on and let's get back out there. If one thing can go right tonight, it's that you can keep the crowd engaged, even with the shit show we've got on our hands."

"Don't worry," Mark assured her. "I'm a final round kind of guy. I got this."

"Final round?" A crease formed in Marisol's brow. "Did you really think this was it?"

Mark's mouth hung open like a dead fish.

"Honey, we're going into the lion's den."

CHAPTER 14

Before Dawn even had the strength to open her eyes, a muffled yet delicate symphony invaded her consciousness. It was as if someone had stuffed cotton balls into her ears and yet as she heard the music more clearly with each passing second that the sedative began to wear off, it was comforting to hear such beautiful sounds after a night of such terror.

She wasn't even alert enough to remember her last conscious moments, to recall that the nightmare was far from over, or that it was merely beginning.

She heard soft singing from somewhere in the room and smelled something cooking, something sweet and savory all at once, and her stomach growled angrily at her. She felt warm hands on her legs now and she was finally able to open her eyes, but was still too tired to move. Through her blurred vision she could see a man standing at the foot of the hard table she lay on and confusion set in. Was he washing her legs? She realized she'd been stripped, dressed only in her bra and panties, and as she willed herself to move she soon found that she was strapped tightly to the table and so would be going nowhere. She managed to turn her head to the side and her vision began to clear, but what she saw only made her wish she hadn't regained her vision at all.

There was another table in the room with another woman strapped to it. Blood stained and oozed down the cloth she was laying on and only her torso needed to be strapped down; her arms and legs were gone. It was then that Dawn came to the realization that nobody had been singing in the room…Dahlia had been sobbing this entire time.

Dawn jumped, startled, as Charming Charlie Whitmore's face filled her entire field of vision.

"Awake, are we?"

Spastically, Dawn tried to escape her bonds. He chuckled, that light, airy laugh that had captured so many hearts before ripping them out.

"They use this to hold me down when I'm bad. And that one your friend's on when I'm good. Much as I do adore watching someone as...shapely as yourself resist, you ought to know it's not going to do you any good. And I should probably add...you might cause yourself to get cut unnecessarily."

He held up an open straight razor and Dawn froze, petrified.

"That's a good girl," he said, pulling the cold, dull side of the blade across her face.

She began hyperventilating as he traced a curvy Nile-like river down her neck and all the way down her torso before finally stopping in between her legs. Only a thin strip of fabric stood between her and rape. Somehow that didn't seem like Charlie's usual style, but who could predict the actions of such a madman?

Instead of feeling the razor cut through her panties, though, she felt it drag along her upper thigh. She glanced down. After washing her, he was now shaving her legs.

"I like to think of myself as cultured, but one thing I've always found rather off-putting about European women is their, shall we say, hygiene habits. In this one regard I far prefer the domestic vintage to anything abroad. Although you, Ms. Churchill, have been badly neglecting your lady garden. It's a bit like the Amazon down here."

She felt her face grow hot. Despite her dire circumstances, she was no less embarrassed, but she forced herself not to strain or try to escape. If she fought him and he cut her, whether by accident or a sense of revenge, she couldn't afford to start losing blood, not over something so petty. Her situation seemed hopeless, but the need to make what few right decisions she could asserted itself.

She deliberately slowed her breathing, both to stop from jumping around and to get her wits back about her.

"Where have you taken me?" she asked.

He gestured at the door, which, though hanging open,

clearly belonged to a cell. He started on her other leg.

"Welcome to my humble abode. This is where they keep me in storage when I'm not needed, the cages below the arena where the killers are kept. Paddocks for animals at the most basic, though they can be well appointed if one makes it worthwhile for them to do so. A gilded cage, they say, is still a cage, but it seems to me that, with apologies to the Bard, all the world's a cage. Certainly, in our current sociopolitical climate."

"What did you do with her arms and legs?"

"They're over there," he replied, not gesturing in any direction.

Dawn scanned the room and spotted a small kitchenette in the corner. It was surprisingly well-stocked with a virtual buffet of spices, fine cutlery, and cast-iron pans and implements, as well as all manner of obscure measuring and preparation tools. Four hooks dangled from the ceiling, each holding one of Dahlia's sensual, but quickly paling limbs. The jagged end of each limb pointed toward the ground, where blood was dripping into a tray Dawn had to assume was expressly for the purpose of collecting blood from fresh meat based on the whole rest of the setup. But for some reason the dangling limbs didn't strike Dawn as the strangest thing about it all.

"They let you cook?"

He chuckled as he lingered overlong on shaving around her bikini area.

"Some monsters need whips and chains to stay in line. Other monsters are easier to keep satisfied. I'm a bit of a gourmand. A few classic volumes of Proust and a bottle of Chateau Lafite now and then and I'm happy to linger here. Oops."

Despite her attempts to keep still and the apparent care of his ministrations, Charlie had still managed to nick her soft skin. He reached down, his eyes wide like a moth drawn to a flame, and caught the single drop of blood on the tip of his pinky. He suckled at his fingertip and then threw his head back in rapturous joy, as though it were more delicious than whatever crazy vintage of French wine he had been talking about earlier.

"What do you want from me?" she asked.

"Just a bit of company for a meal. You must be famished, after all."

"I'm *not* hungry," she said flatly.

He let his lower lip quiver like a child's as he grabbed a copper-colored pan from his collection.

"The lady doth protest too much, methinks. Certainly, you're surrounded by a veritable cornucopia of grotesqueries, and that's enough to put most folks off their appetites, but you're of hearty Geiger Land stock. When was the last time a bite of food even crossed your lips?"

Food. She thought back to the meal that had been served to her before she was thrown into the arena, countless hours of running and fighting ago. Her treacherous stomach rumbled to remind her just how hungry she actually was.

"I thought as much," he said after she didn't respond.

He rounded Dahlia's gurney.

"Bastard," the assassin whispered, unable to stop the flow of tears, "I'll kill you."

He patted her gently on the side of the head.

"Now, now," he said, "You wouldn't harm an unarmed man, would you?"

Bucking her torso, she spat at his face and it struck surprisingly true. His expression unchanging, Charles reached up and wiped a particularly thick nugget of mucus away from his forehead.

"Let me grab a bottle of wine. I think I may get legless tonight."

Humming some classical music Dawn didn't recognize, Charlie returned to the kitchenette and pulled the cork out of a half-empty bottle of red wine and took a swig. He poured some of the wine, along with some olive oil and some pepper and oregano, into the copper pan before returning to Dahlia's table. He grabbed her by the breast to hold her as still as her wild bucking would allow and began to carve into her with an electric carving knife with an astonishing, almost surgical precision. Dahlia's wild, increasingly panicked shrieks of pain rose to a crescendo.

Finally, his face spattered with blood, he reached into her

newly cut orifice to retrieve his prize. Dawn wasn't a doctor, but she recognized a liver when she saw one. He dropped it in the pan and returned to humming his favorite aria over Dahlia's muffled, dying sobs as he began to fry up her liver.

A clattering outside the cell made Dawn suddenly turn away from the kitchenette and stare feverishly outside.

"What's that?" She asked with alarm.

Charming Charlie didn't look back as he answered, all his attention focused on crafting a perfect meal for himself and, it had been hinted, Dawn.

"That'll be the camera crew that the queen sent down here. Such a voyeuristic society we live in. I'd wager they had quite a time finding the place."

CHAPTER 15

"Oh, you owe me big time, Jimmy, you prick," Cameraman 1 muttered as he descended the cement steps that led to the bowels of the arena.

"Yeah, and then *you* owe *me*." Cameraman 2 reminded him, making a face and then mimicking his companion. "'*Oh, Jimmy, we'll get better coverage from multiple angles, I'm gonna need a hand down there.'* Ya big pussy, had to drag me into this because you're too scared to come down here by yourself."

"Am not!" Cameraman 1 protested. "I- I just care about the production quality of the show...ya know? I'm not trying to stay in this position forever."

Cameraman 2 rolled his eyes, unconvinced. "Yeah, yeah, whatever."

They continued their trek down another set of stairs before hitting the sublevel. An armed guard stood waiting by a heavy set of metal doors and nodded a greeting. He beat twice on the door with his fist and a loud click announced the doors had been unlocked. The guard pulled one of the doors open and ushered the cameramen through.

"Wait a minute, you're not coming with us?" Cameraman 2 asked, his eyes wide.

The door slammed in his face and a second armed guard grabbed his wrist and pulled upward. He shoved something into his hand.

"Key to the cells."

"Uh...and why exactly do we need those?"

"You're supposed to be up close and catching the action, what do you think?"

Cameraman 2 stared down at the dirty key in his shaking hand.

The guard gave him a hard shove.

"Best of luck, now get moving." He raised a rifle and motioned for them to move forward.

"B-but we don't...." Cameraman 1 looked at his companion and then back to the guard. "We don't have any weapons! You have to come with us!"

"I said *move it!*" The guard barked and both cameramen jumped.

They quickly departed down the hall, palms sweating, nearly dropping their equipment. As they were about to turn a corner, the guard called out to them.

"Hey!"

Both men turned in unison, confusion and fear plastered on their faces.

"Try not to die!"

"Seriously?" Cameraman 1 squeaked out.

The guard chuckled. "Sorry, I've always wanted to say that."

Cameraman 2 sighed and gave his buddy a nudge, urging him to continue.

As they moved down the damp hall, the lighting began to deteriorate and the men, scared as they might have been, knew they had a job to do.

"Camera 1, lights on."

Cameraman 2 sounded off in turn and soon enough Jimmy's voice crackled through their earpieces.

"How we doin' down there, fellas?"

"This is Camera 2, fuck you, Jimmy."

There was a brief pause. *"Good, glad to hear it. Let's keep the talking to a necessary minimum and remember, watch the language, boys. We've got kids watching."*

The camera crew crept forward, aware now that they were entering uncharted territory. Never before in the history of the show had a crewmember ventured beneath the arena. Even the guards assigned down here fought tooth and nail to get out of the assignment. Sending cameras into the cells had never been warranted, but this episode was really turning out to be something for the history books. Shrieks of laughter, whistles, and cat-calls floated to the men's ears as they passed by rows of cells containing some of the deadliest and most vicious killers known to man. How The Producers had acquired such a collection, no one would ever know, but it didn't really matter...it was a collection unrivaled.

The camera panned left and the light fell upon a young woman, no older than eighteen. Her blonde hair was up in pig tails, stained with what one could only presume to be blood.

"Hey, sugar." She whispered, smiling from ear to ear, revealing a razor-sharp set of shiny, filed teeth. She grabbed onto the cage with her equally revolting fingernails, filed to a piercing point and filthy as the day was long.

Cameraman 2 recoiled and returned his attention to the task at hand: find Charming Charlie.

As they continued down the hall, breathing through their mouths to avoid the foul stench of the wretched place, they passed by all sorts of human atrocities, letting the camera linger only for a few moments on each one as Jimmy informed them through the earpiece, *"the crowd is fucking loving this!"*

The cameramen realized there were many run of the mill copycat killers: several gimps howled and humped their cages; a few animatronic murderers sat dormant, only their lifeless eyes glowing in the dark; chainsaws filled the air with noise as some of the killers challenged each other from within their cells.

They'd nearly reached the end of the hall when they noticed a significant change in atmosphere: the lighting was better, the smell was almost mouthwatering, and instead of the shrieks and taunts of dozens of mass murderers, their ears were greeted by the sweet sounds of soothing, classical music.

The cameramen stopped dead in their tracks when they realized, to their surprise, Charming Charlie's cell door was wide open.

"You go first," Cameraman 2 said.

"No way," Cameraman 1 responded. He opened his mouth to complain, but was interrupted by some sort of mechanical whirr, followed by tortured, bloodcurdling screams.

"Yeah, you're definitely going first." Cameraman 2 said, pushing his coworker forward.

"You guys are killin' me here! You're missing all that sweet action!" Jimmy's voice crackled through. *"If we just missed Charming Charlie killing Dahlia you guys are fuckin' toast."*

Cameraman 2 groaned, deciding against firing back at Jimmy. He took a few steps forward but didn't make it past the next cell. A hand shot out and grabbed him by his shirt, pulling him up hard against the cool metal. His camera clattered to the ground and his unidentified attacker reached their other hand out and placed it over his mouth, muffling his cries for help.

"Gracias," a voice whispered from behind him, and the hand gripping his shirt moved swiftly to his neck, dragging a scalpel artfully across.

The cameraman began to choke on his own blood, his hands flailing wildly, attempting to grasp at his open throat, but he was losing blood so quickly he was too disoriented. His attacker let go when his body began to go limp and in his dying moments he felt hands all over his body; they felt his pant legs, patted his sides, and dug into his pockets.

Finally, the attacker had found what he was searching for, pulling the cell key from the cameraman's right front pocket.

"Buena suerte…" the killer said, admiring the key in his hand with a smile. "I am lucky not to have to kill both of you."

Cameraman 2 looked up at his attacker through tearful eyes, he could see him now, dressed in dingy medical scrubs, a surgical mask covering his nose and mouth.

The man knelt down once more and reached back through the cage, placing his hand over Cameraman 2's eyes.

"You sleep now."

Cameraman 1 had simply assumed his clumsy coworker had tripped and dropped his camera; hearing nothing else out of the ordinary, he'd continued on toward Charming Charlie's cell. When he spotted Dahlia, limbless and dying on the tabletop, his stomach turned and his vision blurred. He spun on his heels to have Cameraman 2 take over, but froze in place when he realized his fellow crewmember was lifeless lump a mere fifteen feet from him.

Whoever had killed him had done it with silent expertise. Jimmy squawked angry words through the earpiece that the cameraman couldn't comprehend in his shock. His eyes darted back and forth between Charlie's cell of horrors and the deadly mysteries behind him. He felt a wave of panic come over him and fought the bile creeping up his throat.

"It seems we have a guest," Charlie said, tending to the meat before him.

Cameraman 1, startled, turned back toward Charlie's cell, his mouth open, but unable to speak.

Charlie waved the man in.

"Don't worry, young man. I've got enough on my plate as it is." He chuckled to himself, closing his eyes for a moment before checking his expensive wristwatch. "Besides, I wouldn't tarry for long out there, it's almost time for the doctor's dinner."

CHAPTER 16

Dawn wanted to shout a word of warning to the skinny little boy with the camera rig, but it was already too late. A shadowy figure was behind him and as he whirled around, the lumpy pile shoved the cameraman into the cell and to the concrete floor, falling on his tailbone.

As the boy hissed in pain the shadow figure—Charles had called him a doctor—limped into view. He carried a corpse, slung like a sack of potatoes over his left shoulder.

"Ms. Churchill, may I present Dr. Feelbad, my next-door neighbor in this…delightful domicile. Young man, if you're not going to do a creditable job of recording these proceedings, I'm going to feel obliged to do so myself."

The cameraman looked like he was watching a tennis match as his eyes darted back and forth from the charming cannibal at the stove to the hulking surgeon blocking the door. If Dawn had to guess, it seemed like someone was shouting at him in his earpiece, because he kept nodding and finally raised the camera and attempted to bring himself to his feet.

"Much better. You know, Doctor, it occurs to me I have no idea what your real name is. Is there something you'd prefer to be called? We are on live television, you know."

Doctor Feelbad shrugged and unslung the dead cameraman from his shoulder, dropping him onto a crushed leather couch. The blood still bubbling out of the dead man's corpse didn't seem to bother Charlie, who, although his tastes were refined, did not seem to be fastidious about his surroundings.

Cameraman 1 scrambled out of the doctor's way as he walked over to the table that bore the somehow still-living Dahlia. He took her face by the chin, turned her head left and right, then shone a pocket light into each of her eyes.

"Get your fucking hands off of me!" Dahlia hissed.

Feelbad didn't react.

"*¿Anestesia?*"

"What, on her?" Charlie asked. "No, of course not."

The doctor gave an impressed grunt and then slunk south-ward, prodding and poking at the gaping hole in her torso.

"Impressed she's still alive, I take it? I know I'm not a profes-sional like yourself, but I do have a lot of practice. And I like to think of myself as an artist."

Charlie turned deliberately to flash his winning smile at the camera. It was an applause line. This was all a big show to him. Charlie turned the heat down on the frying liver and joined the doctor beside Dahlia's deathbed.

"See anything you like?"

The doctor shrugged. "It is good work."

Charlie wrapped his arm jovially around Feelbad's shoulders.

"Oh, no, no, my dear boy, I mean do you see any particular cut you'd like? Guests are treated like kings in my cell."

"Are they?" Dawn regretted saying it as soon as the words left her lips.

Charlie's dark gaze fell on her.

"Welcome guests, yes."

Doctor Feelbad clapped Charlie on the shoulder heavily a few times.

"*Comer, comer, por favor.* Eat without me. I just take a look."

"Suit yourself." Charlie said with a bit of a constipated tone. "Don't say I didn't offer you anything."

The doctor nodded and continued poking and prodding at Dahlia's wounds. Then Charlie turned his full attention to Dawn. He walked over to her, a serving knife and a long honing steel in his hands. He ran the knife repeatedly against the steel.

"What about you, Ms. Churchill? Since you're so concerned with how I treat people in my own home, would you care to join me for supper?"

She stared into his face. Her plan, such as it was, to regain her composure and try to work out how best to move forward had essentially worked. What she had picked up was that Charles Whitmore was obsessed with appearances. It was the tawdry blend of seeming civility and Neanderthal violence that made him so popular. But he was essentially playing the part of the elegant gentleman sociopath.

Survival, and staying intact, meant playing along. If she played her part in his little game—assuming that part didn't mean immediate dismemberment as it had for Dahlia, who presumably had presented a true threat to him had she gotten loose—she might survive for long enough to find an opening for her escape.

"Is that a sincere offer?" she asked.

Charlie perked up. "Of course."

So, she was playing her part correctly.

"I'd be happy to join you," she said, "but if you don't mind, I'm not hungry."

"Oh, but I insist! I certainly understand if this fare isn't to your liking. Not everyone prefers pâté. At least have some wine and cheese."

After a moment's hesitation, she agreed.

"All right."

"Well, that's fine. That'll be some fine entertainment. I'll set you a place."

He began to walk away, but stopped and placed his hand in his chin. He turned back to Dawn.

"Tell me, which is your dominant hand?"

"What?"

He smiled.

"Are you a rightie or a leftie?"

Dawn paused, wondering if this was a trick. Then again, he had her completely over a barrel, and could do whatever he wanted to her regardless. Obviously, she was taking too long.

"It's not a difficult question, is it?"

"No," she agreed, "But I do question your motives in asking it."

He laughed lightly.

"Nothing so sinister as all that. I just need to know for the place settings, my dear."

It would be just like Charming Charlie to worry about something like that, but something about it still didn't sit right with her. She supposed if she had to use a right-handed salad fork or whatever she'd find a way to make do. Southpaws always had to be effectively ambidextrous anyway.

"I'm right-handed," she lied.

Charlie nodded at the information and returned to the kitchenette and began slicing the liver and pulling out some fancy cheeses and crackers, toting it all over to his dining table along with dishes and all the appropriate cutlery.

Dahlia's tone had changed considerably.

"Will you just kill me?" she begged miserably.

The doctor looked up from his fiddling with her organs and glanced at Charlie.

"Oh, no. No no no." Charlie shook his head. "I'm quite content with her as she is."

Doctor Feelbad turned back to Dahlia. "He is the boss."

With a cheese knife in hand, Charlie approached Dawn's slab and cut first one bond, then the other, leaving her free but with the leather cuffs still around her wrists. He helped Dawn to sit up.

"Dahlia's always been rather uncouth to me, as I recall. You see, Ms. Churchill, there is a difference between the way I treat a lady of culture and substance and the way I treat a Philistine."

"I can see that," she agreed, deliberately forcing herself not to shudder in his embrace.

"Yes, a difference, but not much of one."

Dawn shrieked in pain as she felt the double prongs of the cheese knife slip into her flesh, perfectly couching in the socket of her right elbow. With a vicious backward yank, Whitmore sliced through tendon and flesh, almost entirely severing her forearm from the rest of her body. She was shocked that he was capable of doing that with such a tiny instrument. He was an "artist" indeed, though she was having trouble recognizing the beauty of it as it was happening to her. He jammed the knife back into the hole he had made and, with no more than a flick of the wrist, popped the forearm out of the socket and let it drop to the ground completely.

"The right tool for the right job," he whispered in her ear.

The Doctor threw his hands up, almost like an act of defeat and sat at the table, pushing aside the place Charlie had set for him. He began protesting in Spanish, almost as if he were scolding Charlie, motioning to the arm on the floor and the wound spurting blood from where the arm was removed. Dawn cried in agony and the cameraman retched in the corner while attempting to keep the gruesome scene in focus.

"Doc, while you know I absolutely adore your company, I simply cannot understand a word you're saying." Charming Charlie called over his shoulder while he fashioned a tourniquet to staunch the bleeding. He ran a hand over Dawn's head, giving her a gentle caress. "Now, now, you'll be just fine, but you must understand I don't appreciate being lied to. It was time to teach you a lesson."

"Why the arm? How will she eat now?" The Doctor asked, still appearing annoyed with Charming Charlie's decision.

Charlie turned to his friend. "She's a liar!"

He searched his brain for the right word.

"*Mentirosa.*" He pointed at Dawn and then to her right arm on the ground before lifting her left arm. He waved it at the doctor. "She'll be able to eat just fine."

"Ah, *si*, okay." Doc nodded and stood up, approaching the table Dawn still sat upon. "*Dejame ayuda.*"

"No, don't be silly," Charlie waved him off. "Please, sit. Pour yourself a glass of wine, you deserve it. After all this time, here you are, a long-awaited guest in my home. It's nonsense to think I'd have you working."

Doc considered it and then nodded, obliging. He returned to his seat and poured himself a generous helping of wine, bringing it up to his nose and inhaling deeply. Charlie smiled in kind, taking great pleasure in watching the doctor imbibe.

Dawn was on the verge of passing out, but Charlie kept her upright.

"Now, you see, you have no choice but to eat. Your body needs the protein."

Dawn slumped over again, Dahlia coming into view. How the woman was still alive was beyond her comprehension, but there she lay, moaning in misery. Dawn couldn't help but wish she had the energy to get up and kill the woman herself. No one should have to suffer like that, even a cold-blooded assassin like Dahlia.

Charlie took notice of her concern and chuckled.

"It appears you're feeling what... sympathy for the devil?" He raised an eyebrow and looked at Dawn almost like a father would look at a child he was disappointed in.

"You've got an arm off and you find yourself slowly coming to the realization that you will be a part of my main course in more ways than one and yet..." he paused, caressing her again, and clucked his tongue. "Dahlia is an imposter of the craft. She may be graceful and have quite the exterior, but she is no better than the robot your elderly friend so tastelessly dispatched. She takes no pleasure in the art she practices, there is no mindfulness about what she does. She is simply a machine, in her own way, and I possess no adoration for someone so savage."

Dawn's head spun and her face began to grow pale. Charlie continued to speak, about what Dawn couldn't be sure, but it was probably more about his dislike of Dahlia. She felt herself beginning to fade. Her eyes moved to the cameraman who had found his second wind and was keeping the footage rolling, and then her gaze fell upon the quiet doctor, sitting at the table by himself, sipping wine and observing the scene before him. His eyes met hers and he narrowed them, a crease forming in his brow as he cocked his head.

"She will pass out." Doc said, interrupting Charlie's mind-numbing monologue.

Charming Charlie looked to his friend with a smile and nodded, laying Dawn back on the table.

"You're the expert, Doctor. You know better than I." He crouched for a moment and retrieved Dawn's severed forearm from the floor. "Let's trade places then, shall we? I'll tend to my meats, while you tend to the patient."

Charlie returned to his kitchenette, humming softly to himself, every now and again giving commentary to the cameraman, describing what he was doing as if he were hosting his very own cooking show. The doctor inspected Dawn's wound. Luckily the amputation was done with such precision he could actually salvage what remained of her arm. He wondered if the work he would put into the sutures would be worth it if his neighbor's intentions were to serve her up to the same fate as the other unfortunate woman in the room.

The doctor sighed. He admired Dawn. She'd made it incredibly far in this game.

The ridiculous show The Producers and everyone else upstairs put on month after month was a display of fatuity he did not enjoy. It was rare that he was chosen as one of the participating killers, and when he was, he couldn't lie, he enjoyed the game for what it was; letting off steam after weeks or months of lying dormant in a cell with a long-winded cannibal as his only friend. But he didn't enjoy the spectacle of it all. He wasn't truly enjoying himself; his heart wasn't in it.

Though he pretended not to understand Charming Charlie most days, he knew more English than he let on, and his friend made perfect sense when he spoke of his disenchantment with those who didn't enjoy the art of killing and simply committed murder for the sake of murder. Perhaps that was why the two had bonded. They were both intelligent, educated men in their old lives outside these cages. The doctor knew that he wasn't happy in this prison cell, and even when they let him out to play, that wasn't nearly satisfying enough.

Doctor Feelbad found himself, as he tended to Dawn's wound, wanting more. He imagined himself back out in the Geiger Lands, collecting his patients and performing his surgeries. He truly wanted to help those with misfortune; the mutants, the dying, the deformed...he was a doctor, after all. Sure, some of his patients protested and didn't see the good he was doing them, but those that refused or went as far as to force his hand always had a place in his body farm. He smiled as he remembered life out in the GL. Once upon a time the doctor was a good man, and then the war came, and madness with it.

"Why are you smiling?" Dawn asked, the pain in her voice obvious.

"I miss my old life."

Dawn managed to nod. "Me too."

He asked her something in Spanish and realized she couldn't understand him.

"What would you do? If you could leave?" He repeated himself in English.

"I would help my friend Tim out of the maze upstairs. I would find a way up to that platform, I'd climb that god damn tower if I had to...but I'd get there. I'd make sure each and every one of those monsters never did this to another human being. I'd put a bullet right between each of their eyes and I'd shove that despicable bitch right off that platform and watch her skull crack open on the arena floor."

The doctor's eyes went wide and he grinned, he admired Dawn even more now. The girl's eyes were flashing, conflicted, like she didn't want to think of herself as a murderer and yet couldn't deny the impulse all the same.

"This *puta* you speak of, who is she?" Doc asked, an eyebrow raised.

"Marisol Martinez," Dawn answered, as though speaking the name left a bad taste in her mouth.

A loud clatter startled the two and they turned their attention to Charming Charlie who had dropped several pieces of flatware along with some pans to the filthy ground at the mention of the queen's name.

Doc laughed, quietly at first, but could barely contain himself as he watched Charlie silently seethe in the corner.

He turned back to Dawn, wiping tears of laughter from his eyes.

"Uh oh," he warned, "you said the magic words."

CHAPTER 17

"I don't get it," the cameraman said, and instantly he realized he had been so distracted by the drama unfolding in the room he had forgotten just how precarious his situation was.

Charlie whirled on him; his full, laser-like attention now fixed on the boy. He approached, but he was also approaching the camera, and Dawn could imagine his leering visage growing larger and larger on the screens in the arena above.

"What's your name again, boy?"

The cameraman's lower lip quivered, but he seemed to be having trouble saying it, or else didn't want to invoke his own name in the manner of an old superstition.

"Nevermind. I don't care, and neither does anybody else. But the Queen of Texas…now, that's someone I *do* care about."

Charlie grabbed ahold of the camera and practically shoved his face into the lens.

"You hear me up there, Marisol? I admire you for putting this all together. No one's fooled, you know. You make a big show of equality among The Producers, to spread out the blame in case your backs ever get put against the wall I would imagine, but we all know this whole business was your idea and you roped your three semi-literate comrades into it."

His work done, Doctor Feelbad helped Dawn to sit up. Dahlia's sweetmeats were burning on the stove, which didn't seem like Charlie's style at all.

"What's his issue?"

"*No lo sé.* He always gets like this when someone brings up the queen, though."

"It all started with you and me, didn't it, Marisol? The only woman who ever bested me in the wild. And then you locked me up. No cops, no doctors, no nothing. Just this wacky idea of yours. Your entire fortune is built on my back, Marisol, make no mistake. Have you already cut away? Is it already a commercial? Sanitized pap for the mindless masses? I know *you're* still watching, though, aren't you?"

Charlie snatched the camera out of the young boy's hands, with a skill that suggested he could have been a ninja.

"Let me show you. Let me show what I'm going to do to you, Marisol." He turned. "You. Boy."

The cameraman froze like a rabbit in the headlights.

"Me?"

"Yes. Grab that cheese grater over there. And would you turn off the stove? I think my meal is done."

Hesitant, the cameraman walked over to the kitchenette, careful never to turn his back on Charlie. Charlie raised the camera to his shoulder and followed along. The boy turned off the stove and then took a bell-shaped cheese grater from a nail on the wall. He offered it tentatively to Charlie.

"Oh, no. Not me. I'm just a passive observer. I'm just carrying the camera. I bear no responsibility for what goes on. I have no control over what I record. *You're* Charming Charlie Whitmore, and you're about to show Queen Marisol exactly what you're going to do to her when...not if...you get her in your clutches."

"I...I don't..."

The cameraman looked lost. Charlie took a step forward.

"The name of the game is *Try Not to Die*. You don't seem like you're trying with all your might not to invite the wrath of a serial killer down on you. It's funny, isn't it, how a simple flip of perspective can change you from an innocent bystander to a willing participant so quickly. Now, what do you think Charming Charlie is going to do to Marisol?"

Charlie gestured at Dahlia, still breathing, still sobbing, beyond all hope of ever being whole again. The cameraman tentatively stepped over and loomed over the woman's body.

"He would grate her some cheese?"

"Try again."

"He would...just...grate her?"

"He would grate her some head cheese. Have you ever had head cheese, young man?"

The cameraman shook his head.

"Well, it's actually not a cheese at all, but I think you're about to find that out. Are you watching, Marisol? I know you are. I know you're too vain not to. And too vain to come down here personally and deal with me. Do it, boy! Now!"

The cameraman swallowed a lump in his throat and took the cowbell-shaped instrument in his hands.

"I'm sorry," he said to Dahlia, "I have no choice."

"You have a choice," she replied, "You choose to be weak."

Turning his head away so he didn't have to look, he brought the cheese grater down and just barely cut into Dahlia's cheek, leaving half a dozen tiny, scoop-like cuts that barely broke the skin.

"Don't look away!" Charlie shouted, circling around the side of the table, "You think Charming Charlie Whitmore looks away from his victims? He looks them in the eyes even as he's gouging them out. Now press harder! And pay attention to what you're doing!"

Unable to hold back the tears now, the cameraman looked down at Dahlia, a killer, and yet reduced to a pathetic rubble of humanity. He sliced again, this time against the grain, and drew blood. Then he ran forward again, gouging great chunks out of her cheek. Then again and again, he sliced away long troughs in Dahlia's face as she screamed, cutting into soft bone and eye. By the time thirty seconds was up, he too was sobbing as he wildly swept back and forth, sending chunks of human face splattering all over the small cell.

"This is what I'm going to do to you, Marisol! I dream of it every night! I wake up to visions of it every morning!"

Dahlia was long dead, but it only ended when Charlie turned off the camera and slapped his hand down on the boy's shoulder.

"That's enough. She's gone now. The camera's not rolling anymore. You did well, young man."

The boy dropped to his knees, chest heaving.

"Is it all right if I keep this?" Charlie asked, patting the side of the camera.

The cameraman nodded.

"All right. Good man. You acquitted yourself well."

"Does that mean I can go?"

"If you like. Although I don't think you'll get very far without your legs working."

The boy looked down.

"My legs are fine."

Charlie crouched down and took a look.

"Oh. My mistake."

He slipped a paring knife through the boy's spine, severing the cord at about kidney-level.

"Now they're not, but do still feel free to try and run. That might be fun to watch."

Charlie stood and turned back to Dawn and the doctor as the cameraman's yowls of pain filled the room.

"Now, I feel like I have been neglecting my guests."

"I can get you Marisol Martinez!" Dawn blurted out.

Charlie cocked his head. She was breathing heavily, and blood loss was preventing her from thinking entirely clearly, but she still thought she could see a way out of the wilderness.

"Can you now?" he asked darkly.

CHAPTER 18

"What fresh hell is this?" Marisol screeched through clenched teeth.

Her voice was beginning to grate on Mark's nerves. There'd never been a show where she would just leave him alone and let him work. The crowd was eating up every second of the footage, screams of excitement could be heard all around the arena, even louder now that Charming Charlie had gotten hold of the camera.

The sociopath was rambling on about the queen, making accusations and empty threats. Mark took a peek back at Marisol's cohorts and found them unamused. The other Producers looked more bored than offended by Charlie's speech. They knew Marisol usually received, and accepted with open arms, the credit for anything related to *Try Not to Die.*

Mark continued to overact in response to the things Charlie was saying, really hamming it up. It was only when the cameraman had taken a cheese grater to Dahlia's face that he wasn't sure he'd be able to keep up the act for much longer. The audience jumped to their feet, whooping and hollering as Dahlia's gut-wrenching screams pierced every eardrum in the arena. Mark couldn't peel his eyes from the screen. Specks of blood decorated the camera lens and Charlie's narrative during the grisly act was only fueling the crowd's fire.

"They love him," Marisol said, her fists balled up at her side.

"I thought that was the point," Mark replied into the earpiece.

The crowd erupted in applause when the cameraman had finally completed the task at hand and the footage stopped rolling.

"You saw it here first, folks!" Mark shouted. "Dahlia has been bested by Charming Charlie himself!"

The off-screen announcer's voice transitioned everyone into the next commercial break and Mark turned around, exhaling loudly, his stomach in knots. The Producers seemed to be fighting amongst themselves so he made an executive decision to slink back to his dressing room before any of them could notice.

"Who does he think he is? *Nobody* insults me like that! *Nobody* threatens me!" Marisol shouted at her husband. "I made him into the celebrity that he is today! He'd be nothing but another loser roaming the GL peddling tainted meat if it wasn't for me!"

Derron cringed. She was screaming into his ear.

"Are you even listening to me?"

Derron nodded so hard his head looked as if it might snap off. "Oh, yes, dear. You're absolutely right."

"So, what's the plan now?" Jacob asked through a mouthful of food, a piece of greasy chicken flying from his mouth and just missing Marisol's face.

She glared at him and he grabbed a napkin.

"We're going to have to keep improvising." Amy chimed in. "Who do we have on staff that's expendable?"

It had happened a few times before when the killers had disposed of the contestants too early on in the game. Random staff members were selected to fill in for the contestants if need be. Most of them were happy to oblige while others simply said nothing, knowing that any word of protest would result in a fate worse than death.

The lull in the crowd suddenly came to an end, surprising everyone on the platform.

"What am I missing?" Marisol asked, still seated, her head in her hand. "Did one of our sponsors start murdering people in their commercials?" She motioned to the crowd. "These morons will clap for anything that dies."

"No," Amy said, rising from her seat and peering down into the arena. A grin spread across her face and she hopped up and down, pointing. "We've got a live one! The cue ball is still alive!"

Marisol rushed over to Amy's side and raised her eyebrows.

The disoriented Tim had finally woken up from the blow to his head. Everyone had assumed him dead from the amount of time he'd lain dormant. He looked around, confused.

"This is good," Marisol said, patting Amy on the shoulder before heading off stage to find Mark, she tapped the earpiece.

"Jimmy, send out a few of your most useless staff. We've got a show to put on, I doubt this cue ball will last much longer on his own. Let's make it exciting."

"10-4. Which killer am I releasing from the Barn?"

"I'm not picky, just remember... *exciting*, this needs to be exciting."

CHAPTER 19

Charming Charlie sat at his dinner table glaring down at the overcooked food before him.

"Why don't you cook something else?" Doc pointed at the other hanging limbs.

Charlie frowned and pushed his plate away. "Suddenly, I'm not quite as famished as I thought I was."

He turned his attention back to Dawn, who lay on the table with her eyes closed. She wasn't asleep, but Doctor Feelbad had convinced him she needed a few minutes of rest when Charlie had begun to fire off question after question about how she planned to deliver Marisol Martinez into his hands. He tapped his fingers on the wooden table, growing bored.

"How long are we giving her? Need I remind you we don't have time on our side?"

"What is her name?" Doc asked.

"Dawn Churchill." Charlie responded flatly.

"Dawn," Doc said softly, giving her a light squeeze on her good arm. "Time to get up."

Dawn's eyes popped open and she took the doctor's hand, allowing him to help her into a comfortable sitting position.

"Ms. Churchill," Charlie started, rising from his seat and slowly approaching. "I am by nature a patient man, but that is not the same thing as being a fool, or one to easily suffer these delaying tactics."

Dawn struggled to keep from rolling her eyes, she'd finally come up with what she believed was a solid plan and didn't want to ruin it by displeasing her host.

"Well, first, I'm going to need help getting back up there."

"Consider it done." Charlie folded his arms over his chest.

"Okay, well, I'll need some weapons. It'll make it easier to blast my way through any obstacles I might come across." She looked down at where her right arm once was. "Preferably one I can handle with only one hand...considering my handicap."

"*Si, bueno.*" Doctor Feelbad nodded. "I can handle that."

"What else?" Charlie asked.

"I know there's an elevator that takes The Producers and the other staff up to the platform. I just need to get access to it and I'm sure I can make it there. Once I'm up, it'll be easy to dispose of the fat one, the queen's husband seems weak—"

"Yes, he is quite a poor excuse for a man." Charlie interrupted. "It's beyond me why she chose to wed someone so wholly inadequate. Then again, perhaps it's my own fault for putting the fear of competent masculinity into her."

The doctor gave him a sideways glance and shook his head.

"However," Charlie continued, "Miss Green is truly a force to be reckoned with. She's a gunrunner and firearms expert, which means you can expect to be dealing with a crack shot who will be armed to the teeth. Between her and Marisol's goons you'd practically need an army to get from here to there."

Dawn thought for a moment. Maybe killing all The Producers wasn't something she was quite prepared for after all. She was quiet for a few moments more, the howls of other locked up psychopaths filling the air, and a new idea altogether popped into her head.

"We have an army. An army of the greatest killers on the planet. That is, if any of them are trustworthy."

A dark smile spread across Charming Charlie's face.

"I can think of a few."

"Okay, great." Dawn nodded. She was nervous, and couldn't believe she was colluding with slashers. "Now, what are we going to do about my arm?"

Charlie began to head for the cell door and called back over his shoulder.

"I'll be procuring Ms. Churchill some backup for her endeavor. Doc...work your magic."

CHAPTER 20

"Dammit, I can never pronounce this right. Remind me again, is it 'abba-donna' like the old pop group or 'A-bay-donna'?"

Camila and Wendy exchanged glances before looking back at Mark and shrugging.

"You know what, nevermind. Get out, get out, get out!"

Mark flapped his hand back and forth, dismissing the dancers from his dressing room. He grabbed his forehead. His temples were throbbing.

"Hey, wait a minute." He looked at the stagehand who was following the dancers out of the room. "Where are *you* going?"

"Uh…" the twenty-something had the look of a kid who had been caught with his hand in the cookie jar, "aren't all stagehands supposed to report to the arena?"

Mark jumped out of his chair and stuffed a wad of money into the kid's pocket surreptitiously.

"Listen, I won't rat you out if you can snag me a bottle of booze from the Producers' stores. But, you know, I'm not supposed to drink on the job, so it can't look like I'm drinking on the job."

"Coffee, two sugars, no cream; got it, Mr. Winters!" the scared young man announced loudly for anybody outside who might be listening.

Mark clapped him twice on the cheek and then gave him the "shoo" motion. He returned to his seat and hung his head in his hands. Outside, the crowd was talking excitedly, and it seemed like every single one of them was shouting in his ears.

One of the dancers stuck her head back in the door.

"Uh, I know you said to get out, but…it's time to go, Mark."

"Yeah, yeah," he said, rising.

As he was about to step onto the stage, the young stage-hand reappeared, half-running to move quickly, but trying not to spill the mug of liquid he was carrying. He pressed it into Mark's hands and Mark could immediately tell from the cool-ness of the mug that an appropriate portion of it was chilled vodka, cooling off the costume layer of hot coffee.

"God bless you, kiddo."

He stepped onstage. As it descended, the lights in his eyes seemed obscenely bright, but he was too much of a professional to blink or shield his face like he was hung over.

"Hey, there, folks! Wow! What a night! What can I say? I don't think I've ever seen anything like this in all our history. *Try Not to Die*? More like *Try Not to Watch*, am I right?"

The idiots barked and clapped their hands like seals, and Mark had to refrain from rolling his eyes.

"One of our contestants is incommunicado. And Charming Charlie Whitmore has one of our cameras. It's off right now, but I promise we'll let you know as soon as the feed starts running again. You know Charlie, he loves to put on a show for you folks. So I wouldn't worry about that. But our sponsors aren't paying for dead air, and we've still got one contestant in the ring."

Mark stopped and planted his chin on his fist, as though he were thinking hard.

"But you know what? Ah, nah, they'd never go for it."

The crowd started shouting "What?" and "Tell us!"

Mark set his delicious, life-saving mug onto a stool and held out both of his hands like a pauper.

"No, no, I don't even want to bother them with it."

The crowd got even more frenzied, and Mark cupped his hand over his ear as if he couldn't hear them.

"Well, if you really insist…and I mean *really* insist…I guess I can ask them."

The crowd started shouting "We do" and "Ask them." It was just like playing with trained monkeys. They didn't even know what they were asking for, but they knew they wanted it more than anything ever.

"Well, all right then."

Mark turned and looked at the Producers' box.

"I...I feel bad asking, ladies and gentlemen, but you see how excited the crowd is..." he held out his hand to let them whoop and holler their agreement. "It's just...I think it might be better if we had a few more surprise contestants."

The Producers leaned in and formed a fake huddle for a few moments, probably talking about caviar or the weather or something, because it sure wasn't them making a fucking decision about something they had already ordered him to do. When the bullshit was complete, Marisol emerged from the huddle with a smile on her face.

"I think we can help out with that, Mark. In fact, a few of our staff members have *begged us* to let them join in on the fun and, well, we *do* like to take care of our people."

Mark slapped his hands together in mock excitement and rubbed them quickly, as though starting a fire.

"All right! Let's meet some of the crew who make this show possible!"

The green room door opened and six staff members exited. Four were stagehands, like the one Mark had saved, all fresh-faced and healthy-looking young specimens of the GL whose well-to-do parents had pulled strings to get them donkey work away from the irradiated farms. The fifth looked to be an accountant judging by her thick glasses, pocket protector, and the thick bun her hair was done up in.

The last one was one of the security goons who took care of the Barn and cells, moving the contestants around. He was unarmed, naturally, though still wearing his body armor and mirrored sunglasses. He wore a smirk that suggested he may *actually* have volunteered for this mission, looking to test his muscles and guts on the slashers who had probably given him so much abuse for however long he'd worked there.

The staff members waved to the audience, who cheered wildly. The cue ball was off hiding somewhere, which made Mark scowl, but it wasn't like he'd be able to hide forever.

"So now that we have our heroes, let's meet our next slasher."

The big screen behind Mark lit up.

"Standing four feet, two inches tall and weighing in at a

dainty fifty-six pounds, our next killer is thought by some to be the daughter of..." Mark lowered his voice significantly, "The Devil."

He let his eyes rove over the stands, which had suddenly gone quiet.

"But others say she's just a terrible, naughty little girl. All we know for certain is that her kill count at eight tender years of age stands at a whopping fifty-three kills, forty of them in the wild!"

The crowd erupted into applause. Personally, Mark thought it was kind of bullshit. The kid had slashed a few throats, sure, but most of her kill count was due to the fire she had set at her orphanage.

Now he was back to the tricky pronunciation question. He decided to just pick one and go with it.

"Ladies and gentlemen, I give you...Abaddona!"

The barn door opened and a tiny child emerged wearing a tattered dress that had once been white with blue polka dots, but was now turning grey. She stepped out slowly, in bare feet. Her hair was bright red and her skin was as white as a sheet, except where it was speckled with freckles, particularly around her cheeks and up and down both arms.

She wore a mirthless grin and her green eyes were strikingly dead, utterly devoid of human emotion. She carried a dead rabbit, which was festering and surrounded by a cloud of flies, but the way she coddled it in her arms and petted it like a baby anyone watching would have been forgiven for thinking it was still alive.

Two of the security guards stood behind the young girl, each holding a powerful electroshock gun mounted at the end of a pole. It was clear they wanted to keep their distance from the little moppet and just shoo her out into the arena.

Abaddona turned slowly around, which made the goons jump and crank their stun weapons up to maximum intensity.

"Thank you," she said slowly, in a wan voice, "for escorting me."

The two goons backed up into the Barn, never taking their eyes off the little monster. She raised her hand from the dead rabbit and didn't wave, but simply stood there, hand extended in silent farewell. Mark kept waiting for something awful to happen, but the goons managed to make good their escape. The tension was overwhelming, nevertheless.

Mark waited for the slasher to make her move, but she simply stood where the goons had left her, just outside the Barn, patting her bunny and singing a lullaby in a low, barely-there voice that nonetheless seemed to be just audible in every corner of the arena.

The stagehands who had just entered the arena scampered in four different directions. That left the accountant and the security goon. The goon took off his sunglasses.

"Is this really it? A little girl? Come on, we can take her."

He gestured with his head at the ginger menace, who was making no aggressive move or, indeed, even seemed to be aware of what was going on around her. The accountant pushed her glasses back up on her nose.

"Um, you heard her stats the same as I did. I'm not eager to tangle with that."

The goon waved his hand at her dismissively.

"Never mind, then. I'll take care of this one myself. At least I know what good you are in a pinch. Don't come to me if you need help when they drop Denney or The Goat."

The accountant nearly jumped at the mention of the arena's most dangerous denizens. The goon cracked his knuckles and made a beeline for Abaddona, only going out of his way to step around a bear trap.

The goon stopped just short of Abaddona. She still seemed so out of it, staring blankly ahead, humming to herself, petting that rotting animal. He wondered what would be the best way to dispose of her since he didn't have a weapon; he might have been on *Try Not to Die*, but the thought of beating a child to death was too much, even for a show like this. He decided on swiftly breaking her neck and as he reached out his hands, an odd feeling spread up through both his arms. He managed to bring his hands to the girl's throat, but was unable to work his fingers. He looked down only to find that both wrists had been sliced straight through the tendons. Dark crimson dripped onto the little girl's shoulders and she finally looked up at the goon's horrified face and giggled.

The little girl had moved so quickly that even the audience hadn't seen what happened. It was only when a slow-motion playback on the big screens revealed her actions that the audience went into a frenzy. The enormous screens showed Abaddona slip out a razor-sharp knife from inside the bunny's belly and with lightning speed, slice through into the goon's wrists like butter, almost as though she'd done it a thousand times.

The goon dropped to his knees, staring at his open wounds, his eyes wide and his face pale. He would soon bleed out. The accountant shrieked behind him and Abaddona turned her attention to the woman.

"Pretty lady, wanna play?" Abaddona cocked her head and smiled, holding the rabbit out in front of her.

The accountant shrieked again and tore off in the opposite direction while the tiny yet terrifying child skipped after her, humming the same song over and over.

"You know what they say," Mark said into the mic. "The bigger they are, the harder they fall!" He pointed at the goon lying on the floor, slipping into unconsciousness.

"Let's keep a close eye on the rest of our contestants! I have a feeling this little one's got a lot more in store for us!"

The crowd cheered and chanted for Abaddona as she skipped around the maze, avoiding traps with grace and admiring them with childlike wonder. Every so often it appeared she was speaking to the rabbit, sometimes scolding it.

"This is one future serial killer that's had a hell of a head start in life! Am I right?" Mark commented, eliciting a laugh from the crowd.

Abaddona finally rounded a corner and found that the accountant was trapped at a dead end, a sort of cul-de-sac. Cardboard cutouts of homes decorated the area, making it appear as if they were in some pre-war suburbia.

"There you are!" The little girl shouted with glee.

"No! Get away from me!"

The accountant cried out in terror, clawing at the walls, desperate to flee. Her glasses were crooked on her face, her bun was coming undone from the top of her head, and she looked like she'd been in the maze for hours as opposed to just a few minutes.

Every time the accountant made a move left or right, Abaddona would mimic her, stepping this way and that, giggling, enjoying this new game.

"Stop doing that!"

"Stop doing that," Abaddona mocked.

The accountant cried out with frustration, still searching for an exit, and the little girl imitated her movements and cried out, letting a giggle or two slip in between.

"Why are you doing this? Just leave me alone! Please!"

Everything was repeated, from the words down to the inflection; naturally, the crowd thought it was a hoot. The accountant screamed at the crowd, shouting insults and cussing them. Abaddona didn't repeat the swear words, instead she brought her hand up to her mouth and feigned shock.

"I'm not allowed to say those things," she giggled.

"Oh, is that right? You ugly little shit?" The accountant asked, turning her attention to the little girl. "What the fuck do I have to do to get you to leave me the fuck alone and go after one of those other assholes? I can go through every god damned bad word in the book, I've got all night, bitch."

Mark winced. The broadcast was on a seven-second delay, and he could only hope Jimmy was editing out the language in time. The last thing they needed was a fine.

The crowd booed the accountant, but she kept her scowl fixed on the little girl who actually appeared sad. She hugged her dead rabbit into her chest and whispered something to it, then looked up at the accountant.

"We just...we just wanted someone to play with us." The little girl rocked from side to side, even going so far as to stick her thumb in her mouth.

The crowd let out a collective "aww" and the accountant rolled her eyes.

"Okay, fine! If I play with you, will you go away?"

Abaddona nodded and smiled, hopping up and down with glee.

"Okay then... what game do you want to play?"

Abaddona thought for a moment and then shouted out "Simon Says!" The crowd cheered in response, and the game began.

"Simon says: hop like a bunny!"

The accountant sighed but obliged, hopping in place like a bunny, the crowd falling into hysterics.

"Simon says: hop forward three times."

The accountant hopped forward three times.

"Simon says: hop twice to the left and forward two times."

The accountant did as instructed.

"Simon says: hop to the right four times."

Again, the accountant hopped.

"Take a step backward."

The accountant stepped back and then realized her mistake.

"Uh oh!" Abaddona shouted, giggling along with the crowd. "I didn't say *Simon says!*"

An expression of terror came over the accountant's face, but only for a brief moment as a guillotine released from above her and handily split her into two clean pieces down the middle.

The audience cheered for Abaddona and she waved at the collapsing chunks of the accountant before skipping back the way she came, eager to find her other playmates.

CHAPTER 21

Dawn awoke, not with a start, but in a fog. She wasn't thinking clearly, but some animal instinct inside of her reminded her that she was in danger. She tried to jump up, but found it hard to even sit up, and was having trouble propping herself. Something was wrong with her arm.

She looked around, feeling confused about her surroundings. She vaguely remembered the daintily-appointed appearance of Charming Charlie Whitmore's cell, with its crushed leather sofa, kitchenette, and small dining area; this was definitely not the same cell.

The place was dingy, with exposed pipes that seemed to be constantly leaking. A large light shone above her head, and all around her were trays full of bloodied surgical instruments. The operating theater was surprisingly spotless compared to the rest of the cell.

"Easy, easy, *pepita*."

Doctor Feelbad loomed over her, his surgical mask still covering most of his features, but his eyes shining with a soft, almost maudlin sadness. Groggy, she reached up to try to pull down his mask, but he stepped gently aside, dodging her with all the deftness of a Mack truck.

"*Descansas*," he said. "Relax. You are young and strong but *cirugía* is hard on us all."

She thought for a moment. "Surgery?"

His scrubs and apron were spattered with fresh blood, and he wore gloves that looked more like rubber dishwashing gloves than latex surgical gloves, and they, too, were coated with crimson. Her blood, she realized.

"What…did I get hurt or something? I mean, worse than losing my arm?"

"You don't remember. All right, prepare yourself. I replaced your arm with a prótesis…ah…prosthetic."

Dawn's mouth hardened. She swallowed a lump in her throat and wiggled her right arm. It felt off balance, much too heavy.

"I don't want to look."

"It's okay," the doctor said, stroking her hair affectionately, and then suddenly remembering himself and pulling back. "Take your time."

A jumble of memories came back to her. The walk home with the heavy bag of loot. Her neighbor screaming. Trying to make a run for it. Marisol Martinez. Entering the arena, the game show. Charming Charlie's leering grin, and a conversation with the doctor in muted tones. A pact with dark forces. It may as well have been with the Devil himself.

She raised her arm. Where Charlie had severed it at the elbow, a cup-like prosthetic covered the jagged edge. Below that was a cleverly constructed hinge which allowed for some vertical movement and apparently 360 degrees of horizontal swiveling, as well as locking the arm into place. Except the lower arm wasn't an arm or a prosthetic of any sort. It was a shotgun.

"Holy shit!"

It wasn't a cry of anger or even shock. It was one of amazement and grim determination. The doctor's face was still covered, but he looked like he might have been smiling.

"You are, uh, re-armed."

She shook her head. "I thought the one nice thing about you was that you didn't know enough English to make puns."

He was definitely smiling now.

"I know more than you think."

She looked him up and down.

"You've got more layers than an onion, Doc."

He reached out to help her as she swiveled her feet over the side and stood up. She took a few steps forward. She still felt groggy, but not particularly weak. She'd need to be strong for what was coming next.

"Has it been long?"

"No, not very long."

"I'm surprised they haven't sent any guards after us."

"They sent them."

Getting a feel for her feet again, Dawn walked to the doctor's open cell door. The hallway was littered with bodies. One goon had a scalpel shoved directly into his forehead. Another had been sliced from neck to crotch with a surgical saw. Each of them had been gruesomely mutilated and Dawn got the impression that the Producers had either run out of goons or given up on sending more. So Feelbad had been acting in a double capacity this whole time as her surgeon and her guardian—albeit demented—angel.

She tested out her arm, getting a feel for how pulling on her muscles in a certain way which before would have caused her fingers to clench or her elbow to bend now caused the shotgun to turn up and down, side to side.

"Does this work?" she asked.

Feelbad shrugged. He walked up to her and unlocked the break action on her new forearm, inserting a red shell into one barrel.

"Wouldn't be much use if it didn't."

She turned and pointed down a hallway, spotting a light fixture which was flickering. Trying her best not to use her left arm to adjust it, she aimed and even pulled the trigger using just the wreckage of her right upper arm and shoulder. She missed the lightbulb, but the weapon discharged with a satisfying crack.

"Oh my," a familiar, lizard-like voice intoned, and if Dawn had had a second shell she probably would have discharged it. "I was worried more security guards were en route, but I see it's just you, up and about, Ms. Churchill."

Charming Charlie stepped into view, coming down the hallway. And he wasn't alone.

To his left and right hopped along two men dressed in apparel she was once up close and personal with: head to toe leather and zippers everywhere. Around the gimps' necks were tight metal collars and Charlie held a chain in each hand. Behind him was a massive shadow that towered over him. As the group stepped into the light cast by the fixture she'd missed with her shotgun earlier, she could now see that the massive shadow was the scariest looking man she'd ever seen.

Standing at nearly seven feet and sporting a scar from scalp to chin over his right eye, he carried a chainsaw that seemed bigger than Dawn herself. His biceps were bigger than her torso and his shirtless chest revealed untold stories of countless wounds from long ago that had since healed and formed wretched, purple scars.

"Holy shit," Dawn muttered under her breath.

"Rather striking, isn't he?" Charlie smiled and looked up at the man behind him who simply grunted in response. "This is Big Gus, and these fine young specimens are your attack dogs." He pulled just hard enough on the chains to force a growl from each gimp. "They follow basic commands and they're loyal to the death. Marisol trains them that way."

Dawn didn't know what to make of it, her eyes flicked between each killer surrounding Charlie and she felt sweat forming on her upper lip despite the cool climate of the sub-level cells. Sure, she'd managed to survive an evening with Charming Charlie and Doctor Feelbad, but they at least seemed to have their wits about them. The gimps and Big Gus on the other hand, well, that was a gamble she wasn't exactly feeling good about.

"Oh," Charlie put a finger up. "There's one more thing."

He stepped to the side and revealed a short, young woman who had been standing between him and Gus.

"Hiya, sugar!" She said with a Southern lilt and a cheerful wave, her blonde pigtails bobbing side to side.

Her fingers might as well be talons, Dawn thought, hoping she hadn't cringed at the sight of the girl's ferocious teeth.

"This is Razortooth," Charlie said.

"Raze, please," the girl said, a crazed look in her eye.

Charlie rolled his eyes, a decadent, patrician gesture.

"Keep an eye on this one, Ms. Churchill. She's certifiable. And that's coming from me."

Raze hissed at the insult, baring her teeth, and Dawn took a cautious step back.

"So I'm supposed to trust that none of these people are going to kill me as soon as we're back up in the arena?"

Charlie snickered, setting down the chains and approaching Dawn.

"You don't know that they won't kill you *before* you get up to the arena."

He was close enough to her now where with one smooth movement he could end her life. She knew how dangerous he was, but she also knew she couldn't back down now. She inhaled deeply, straightening her posture, and looked him in the eye.

"All right," she said.

"Good girl," he replied, the corner of his mouth twitching slightly.

He lifted a hand but she didn't flinch, refusing to show any sign of weakness. His fingertips brushed her cheek, taking a lock of her blonde hair and tucking it behind her ear. Normally she would have recoiled, but she remained calm, and instead simply closed her eyes. He inhaled her scent as if he were savoring the smell of a sweet roast, reminding her that he'd skipped dinner. She wasn't out of the clear yet, she had to stay strong.

"Take this."

She opened her eyes and saw a small earpiece in his palm.

"What's that for?"

"Ah, my dear, it's my show now, even if they don't know it yet. And you are the star."

She plucked the earpiece from his palm and placed it in her ear.

"How do I know if it's working?"

"You'll know." He went to the doctor's side and patted him on the back. "Good work, my friend."

"*Gracias*," Doc replied. "Some of my finest work."

Feelbad lumbered forward and gave Dawn a small satchel. Peeking inside she said, "That's a lot of shotgun shells."

"*Si*, you will need them."

He waved her on, pointing at the chains on the ground before her. She bent down and retrieved them. It would be tough hanging onto them with only one hand, but she'd find a way to manage.

"Go on, then," Charming Charlie said. "You don't want to be late for the festivities."

She nodded, a knot forming in her stomach as she stepped toward Raze and Gus, but they stepped aside, allowing her to pass, and then soon fell in step behind her.

"Do yourself a favor and let the girl handle the guards." Dawn heard Charlie call out to her. "She's quite good with men."

CHAPTER 22

Tim ran his hand furtively over his pate, like he was polishing a bowling ball. It was a nervous tic, one he hadn't indulged in for years, since it used to get him endless torment from his schoolyard playmates, but now it was back in full force.

He wasn't a fighter. Never had been. Even back in those days when he'd been teased, he'd run and hide rather than settle things with his fists. He was good at hiding. He liked to think it made him clever. And he wondered now, hiding beneath the porch of a fake home in this mock neighborhood within the maze, if he could hide for long enough, would The Producers and the killers forget about him? Or would things only get worse?

With Dawn he had felt like someone had been there who not only knew what she was doing, but thought like him, wanted to survive like him. But now Dawn was gone, dead, taken by Charming Charlie and subjected to some horrific fate beneath the arena.

He went from rubbing his head to slapping it. Slap, slap, slap. Trying to restart whatever brain was in there, clear out the cobwebs that always seemed to obscure from him what seemed so obvious and easy to everybody else.

Something like a giant spider scrambled down under the porch alongside him.

Shit shit shit!

Tim started scrambling against the rubble, worried now that his safe space had turned into a deathtrap.

"Hey," a jaunty voice said, and a young man in glasses crawled next to Tim, raising his hand in a halfhearted salute.

Tim relaxed, letting his heartbeat and breathing return to

normal. It wasn't the slasher girl. It was one of the stagehands Marisol had forced into the arena.

"Hey," Tim replied, an awkwardness setting in.

"Everybody's wondering where you are."

"Well, let them wonder. If they don't know, then that creepy little girl doesn't know, either."

The stagehand brightened up.

"That's good. That's a real good way to look at it. Your name's Tim, right?"

Tim scanned the horizon furiously. All the action was out of view, which meant he didn't know what was going on. He had been gauging from the screams of the crowd and what he could hear over the loudspeakers what had been happening after the little girl had killed the accountant and the four stagehands had scrambled. But now he had an eerie sense of foreboding in his stomach, like he wasn't the one hiding away anymore.

The stagehand nudged him in the side. "Hey."

"What?" Tim was growing frustrated by the man's mere presence.

"You're Tim, right?"

"Yeah, man. Listen, if you're going to hide here you need to keep it quiet."

"Yeah, I will, it's just...I want to tell you my name, too. If nobody knows my name out here it's kind of like I'm anonymous, and if you're just an anonymous guy then you can die at any second, right? But if you at least have a name, then..."

One of the floorboards above them creaked. Tim clapped his hand over the stagehand's mouth. The floorboard creaked over and over again, as though someone were standing on it, rocking back and forth on the balls of their feet. Tim and the stagehand lay absolutely still, tangled in each other's embrace, the only movement the beating of their hearts, which seemed wildly out of place in the otherwise utter stillness.

A low voice—a child's voice—began singing.

"Ring around the rosie..."

Tim glanced up through the floorboards to see the little ginger girl, skipping along, a yo-yo in her hand bouncing up and down in time with the music. Tim slowly loosened his grip on the stagehand, preparing to dart out from under the porch.

"...*pocket full of posies*..."

The stagehand whispered, "It's just that..."

Tim looked at him with a disbelieving death stare.

"...if nobody knows my name..."

"...*ashes, ashes*..."

Tim jammed a single finger upward, indicating that the slasher was now mere inches above them, her entire visage visible through a knothole slightly larger than the gaps between the boards.

"Just let me tell you..."

"...*we all fall down!*"

The yo-yo dropped down through the knothole and with unbelievable deftness, the string wrapped around the stagehand's neck twice before coming to a stop. A girlish giggle slipped through the floorboards. Tim looked up and jumped as an eyeball appeared in the knothole.

"Found you!"

Tim scrambled haphazardly to get out from under the porch, sending gravel flying behind him. He looked back and saw the stagehand's face turning a deep shade of purple as the yo-yo string cut into his throat. He was trying to mouth something, tears streaming down his face.

When Tim was out from under the floorboards, he looked up and found himself only a few feet away from Abadonna. She turned and looked directly at him, temporarily loosening her grip on the yo-yo with the improbably strong string. Tim heard a ragged gasp and he looked back under the porch to see the stagehand had managed to pull the string away from his neck a quarter of a centimeter.

"My name is..." he gasped.

But then he said no more. Abadonna yanked especially hard and the string sliced right through the stagehand's neck. Glistening with blood, Tim could now see that it hadn't been simple toy string, but rather piano wire.

As Tim scurried off, his heart racing, he could hear Abadonna giggling. With the goon, the accountant, and now one of the stagehands dead, that left Tim and three other contestants. It was only a matter of time before they all met similar fates at the hands of that maniacal child. Tim just hoped he could outlast the others.

He rounded a corner and cried out, stopping short just in time. A few more inches and he would have ended up with his face inside someone's gaping torso. One of the stagehands, oblivious to the numerous booby-traps, had stumbled into the wrong hallway. Six long, wooden spikes, that had undoubtedly surprised him when they suddenly sprung from the walls, kept his body suspended off the ground. When the spikes had lifted up and retracted, they'd malfunctioned, ripping the poor stagehand right open. A dark puddle of blood was still gathering beneath him, so Tim knew he hadn't been dead long.

Make that me and only two contestants, he said to himself, crouching under the death trap in order to pass.

Possessing no grace, Tim slipped in the puddle of blood and fell forward. Out of instinct, his hands reached out for something to keep from falling and he ended up grabbing part of the stagehand, ripping him open even further. Tim landed hard on his ass in the puddle of blood, and to make matters worse, intestines spilled out from the torso above him, covering him in gore.

Tim slapped the intestines away with both hands, but they just kept coming back and hitting him in the face. Shrieking, and trying not to vomit, he grabbed hold of one of the wooden spikes to pull himself back up to his feet, but it snapped in half, the body half-falling on top of him, further adding insult to injury.

"Oh, come on!" he screamed as more viscera and post-mortem fluid covered him.

He finally crawled out from under the disgusting mess he'd *sort of* helped create and thought of stripping all his clothes off before continuing. He wondered what would be worse: spending what little time he had left covered in someone else's blood and bodily fluid or dying in his birthday suit. He seriously considered the birthday suit, but decided against it, simply removing his shirt and cleaning himself up as best he could. He tossed the filthy shirt to the ground and spotted the piece of wooden spike that had snapped off.

He bent over to retrieve it and waved it around as if he were attacking an invisible enemy.

Might come in handy.

As he pressed on, he heard distant screams, but not the typical screams of torture or death, these were more nerve-wracking and annoying. He heard Mark egging on the crowd, enjoying whatever was going on far too much.

"Where oh where could our contestants be? I sure hope they don't keep our poor little Abadonna up past her bedtime!" He mispronounced her name again, laughing.

Evidently, the psycho-child was throwing a temper tantrum. When Tim was finally able to get a better view of one of the projection screens, he could see that she'd retrieved the severed head of her last victim and was beating it repeatedly with both of her fists, screaming that she was tired and didn't want to play anymore.

"You hear that everyone?" Mark asked the audience. *"Abadonna is ti-yawed!"* He said in a baby voice.

The psycho-child shrieked in response, throwing the severed head—along with her dead bunny—down the hall she was in.

"Woah, somebody's cranky! What do you say, folks? Should we help her out?"

The audience agreed and Mark put a finger up to his mouth as if deep in thought, a *hmmm* escaping his lips.

"Aha!" He shouted, jumping up and landing in a half-squat, pointing down into the arena.

An alarm sounded and the lights in the hall Tim was in began to blink.

"Oh, shit."

CHAPTER 23

Dawn glanced up and up at Big Gus. The mountain of a man was staring forward, grimly, his eyes dull and vacant.

"Uh...so, why are you helping me?"

If he heard, he gave no signal. He just continued plodding forward. Dawn nearly had a heart attack as she felt something heavy jump onto her back and ride her piggyback. She felt Razortooth's hot breath in her ear and felt the freaky young woman's hands running up and down her belly and breasts. Her legs were locked around Dawn's waist. Dawn froze in place and waited for the deathblow to come.

"He doesn't talk much," Raze said.

"Much?" Dawn asked as Raze's sharp nails found purchase in her sternum, cutting through Dawn's tattered shirt, but not quite breaking the skin.

Raze cackled maniacally and squeezed tightly, an attempt at a warm hug, Dawn would've guessed.

"You've got me there. I've never heard him talk at all and we've been neighbors for going on two years."

Dawn glanced back at Gus, who, though he had stopped when she had, was showing no signs that he had heard anything they were saying, or, indeed, that they were even talking about him. Raze kicked her heels against Dawn's pelvis and neighed.

"Come on, horsie! Why'd you stop?"

Dawn gritted her teeth together.

"Do I really have to tell you?"

She peeked around from her vantage point on Dawn's back to get a better look at her face. She couldn't see her own expression, but imagined it was a mixture of grim resignation and white-knuckle fear.

"You thought I was going to kill you?"

Dawn turned her head, teeth still rigid, and nodded robotically twice. Raze reached out and touched her cheek. "Baby girl, why would I kill you? You're one of us now. We've got to look out for our own. Isn't that right, Gus?" With a spritely hop, she disembarked from Dawn's back and walked around to take Big Gus's giant hand in her own. His fingers were like sausages and it occurred to Dawn that he probably could have crushed Raze's daintier, dirtier paw into paste. Instead, he held fast and let her lead him forward like a child taking his mother's hand to cross the street.

Dawn reached up and touched her own face, feeling the indentations of Razortooth's fingernails where she had touched her. They could easily have been inch-deep, face-wide furrows, but instead she had been gentle.

"One of us," Dawn whispered.

It was a horrifying thought. But looking down at her prosthetic shotgun arm, and thinking back on all the damage she'd already done in the arena today, it wasn't as though the madwoman was wrong. In fact, she had been entirely cogent. Maybe she even had a point. Maybe it wasn't so scary a thought after all. In a world like this, what other answer was there but to go mad? Maybe it was the only sign that you were still sane. Maybe it was the people out there, the ones cheering in the stands and organizing this whole horrific game show madness, who accepted the apocalypse and all that it implied, who were well and truly mad.

"You coming, beautiful?" she heard Raze's voice waft down the hall after she and Gus had turned a corner.

"Yeah," Dawn said, first to herself, then repeating it to her partners. "Yeah, I am!"

CHAPTER 24

Tim stumbled and fell backwards, flat on his back. His heart was thundering and the alarms seemed to be everywhere, even inside his skull. He began flailing back and forth like a turtle on its back, then shrieked in alarmed pain. Something was piercing his back.

He scrambled to his feet and looked around the arena, trying to get his bearings, but a wave of amnesia turned the hooting faces of the crowd into a sickening sea of color like a van Gogh painting. He pinched his eyes shut and tried to control his breathing, focusing, as he had when he had been bullied as a child, on a place that made him happy.

His grandmother's house. Not his parents'. That had been a place of shouting about unmet expectations and beatings with hairbrushes and wooden spoons, but his maternal grandmother had always been kind to him.

"Timothy," she would say—and she was the only one who ever called him by his given name instead of *Cue Ball* or *Weirdo*—"you don't worry about what anybody says. You just worry about being a good boy and the people who matter will come along."

Yeah, they had come. Maybe a bit too late. Dawn and the old lady and the albino girl and even the little guy. Even the nameless kid under the floorboards had been pretty nice when the chips were down. And where were they all now? He sighed. It had never been easy for him to make friends, and now he was all out of opportunities. He thought of his grandmother's pork stew, the kind that only she could make, even if it did have turnips in it. Maybe the turnips were part of the charm. A little something gross to remind him of how much he liked everything else.

The pain in his kidney dulled to a low ache and he felt like he was starting to get a grip on himself. He reached around his back and scrabbled to grab ahold of whatever was there. Biting his lip, he yanked it out and clutched his back where the wound had been made. The stick he had yanked from the booby trap was now dripping with his own blood, and his kidney was probably ruined, along with his charbroiled half-hand and per- forated upper arm. He was starting to wonder how much more damage he could take before his body would just give up and deny the audience the gruesome dismemberment they were all hoping lay in store for him. Still, as a child of the bomb and a resident of the Geiger Lands, he was nothing if not resilient.

The alarms were still blaring, but either they had deafened him to the point where they seemed like little more than a dull roar or else he had just gotten used to them. He looked up at the crowd, who were laughing and jeering and calling for his blood, but that just made him feel woozy so he looked away. He was starting to feel lightheaded. So much blood loss. This was defi- nitely not good. He tripped and fell, this time on his face. Looking back, he saw a crumpled body on the ground missing a head. It was a girl's and he started to panic. He scrambled back and flipped it over, but she wasn't dressed in Dawn's clothes. Instead she was wearing smart business attire. Another one of the stagehands.

Tim balled up the hem of the dead girl's shirt and ripped away a huge swathe of the material, inadvertently exposing her bra.

"Oh, sorry," he said, and attempted to cover her back up.

The crowd was laughing hysterically at him. He looked up at them. It did seem a little silly, worrying about a decapi- tated woman's dignity. Then again, maybe lack of dignity was what was wrong with the Geiger Lands. Life was cheap here and nobody seemed to respect anybody anymore, except at the point of a gun.

He struggled to flip the girl over, so at least her breasts would be covered from the leering, laughing crowd. He balled up the cotton he had ripped away from her shirt and pressed it into the wound in his back. With his other hand, he raised his fist and shook it.

"We're people, you know! And we have names!"

"Really? What's your name?"

He looked up. The little girl, Abadonna, was perched on a catwalk just above him, her legs dangling over the side and kicking through the air. In lieu of the dead rabbit she had recklessly tossed away she was holding what appeared to be the head of the dead woman Tim had tripped over, mounted on a long, white stick. It resembled nothing so much as an oversized lollipop. Completing the illusion, a tiny dribble of blood trickled out of the dead woman's empty eye socket, and Abadonna, without taking her eyes off Tim, stuck her tongue out and licked it off the corpse's face.

"I'm Tim," he said, struggling to his feet. "Timothy Powell. And I have a home. And I have a job. It's not a great job, but it pays. And I have friends, or at least I *did* until you people took them away from me."

Abadonna frowned. "Why'd you leave all that to come here?"

"You think it was by choice?"

The little girl shrugged and the crowd started booing. Tim looked up at them. Their thumbs were pointed downward.

"Stop talking," they were screaming, *"Kill him!"*

"All right," he said, holding his arms wide and letting his pathetic weapon of a sharpened stake drop to the ground. "It's been a long night. Give the people what they want,"Abadonna giggled. "I like you. Your head is shiny."

Tim let out a sigh of exasperation.

"Just kill me already!"

"Catch!" The child yelled, throwing the severed head to Tim.

He caught it out of instinct and then shrieked at the severed head in his hands, dropping it to the ground; it landed with a sickening plop and rolled onto one side. Tim jumped back and away from it. He was growing weary of interacting with dead things.

Abadonna clapped and giggled with glee. Tim was also growing weary of the child sitting on the catwalk above him. He knew she was capable of terrible things and had a track record of toying with her victims, but he wasn't in the mood for games.

"Hey!" he shouted at her. "Get it over with!"

The little girl stretched her arms and gave an exaggerated yawn.

"I want to go to bed!" she yelled up at the platform.

The crowd let out a collective, "Aww!"

"Now, now, little one." Mark said, his face filling the screen. "You know you can't go to bed until you finish all your homework. Mama Marisol said—"

"I hate Mama Marisol! And I hate you! I wanna go to bed! Now!" She stood up and shouted at Mark's face on the projection scream, stomping her little, bare feet on the catwalk, causing the rickety old thing to shake.

Tim sighed. He hated children.

"You listen here, young lady." Mark put a hand on his hip and tried not to laugh as he scolded her. "You're going to be grounded if you don't listen to your mama. Don't you remember the last time you were grounded?"

Abadonna shook her head wildly, stomping her feet harder and flailing her arms around.

"I hate you! I hate you! I hate you!" She screamed like a wild animal between proclamations of detestation and began to jump up and down.

The catwalk shook violently beneath her, creaking every time her feet slammed back down.

The audience could see how upset the brat was, but, brat or not, they loved her. They began to shout insults at Mark who was growing visibly annoyed. With every attempt to calm the little girl down she seemed to scream louder and her tantrum grew more intense.

"Hey, buddy, a little help?" Mark looked down at Tim, it was his last resort.

Tim bunched his face up. "Fuckin' seriously?"

He flipped Mark the bird and decided, with the evil little princess throwing a fit, maybe he should count his blessings and try to find another hiding spot. He'd been waiting for a sign that he'd thrown in the towel a little too soon.

As he began to make a run for it, a loud crack broke him from his jog and he snapped his head back to see what had caused it. The catwalk broke from its hinges on the left side and Abadonna, mid-tantrum, hadn't noticed quickly enough. The little girl tumbled from the catwalk and Tim cringed as she fell head-first to the ground. For a split-second he thought about sprinting back to try and catch her, but even if he'd been stupid enough to try, it would have been too late.

The evil child landed with a gut-wrenching crack heard 'round the arena and the crowd let out a collective gasp before falling silent. Her body lay limp, her neck bent at an unnatural angle, yet there was still a smile on her freckled-face that sent shivers down Tim's spine.

"And that, kids, is what happens when you don't listen to your parents." Mark commented before the stage began to retract, seemingly surprising him.

An announcement was made introducing the next set of commercials.

The audience began to boo, disappointed and enraged that Abadonna had met such an untimely fate. To make matters worse, the catwalk snapped from its hinges the rest of the way and the heavy object fell on top of the little girl, crushing her into the earth like an insect, obliterating bone and cartilage and sending blood and guts oozing out the sides. The crowd became more enraged and began to point down into the arena at Tim.

Tim made a face and began to run in search of a hiding place before they decided to unleash another maniac into the maze when he realized they were blaming him for the child's death.

"How is this my fault?" he shouted at the crowd and began defending himself, but his shouts fell on deaf ears.

The crowd began to demand Tim's blood and he cringed as he heard some of the things they were shouting.

"Kill the cue ball!"

"The freak needs to die!"

"Cut off his balls and feed them to him!"

"Justice for Abadonna!"

Tim scurried through the maze, desperate to get out of the audience's line of sight, but this area of the maze offered no such refuge. The patrons began to throw things from their seats, and although most of it hit the electric fence and burned up, Tim still winced out of habit. He broke free from the corner of the maze and reentered the main area. He'd go back to hiding under the porch. It felt safe there.

As he sprinted off, an ear-piercing whistle began to blow, even some of the audience members closest to the arena covered their ears and screamed in pain. Tim cried out and dropped to his knees mid-run. He thought his head might explode with how intense the whistle was and he squeezed his palms over his ears. No matter how hard he pushed it didn't help drown out the agonizing sound and blood began to trickle from both ears.

A set of heavily-armed goons marched out in formation and pointed their weapons at Tim. Finally, the whistle stopped. Tim rolled over onto his side and vomited. Several audience members who'd been affected by the piercing noise did the same.

"Grab him. Queen's orders," one of the goons barked at the others.

Tim was too weak to protest or defend himself as two goons scooped him up on either side and began to drag him away.

"Where are you taking me?" He barely managed to get the words out, but neither goon responded. From what Tim could see, they still had earplugs in.

The crowd murmured, confusion setting in. They weren't sure what was going on. No contestant had ever been pulled from the arena before and now two had been in one night.

Tim thought it was actually nice to just relax for a moment, letting the men drag him off to what he assumed was certain death—or worse—but in that moment, he allowed his eyes to close and he let his head fall back.

CHAPTER 25

"This is a motherfucking disaster! A catastrophe!" Marisol shouted at the top of her lungs. "What in the name of fuck could go wrong next?"

"You know, you're never supposed to ask that," Derron chimed in.

Marisol glared at her husband. If looks could kill, he'd be dead twice over.

"Look, I don't know how these idiots are still entertained." Amy motioned out at the audience. "Why don't you grab that thing down there, the Cue Ball, and try out that new toy I got you?"

Marisol looked at her for a moment, confused, but then her face lit up and she nearly squealed. She grabbed Amy's face in her hands and squeezed.

"Oh, how could I have forgotten The Wheel! Thank you for the reminder, darling. You're so fabulous I could kiss you."

Jacob let out a snort. "Can I watch?"

"Shut the fuck up, Jacob," the women said in unison.

Marisol put her finger up to her ear.

"Jimmy, do we still have the special guests on standby?"

"Yes, ma'am," Jimmy's voice crackled through.

A mischievous grin spread across her face.

"Good, do that thing with the whistle and send some people in there to snatch that freak up. Roll two more commercials and have somebody bring out The Wheel."

Mark slapped his own face again.

"They're going to kill me. I know it. Nothing's ever gone off the rails like this before. Nothing."

"More *coffee*, Mr. Winters?"

It was that stagehand again, with his shit-eating grin.

"Yes, for fuck's sake!"

The boy went scrambling off.

Mark shook his head. "What a pain in my ass."

He thought he was going to survive by hitching his wagon to Mark's star. He was the only person in this arena whose fate was in as much jeopardy as the cue ball's.

Camila was rubbing his shoulders, or at least he thought it was Camila.

"It'll be all right, Mark. They can't get rid of you. You're the face of this show."

He glanced back at the dancer, maybe it was Wendy. He decided it didn't really matter anymore.

"Look out there." He pointed out beyond the dressing room door. "How old do you think Marisol Martinez is?"

The dancer furrowed her brow. "I don't know...uh... twenty-eight?"

"She just turned forty, but don't let the word get out if you know what I mean."

The dancing girl stopped squeezing his shoulders.

"Really? How does she look so young?"

Mark sighed and lurched out of the chair, accepting his third or fourth—or who knew at this point—cup of spiked coffee of the night.

"She's never been afraid of a facelift." He chugged down the mixture of vodka and coffee and wiped his mouth, sighing. "Or maybe it's all the blood of the innocents that keeps her looking so good. I always did wonder if that woman made a pact with the devil."

He strutted back toward the stage and prepared himself for what he desperately hoped was the final round of the night's absurd shenanigans.

CHAPTER 26

Dawn and her newly acquired pack of psychopaths came to their first obstacle of the night. She peeked around the corner at a bored guard playing with something. Squinting in the poor lighting to make out what it was, Dawn watched as the guard twisted and turned the multicolored object in his hands, and seeing it made her smile.

A Rubik's Cube? I didn't think those things even existed anymore! She briefly considered asking the guard if she could borrow it, and then remembered with a start that in a few minutes she wouldn't have to.

Dawn spun back around, not even realizing she'd begun patting the head of one of the gimps at her side who was whimpering like an animal starved for attention.

"So what's the plan?" Dawn asked Raze, who, strangely, had begun to take her boots off.

"You just sit back and relax, honey. I got this."

She tossed one boot to the side and started unlacing the second. Dawn tried not to be rude, but she couldn't stop staring; Raze's feet were both ghastly and fascinating.

Just like the young lady's fingers, at the tip of each toe was a particularly razor sharp nail, each point as deadly as the next. Dawn had previously avoided staring too hard at Raze's fingernails, but as she gazed at the deadly toenails, she realized they weren't really nails at all.

It was starting to make sense.

Her teeth and nails weren't discolored or dirty, they just weren't biological material. They were metal. Steel perhaps, Dawn wasn't quite sure, but she was beginning to grow less appalled and more interested. She looked Raze up and down,

seeing now that she was much paler than she'd initially realized, and her legs and arms were completely hairless. Her perfectly arched eyebrows were only perfect because they were, in
fact, tattoos, and the well-groomed mane that sat in impeccable
pig-tails atop her skull now looked a little too perfect; it was a
wig.

Dawn's eyes went wide. "You're a—"

"*Tsk tsk.*" Raze wagged a finger at her. "Don't say cue ball,
it's so offensive."

"How...why..." Dawn cocked her head, her brows drawing
together.

Raze giggled, wiggling her fingers and toes.

"My pops was a good man, he was trying to make things
easier on me when he gave me all this. Problem is, in the GL,
nothing stays easy for long. Pops was real rich, you see, and
what do rich people do these days? They stick together. But he
didn't want anything to do with all this mess, he didn't want to
be a Producer. So that bitch upstairs killed my pops and took
me right out of my own home."

Dawn made a face. "What? You mean..."

Raze laughed, punching tiny holes into the wall with her
steel-tipped fingernails. She began to climb, leaving a trail of
small craters as she scurried up the wall lightning-fast and onto
the ceiling like a giant, beautiful spider. She stopped directly
above Dawn and dropped her head, her pig-tails swinging.
Dawn wondered how she kept the cutesy, blonde wig attached.
Maybe costume tape, but knowing Razortooth, it could have
just as easily been stapled straight to her skull.

"We're not monsters, Dawny," Raze said. "I never hurt a fly
before I came to this place. They made us this way. Even Charlie
only hurt people on the outside that deserved it. Don't let him
fool ya, he's not so bad."

Dawn frowned, trying to wrap her head around it. *The*
Charming Charlie? She thought about how he'd so mercilessly
handled Dahlia, and then it dawned on her that Dahlia really
was a ruthless assassin from the Far East before coming here.
Perhaps she had truly deserved her fate.

She wasn't gullible, but she didn't think that a *crazed maniac* would be having a conversation with her—or helping her for that matter—rather than ripping her to pieces. Could it be that these supposed psychopaths were really the good guys? She thought of The Girl Splitter. He wasn't designed to be a ruthless killing machine. She remembered hearing of the place down in Orlando where the robots came from. Once upon a time it had been the happiest place on earth. Even the robots had been reprogrammed for murder. It was beginning to weigh heavily on her heart as she glanced down at the weapon where her arm once was and considered what Raze had told her earlier.

One of us.

Dawn looked back up at Raze.

"Be back in a jiff!" the small woman said before scurrying off, the slight *tick tick tick* of her claws digging into the ceiling almost inaudibly.

Dawn jogged after her, peeking around the corner again. The guard was still engrossed in the Rubik's Cube, letting out grunts of frustration here and there. Raze moved along the ceiling in silence above him with the grace of an insect. She dropped down in a backflip and landed on his back.

Before the guard had the opportunity to react or cry out, Raze hissed and pulled his head back, chomping down on his exposed throat. She yanked it out and Dawn cringed as she saw the gaping hole spurting blood. Raze spit his Adam's Apple to the floor and went back in for another bite as the guard choked on his own blood. Dawn whirled back around the corner and flattened her back against the wall. Her heart pounded in her chest and she squeezed her eyes shut. She couldn't judge Raze for her actions, but it didn't mean it was any easier to witness.

She opened her eyes back up when she heard the gimps' chains rattle. They were jumping around like excited puppies and Raze was crouched down, trying to calm them. She undid their chains and tossed them to the side.

"You don't need these, silly," she cooed. "Dawny loves us now."

She looked up at Dawn and smiled, blood smeared across the bottom of her face and dripping from her chin. She held out her hand and jiggled a set of keys.

"One down, one to go!"

Dawn couldn't help but return the smile as she grabbed the keys from Raze's hand.

"All right," she said. "Now or never."

She led the way around the corner and started down the hall. The guard lay face up in a heap in front of the door in a pool of his own blood. Dawn spotted the Rubik's Cube a few feet from him and bent down to retrieve it.

"Ooh, you're such a nerd!" Raze gave her a playful scratch on the arm and this time Dawn didn't recoil.

She popped the Rubik's cube into the ammo satchel the doc had given her and double checked that her arm was loaded.

"I guess it's time to see what you guys can do." She said to the gimps at her side as she unlocked the heavy door.

CHAPTER 27

Far down beneath the platform, on the outskirts of the arena, Dawn and her group crept through the old access halls. She could hear the blaring music and the cheering crowd. She wasn't sure how much time they had to get their asses out there, but she knew they needed to keep moving. If the idiots in the audience were still excited about something, that meant that Tim was somehow still alive, and she needed to get to him quickly.

"Hello, Dawn." A creepy, yet familiar voice said.

She'd completely forgotten about the earpiece that Charlie had given to her before she left.

Guess that means it works, she thought

"Do be a dear and press the button on the side for me."

"Oh, right." Dawn muttered, and Raze gave her a funny look. She pointed to her ear and the girl shrugged, continuing to skip along. Dawn pressed the button on her earpiece.

"Hello?"

"Ah, there you are. How I've missed the sound of your voice," Charming Charlie chuckled.

She rolled her eyes. In the absence of his intimidating physical presence, Charlie's highfaluting style of speech just sounded ridiculous.

"How are things coming along? Swimmingly, one presumes?"

"Yeah, everything's just peachy."

"Molto bene. How long until you reach the arena?"

"I'm not sure. We're in the old access tunnels now."

"Splendid. The doctor and I are on our own mission and now that you've disposed of the guards for us we're working on finding a live feed. I wouldn't miss your grand entrance for all the tea in Darjeeling."

There was a brief silence and then Dawn could hear the

doctor and Charlie bickering about something followed by someone shouting.

"And now I must run, Ms. Churchill. We've got our work cut out for us. I'll be in touch. Do me a favor and keep your earpiece on. It makes me feel like I've got a front row seat to all the action." His end of the com went silent.

Raze whistled softly from up ahead and the gimps went running to her. Dawn picked up the pace and jogged after them, glancing back at Big Gus who didn't seem to respond at all. He trudged along at his oafish pace and stared ahead with that empty gaze.

"Gus," Dawn said, hoping to get a response from him.

He remained unchanged and Dawn sighed, leaving him to it.

Raze put a jagged finger to her lips as Dawn drew nearer.

"What is it?" Dawn whispered, crouching down beside her and the gimps.

"The Control Room. That's *one* way into the arena, but I don't think even with Gus that we'll get very far."

Raze motioned for Dawn to take a look and she peeked her head around the corner. At least two dozen heavily armed guards stood around a reinforced door that looked similar to the ones she'd seen in bunkers over the years.

"Why can't we just go in the way I did earlier tonight?" Dawn asked.

"That *is* the way you got in earlier. We'd have to get past them to get to the Green Room."

"Damn," Dawn shook her head. "So what's our other option?"

"The Barn. Everyone in there will be chained up, but it's still risky. *You know who* is in there."

Dawn scrunched her face up. "Who?"

A look resembling fear came over Raze's face and she looked up at Gus who now stood behind them.

"They call him Denney. He's like Gus...but not. He's been here too long. A lot of the guys in the Barn have been here too long: Denney, The Connoisseur, The Goat. We don't tussle with those guys, not even Charlie. Especially not with Denney."

She took Gus's big hand in hers and stood up, latching onto his arm like a frightened child.

"I'm sorry, but I gotta ask...they keep an actual goat in a place called the Barn?" Dawn scrunched her nose up.

"No, silly," Raze said, placing a hand on her shoulder. "He's a nutcase, calls himself The Goat, stands for Greatest of All Time."

Dawn shrugged, "At least he's clever."

"He's a real asshole if ya' ask me, and pretty dangerous."

"Well, don't worry," Dawn reassured her. "We'll get through this together. Which way is the Barn?"

They headed back the way they'd come and took a left down another hall, Raze leading the way once more. Dawn heard the music stop suddenly and panic swept through her.

"We need to hurry!" she shouted. "We need to get to Tim!"

Even Gus responded this time, picking up the pace. As they neared the end of the long corridor, Dawn could hear voices up ahead.

"Who's that?"

"Nothing we can't handle." Raze replied, hopping up onto the wall and climbing up. "Wait for my signal."

She scampered onto the ceiling and disappeared. Curiosity got the best of Dawn and she poked her head out to see what lie ahead. There were guards, just as heavily armed as the ones watching over the control room, but they were more relaxed, a few of them smoking cigarettes and chatting loudly.

Raze carefully made her way above the guards in perfect silence rather than taking them out.

What is she doing? Dawn wondered, and then spotted where she was headed.

There was a guard reading a tattered, old magazine in a chair. A radio sat on the dilapidated table beside him. Raze prepared to leap onto her prey and looked directly at Dawn.

"Now!" she shouted.

The guards collectively looked up with gaping mouths and Raze dropped from the ceiling onto the poor guard in the chair. She clawed into him like a tiger, ripping his throat to shreds.

The gimps tore off down the hall, shrieking in glee, pulling whips from their sides that Dawn hadn't even known were there this whole time. They expertly lashed out at the first guards they came across before they'd had the chance to ready their weapons. The whips wrapped around their throats and both gimps pulled their victims back in unison. The guards desperately clawed at the leather around their necks, desperate for air that would never come.

Dawn nearly shit herself as Gus started up his chainsaw and moved forward. Raze leapt onto her next victim and the guards that weren't being attacked began to fire at Big Gus.

"No!" Dawn cried out, out of instinct.

She almost looked away, not wanting to witness the giant being shot, but she was pleasantly surprised to hear the *ting* of bullets being deflected by the man's enormous chainsaw as he wielded it with expertise.

He sliced into the guard still firing his gun and the man seized, screeching in torture as Gus cut him in two with ease. Before the guard beside him could pull the trigger, Gus kicked an enormous leg out and knocked him to the floor. He brought the chainsaw up and plunged it deep into his torso, decorating the walls vermilion.

As her friends made quick work of the guards, she saw that there was still one left, struggling to pull his handgun from its holster. She looked down at her shotgun-arm and smirked.

"Time to shine."

She sprinted toward him with a warrior's cry and the burly guard looked up with wide eyes, a look of sheer terror on his face. She raised her arm and fired, his face disappearing in an explosion of gore. His lifeless body stayed standing for a moment and Dawn delivered a swift roundhouse kick, sending him flying to the ground.

Her chest heaved and she could hear herself panting like an animal. She jumped when Gus placed a big hand on her shoulder, his chainsaw idling in his other hand. The gimps scurried over to her side, nuzzling her. Raze stood over her last kill with a shining grin.

"You made it, Dawny."

Dawn nodded, embracing the adrenaline coursing through

her body. She moved toward the waiting room door, her hand shaking slightly as she placed it on the handle, and she took a deep breath, throwing the door open.

The waiting room was a dark and dingy place, and Dawn immediately felt overwhelmed by an almost palpable sense of madness and despair as she entered. A half dozen killers had been pulled from their cells and chained to the walls here, queued up and ready to be sent into the arena on demand.

The chained slashers reached toward them at their appearance, but Dawn found that as long as she stayed on the path in the center of the room the goons had outlined with tape, she was out of the reach of any of the killers. Just before the barn doors that opened out onto the arena floor, a mysterious door led to the left. Painted on the door was a skull and crossbones, the universal symbol for danger, though some graffiti artist with a knife had given the skull a floppy clown hat.

Dawn paused for a moment in front of the door, unable to peel her gaze away. The room seemed to exude malevolence and hate, and even after the night she'd experienced, it made her shiver as though someone had stepped on her grave.

"Dawn," Raze pulled on her arm.

"Denney's back there, isn't he?"

Raze nodded.

"He has a private entrance."

She couldn't look away. She raised her shotgun-arm.

"Maybe we should kill him now, while he's chained, so we don't have to face him later."

"Ooh, girl," Raze said, affecting a shiver, "You're cold-blooded. Want me to take care of the Goat while you do Denney?"

Raze bared her talons with a smile. Suddenly a familiar voice echoed through the arena just beyond the doors of the waiting room: Mark Winters.

"Tim..." Dawn muttered, dropping her arm and racing for the door, her crew of misfits following closely behind.

CHAPTER 28

The stage descended with Mark and his dancers. He twirled them both and began one of their practiced dance numbers. He hoped it wouldn't take the crew too much longer to set up The Wheel. His coordination was not on point due to the number of special coffees he'd consumed, but finally, after what seemed like forever, the music stopped.

"Hey folks! Thanks for bearing with us. It has been a whirlwind night of firsts! Am I right?" He paused so the idiots in the crowd could applaud and murmur.

"So, what do ya' say? Why not *another* first for you? It's my absolute pleasure to introduce, courtesy of our very own Amy Green, the brand spankin' new and ever deadly, *Try Not to Die* Wheel...of...Dismemberment!"

The crowd went wild.

A couple of goons pushed a huge wheel, about the size of a playground merry-go-round turned on its side, out into the center of the arena. Tim was attached to The Wheel.

"You all asked for justice for Abadonna. Coincidentally, *Justice for Abadonna* t-shirts are on sale in the lobby for only $27.99! Get yours now!"

Mark thrust back his jacket and partially unbuttoned his formal shirt to reveal his own Abadonna t-shirt. He knew as soon as he gave it a good wash that all the hastily ironed-on lettering would come off, but he didn't really give a shit. He got 5% commission on all t-shirt sales.

"Now, they say nobody can be harder on you than yourself. So let's test out that theory, shall we? We will let Mister...uh..." he thought for a moment before remembering the contestant's name, "Mr. Tim Powell decide his own punishment! Let the Wheel spin!"

The audience began to chant "Spin! Spin! Spin!" and the goons gave The Wheel a nice hard shove. The Wheel itself was divided into about a dozen equally-sized pie pieces, each a different color. At the top of The Wheel was a ticker, and as each segment passed by the ticker, it lit up. The symbols on some of the segments were obvious, others were more esoteric, so Amy Green had provided Mark with a key.

As The Wheel slowed, it very nearly stopped on castration, represented by a playfully prudish fig leaf, but it passed by that and stopped on the purple pie piece, which was marked by, Mark had to admit, an unmistakable nose.

"Oh! And the Wheel of Dismemberment's first stop is…cutting off your nose. Let's hope it doesn't spite your face."

Pneumatic pipes whistled and a multi-jointed robotic arm ending in a pair of what looked like pliers telescoped out from the back of The Wheel. The pliers clamped down on Tim's nose, making him shriek bloody murder. The pliers pulled his nose forward, and a guillotine-like blade sliced downward behind it, shearing his nose from his face. He screamed and his new missing proboscis made him look like a pig.

Mark turned to the Producer's box. Marisol and the others were cackling with glee. He didn't even bother to look for a signal to continue.

"Spin…" he swallowed something in his throat. Normally this never happened to him on camera. He ginned up the biggest smile he could. "Spin 'er again, boys!"

The goons spun The Wheel a second time. Tim was moaning a low, plaintive cry, probably asking for the relief of death while the audience shrieked with excitement. The Wheel came to a halt with the Tim nearly 180 degrees upside down. The pie piece it landed on was yellow, and when The Wheel stopped, what looked like an entire human leg, replete with Hermes' winged ankles, blinked. The pie piece was also where the cue ball's left leg was strapped down.

Mark waited for a pneumatic arm to extend from the back of the Wheel of Dismemberment to chop the man's leg off, but he jumped back in shock when the entire yellow pie piece exploded forward off The Wheel, ripping Tim's leg along with it.

Mark and the audience alike waited in dumbfounded shock for just a split-second as Tim screamed in agony, but a ringing bell startled everyone out of it. The big projector screens were lighting up with dollar, ruble, and peso signs. He ran his hand through his hair.

"Well, well, I guess the yellow slice triggered the bonus game!"

Camila and Wendy, the smiles never leaving their faces, grabbed their t-shirt cannons and began to strut around the stage suggestively. The crowd went wild, Tim, his ragged leg still spurting blood, forgotten on The Wheel for the moment. Mark grabbed one of the marketing packets and held it up.

"One of our sponsors, Farmer Brown's Country Fresh Moonshine, has happily put together six of these prize packages for you folks. First you get a one-size fits all *Try Not to Die* t-shirt, featuring one of twenty of your favorite slashers!"

Mark unpeeled the first layer from the prize packet. He unfurled it. The t-shirt was of such cheap quality he hoped it wouldn't fall apart in his hands.

"Look at that. I got…The Connoisseur! Haven't seen her yet tonight. Maybe we still might. Night's still young, don't you think, Mr. Powell?"

He gestured at the man on The Wheel, who groaned an incoherent response.

"Okay. In addition to that, a Justice for Abadonna t-shirt. Never let it be said that Farmer Brown is not a socially conscious bootlegger. And inside all of that, a bottle of Farmer Brown's… and, oh yeah, a roll of coins adding up to a hundred rubles in various denominations! How about that, folks? We've got six of these for you. All you've got to do…is walk out of the stadium with it."

He signaled for the girls to start shooting. Prancing, more than anything else, they began walking back and forth, holding their hands up to their ears, riling up the crowd. Finally, the first dancer fired her t-shirt cannon, and the payload struck a young girl sitting on her father's shoulder's directly in the face, sending her flying backwards. In the scrum that followed, a six-foot tall man built like a linebacker and wielding a hatchet at arms' length came out on top, daring the other competitors to take the prize pack from him. He made it all the way to practically the entrance before a farm girl with a garrote brought him down.

The dancers made a show of it, pretending to sympathetically listen to the pleas of the shouting audience members, and then, inevitably, firing the prize packs in a different direction. Each time they did, a violent scuffle broke out. Finally, their bloodlust for t-shirts and gewgaws satiated, the audience turned their attention back to the arena.

"Okay, gentlemen," Mark said. "Let's spin The Wheel...one last time!"

The goons gave it a whirl, amidst Tim's labored moans of pain. The Wheel came to stop on a blue pie slice that seemed to depict a stick figure. Mark glanced down at his key.

"Oh!" he exclaimed. "That is...a family member!"

Tim looked up from the dismal place where he was lost. The Wheel of Dismemberment began to hiss and groan and the back of it opened up and discharged a cage, about half the height of a human being and containing a stooped over figure. Once the cage had been discharged, it telescoped out on pneumatic limbs to where the victim could see it.

"Grandma?" Tim said loudly.

The old woman in the cage's eyes widened.

"Timothy! Oh my goodness, my boy!"

She began weeping and tears fell from Tim's eyes as well. The old woman composed herself first.

"It's so good to see—"

But her sentence was cut off as a pneumatic drill press, identical to the ones used to slaughter pigs in abattoirs, shot down from the roof of the cage and drilled through the old woman's head. Her eyes rolled back and her body seized against her restraints. Tim began screaming in horror as the Wheel of Dismemberment simply, and unemotionally, returned the cage to its place.

CHAPTER 29

Mark closed his eyes and let the audience's wave of pleasure roll over him, though he could share none of it. Who knew all it would take to fire up this jaded crowd was an old lady getting brained with a pneumatic drill? While the crowd was distracted he discreetly snapped his fingers at the stagehand, who was lurking around above the stage area. He knew he was going to need to be a lot drunker to keep narrating this.

As the stagehand scrabbled down the access ladder, sloshing more of his drink out than was staying in the cup, the crowd gasped and Mark wrinkled his forehead.

What could be driving these jaded fucks into an uproar?

He looked down into the arena and his stomach turned to ice.

"Mr. Winters? Mr. Winters?"

"Get the fuck out of here," Mark spat, slapping away the stagehand with his drink in hand.

Surprised, the young man scurried back into the rafters.

Dawn Churchill was back in the arena. Not dead, and not hiding anymore either. She was striding with a purpose towards the Wheel of Dismemberment.

The crowd had noticed before the goons standing in the pit had. Shocked out of their complacency, they both reached for their rifles. One dropped immediately, a puff of smoke emerging from the crater where his face had been.

Mark stared in amazement at what he had mistaken for a crude prosthetic arm. In reality it was a fully functional shotgun on a swivel, and without seeming to otherwise manipulate it with her good arm, Dawn pointed it at the remaining goon. She blasted the rifle out of his hands, and unlike in the movies where that always seemed to happen cleanly and painlessly, she had left the man with a stump of a wrist where his left hand had been, and he collapsed to the ground clutching his wound.

"Get up!" she shouted, planting her feet.

"Look, lady, I just work here, I don't—"

"Get. Up." She repeated her words, raising the shotgun to his head.

His eyes swiveled over to the Producers' box. Marisol and the others were riveted on the new development, and thankfully not staring down at him with what he knew would have been murderous glares.

Down in the arena, the goon was struggling to his feet, while still cradling his ruined arm. He was really only a kid, actually, once his mirrored sunglasses were off and he was just standing there. He held out the wreck of his lost limb towards Dawn accusatorily.

"You ruined my arm!"

"It happens," she said grimly. "Now get him down from there."

"Da...Dawn?" Tim was whispering, seemingly in and out of consciousness.

"I've got you, Tim. Don't you worry about it. I'm here now!"

Mark's earpiece crackled to life.

"What the hell is going on out there, Winters?"

"I...I...I..."

Mark clenched his jaw shut. He slapped himself across the face once, hard. He had overcome his speech impediment in the fifth grade. It hadn't come back, not even during times of great stress, ever since. Certainly never while on stage. Certainly, never in public. He swallowed the souls of a thousand garbled words and a thousand laughing children's torments.

"I don't know, Jimmy! I'm watching it the same as you! The question is: can you fix it?"

The line was silent for a moment.

"There's Denney's special entrance. It'd be between the girl and The Wheel."

Mark glanced up at the Producers. They were still watching the action, not him, which thank God for small miracles.

"Let him out."

"What's Marisol going to say?"

"What's she going to say if we let this get out from under us? You want to be hung from piano wire? That's if we're lucky. Maybe we get strapped to that fucking wheel next, or sent down to the gimp farm. We need to unfuck this, Jimmy. We need to unfuck this right now. Release the fucking Kraken."

CHAPTER 30

Dawn gritted her teeth. Seeing Tim like this was doing a number on what was left of her compassion.

"Get him down from there."

"Look, lady, you need to get real," the goon said with a resigned chuckle. "Where do you expect to go? What do you expect to do? Nobody gets out of this arena alive."

"Just get him the fuck down! Now!" she ordered, restraining herself from beating him over the head with her weaponized arm.

Between his missing hand and his missing partner the guard struggled to get Tim unstuck from the abominable contraption. Dawn wanted to say to get his grandmother out of the machine, too, for a proper burial, but grandma was just going to be dead weight, literally. The truth was the guard was right. There wasn't much chance of anybody walking out of there. Not with a corpse in tow, not without either. Especially with the shape that Tim was in.

"*He's right, you know,*" a dark, syrupy voice whispered in her ear.

She tucked a lock of hair back behind her ear.

"Charlie?"

"*The game's not a game. The game's a show. Think about the difference between having a conversation with a human being and reading lines from a script. In a stage play there's the appearance of a conversation, but really the whole thing is already decided far, far in advance by a person…a screenwriter acting essentially as God.*"

She glanced up at the Producers' box. The four miserable fucks were whispering to one another, and now Marisol was calling the host of the show over. Mark looked like somebody had pissed in his cereal, or, more accurately, like he was about to be executed for gross incompetence.

Those people had fixed everything. There was no contest. Not really. Her decisions didn't matter. She was just a rat in their maze. There was no free will, only the appearance of it. When they wanted to change the rules, they did. When they wanted to double- or triple-stack the odds against them, they did.

"How do you change the script?"

"What?" the guard asked, looking away from unbuckling Tim.

"I'm not talking to you," she said.

He snorted.

"Yeah. Just to the voices in your head."

"He's more right than you know. I live with this every day. It's interesting watching a supposedly normal person have to deal with it as well. Now to your point: actors are on rails, or so we think, but they do feed off the reactions of the audience. A particularly well-liked bon mot can inspire improvisation from the actor. And if you know your history, even the Emperor of Rome looked to the mob for decisions when it came time to let particularly well-loved gladiators live or die."

"Thumbs up he lives, thumbs down he dies?"

"Well, historians dispute the historicity of those particular gestures, but, yes, essentially."

"Rally the crowd to my side? How? It can't be done. All they want is blood."

"Huh. And I thought you were so smart, Ms. Churchill. If all they want is blood, then you offer them more blood."

Charlie hissed his final words before the earpiece went silent and Dawn's flesh broke out in goose bumps. Her mind raced, but finally she thought she knew exactly what Charlie was getting at. She turned around and pointed her remaining hand toward the platform above the arena.

"Hey! Marisol!" She shouted, her voice echoing.

Hushed murmurs spread through the crowd and Dawn could feel the electric excitement beginning to build.

Startled, Mark ran away from the Producers and back to center stage, where he straightened his bow tie.

"Oh, it looks..." Mark wiped the nervous sweat from his

brow. "It looks like we've got some action going on now, folks! It looks like..."

But no one was listening to him, their attention was fixated on Dawn as she marched over and grabbed the goon who'd finally finished releasing Tim from The Wheel. The goon shrieked, caught off guard. Dawn dragged him back over to where she previously stood and tossed him to the ground before her, forcing him to his knees, placing the shotgun to the back of his head.

The crowd was more than interested now. Dawn could hear the wicked shouts erupting all around her.

"Kill him!"

"Execute the goon!"

"Blow his head off!"

She stared up at the skybox, a fire in her eyes.

"No." She said, and the crowd gasped, briefly falling silent.

"How about a new mini-game?" she asked, pausing as the audience whispered amongst themselves. "It's called...well, I don't know what the fuck it's called."

"Please, Ms. Churchill! There are children watching!" Mark scolded.

That garnered a laugh from the crowd.

Marisol folded her arms.

Dawn nodded. Of course, it was all about playing the crowd.

"The mini-game is called Get in the Barn. It's where one of the Producers puts her money where her mouth is, and instead of sending out a slasher to do her dirty work, she enters the arena and faces the contestants herself. What do you say?"

Marisol, now standing beside Mark, looked around. The crowd seemed really excited about the idea. The Queen of Texas paused for a moment, cocking her head as if considering it, but then a wicked grin twisted her face in half.

"I say you'd better turn around, Ms. Churchill."

Dawn whirled around as the entire arena suddenly seemed to be shaking. The ground fell away under her feet and she quickly dove to safety. She regained her footing and turned around in time to see the goon scurrying out of harm's reach.

In the dead center of the arena, right smack in between

where she was standing and where Tim still lay on the Wheel of Dismemberment, a circular hole appeared in the ground.

Shit shit shit and double shit!

It dawned on her far too late what was happening.

Entry of the Gladiators was blaring on the loudspeakers.

"Laaaadies aaaaand gentlemen," Mark Winters announced in his very best grand entrance voice against the music. "Let's all put together a very warm welcome for the king of the ring, the master of disaster, the number one killer in the *'Try Not to Die* Barn.'"

The crowd was going apeshit. Every single one of them seemed to be wearing a Denney t-shirt, though Dawn knew that was impossible unless it had just happened in the last few seconds. Then she saw Winters's two dancing girls frantically firing their t-shirt guns to every corner of the crowd. It was turning into a sea of pink shirts, all plastered with the goonish face of the greatest slasher who had ever lived.

"Weighing in at nearly 600 pounds and standing over seven and half feet tall, I present to you the most successful serial killer who ever lived. With four hundred and thirty-seven kills in the wild, eighty-seven of our finest guards, and forty-three contestants...and one visiting dignitary from the Soviet Union..."

The crowd chuckled. Denney's famous exploit of ripping apart the Politburo member who had asked to shake his hand was a staple of *Try Not to Die* clip shows and sizzle reels. Mark continued.

"...adding up to a lifetime total of five hundred and sixty-eight murders, I am very proud to present to you, on behalf of Farmer Brown's Old-Fashioned Moonshine, Hedare Beauty Company, and the producers of *Try Not to Die*...please put your hands together for Denney the Killer Clown!"

Slowly, a building began to emerge on pneumatic presses from the sand of the arena. First, a conical top appeared, then a rotating center portion that dripped with sand from the arena floor. Finally, fully revealed, was a slowly rotating carnival merry-go-round. The horses, camels, and occasional far-fetched animals like dragons and giant seahorses slowly gave way to a single, dark, hulking figure looming in the shadows.

Psychedelic light took over the arena's light system, turning the rotating of the carousel into a drug trip-like experience.

Dawn tried to follow what was going on, but all she could really tell was that one of the horses, a brown mare if she hadn't missed her guess, had come loose from the pedestal, pole and all. The flashing lights made it difficult to see, and Dawn nearly missed witnessing the horse and pole as it flew through the air like a javelin, impaling the one-handed guard.

Dawn tried not to lurch from her discombobulation. The circus music seemed to slow, and with it, the lights went wild, throwing her sense of balance off. Finally, the merry-go-round came to a halt, the lights returned to normal, and the hulking figure of Denney stepped forward in all his glory.

Swaddled from head to toe in a onesie with vertical stripes, and with huge fluffy buttons running down the seam of where his shirt would have been, Denney was very close to eight feet tall. Dawn wasn't sure offhand what the record for tallest person was, but she'd bet that the slasher either came very close or had already claimed it.

And he wasn't a thin seven-plus-feet tall, either. At well over a quarter of a ton he loomed like an outhouse, or like the theoretical brick shithouse of metaphors. His arms were unnaturally long, dragging almost along the ground like a Neanderthal's, an effect which was amplified by his stooped posture, which made Dawn suddenly shudder and wonder what it would be like if the murderous clown stood up straight. At that size, he was certainly a mutant, some hulking child of the fission bombs which had laid waste to the former United States and ravaged the genetic material of the Geiger Landers.

A comically undersized top hat—which, as Dawn thought about it, might have simply been an average sized man's hat—lay cocked at an angle on Denney's head, held in place by a wire under his chin like a child's birthday party hat. And completing the ensemble was a horrible face not Denney's own.

No, Denney's face was hidden under what appeared to be the skinned-off face of one of his latest victims, probably a fatter one, though still stretched nearly to the breaking point to slip over his own like a mask. The reason Dawn thought it was a human face instead of a latex mask—other than the grim feeling of alarm she felt in her stomach—was the flies that still buzzed around, crawling in and out of the mask, apparently not bothering Denney at all.

Somewhat surprisingly, the facemask was painted to painstaking perfection with grease paint. Again, Dawn wasn't sure if some backstage hand did the painting for him, but she had a strange feeling the giant murderer labored over the project for hours, his ham hock-sized hands somehow discovering the dexterity to paint impeccable flourishes to make him look the perfect clown.

Denney lumbered out from under the overhang of the carousel. He eyed Dawn, the eyes in his head visible and cold, distinctly inhuman and reptilian. She instantly felt again the same sense of malign, ignorant wrath she had felt in the Barn, when he had been just behind the graffito-tagged door from her.

I should have killed him when I had the chance.

Denney lurched toward her, his massive hands outstretched like a child's trying to grab at a dolly.

Dawn whirled her shotgun around and fired, once into his chest, then again with the other chamber. Denney halted in place, and for a moment she hoped she had managed to stop the murderous Pagliacci in his tracks, but Denney merely reached down to pat the front of his onesie, which was peppered with tiny holes from the shot. As he patted his front, not a single drop of blood trickled out.

A mutant he was indeed, and one impervious to gunfire it seemed.

Dawn took a few steps backward and glanced over at the holding area where her friends were hiding. It might be time to call upon them. She turned around and looked up at the Producers' box, opening her mouth to speak, but the off-screen announcer interrupted her before the words could even form on her tongue.

"And now, a word from our sponsors."

CHAPTER 31

Dance music played in the background as cameras flashed and a waif-like blonde posed seductively in a studio. Moans and whispers in a foreign tongue intertwined with the music in perfect timing with close-up shots of the blonde smiling and winking at the camera.

The scene cut to the same blonde sitting at a vanity with a myriad of products set out before her.

"When it comes time for my close up, I need a make-up I can trust." She said with a wide smile, picking up a dainty bottle of foundation.

The blonde stood up and began wiping her face with silk cloth and the dance music began playing again, cutting to a scene of the blonde standing in the wasteland with her back to the cameras. She turned around, revealing a disfigured face with hideous burn scars. She smiled wide again and held out her hand, the foundation bottle in the center of her palm.

"Don't just be another product of the Geiger Lands, be a product of the Hedare Company."

She popped open the bottle and began applying the make-up to her face. The scene cut harshly to the blonde smiling and posing for the cameras in the studio once again with beautiful, flawless skin before it returned to her sitting at the vanity.

"You know I wasn't born with it."

She winked at the camera and blew a kiss as a short jingle played and the scene faded out.

CHAPTER 32

"So, you're afraid to face me yourself after all, Marisol." Dawn said. "You have to send an invincible killing machine to stop me? Well guess what? I have one of my own."

Dawn gestured back to the Barn and hoped that Raze wasn't off on one of her head trips. The younger woman seemed to get the idea though, and either gave Gus a shove, or else Gus got the idea all by himself. The hulking slasher, who was nevertheless dwarfed by Denney the Clown, came roaring out, his chainsaw revving, the mere sound of which was driving the crowd into absolute hysterics.

Denney turned at the sound of Gus's appearance. One thing Dawn saw they had going for them: Denney moved slowly and deliberately, like a train switching tracks. He turned just in time to catch Gus's chainsaw in his shoulder. Rather than slice him in half like a knife through hot butter, as it would have to any ordinary human being, Gus's weapon merely rocked back and forth about an inch into Denney's clavicle, discolored blood trickling from the wound. So, he wasn't utterly invincible, but he was still the human equivalent of a brick wall.

Denney reached out and clasped his left hand around the chainsaw, making it catch and halt, and Dawn would have thought severing all of his fingers, but no.

Minimal blood poured from the clown's hand and Dawn thought she heard him let out a chuckle. Denney kicked an enormous leg forward, his foot meeting Gus's stomach, and the chainsaw wielding giant flew backward.

"Fuck." Dawn found herself saying aloud.

She watched in horror as Gus landed on his back. If Gus wasn't a match for Denney, then no one was. They were all screwed. Gus got to his feet quickly though, grunting in anger, and restarted his chainsaw. Denney moved forward and the two giants moved in a circle, calculating one another's moves, waiting for the right moment to strike.

"*I see you've met Denney,*" the voice in her ear said.

"Uh, yeah. Thanks for the heads up, Charlie."

Charming Charlie chuckled. "*Not to worry, old Gus is a bit rusty, but he's been itching for a good fight. I need you to continue your mission, Ms. Churchill, don't forget why you're up there.*"

"I tried getting her to come down. Weren't you listening?"

Dawn was getting irritated, she couldn't keep talking to Charlie like this. Gus needed her help. She wasn't sure exactly how she could be of assistance, but she needed to do something.

"*My dear, did you really think it was going to be so easy to lure the queen from her throne? No no no, that's not how this works. You have to go to her. Simple as that.*"

Dawn rolled her eyes.

"Easy for you to say, but what about Gus? And Tim? I'm not just leaving them like this!"

"*That's the name of the game, Dawn. Keep your eye on the prize.*"

Dawn gritted her teeth, expecting the worst as she watched the clown make his first move. He dropped a shoulder and charged Big Gus, but in the nick of time Gus plunged the chainsaw into the wound he'd previously opened up. The big piece of machinery worked back and forth in Denney's thick, armored skin. The clown attempted to try to remove the chainsaw, but Gus had finally gotten the upper hand: it was in there good. It would take some time, but Gus would get that arm off; Dawn saw a look of determination on the silent man that she'd hadn't ever seen before.

"*You see?*" Charlie asked. "*He doesn't need you. Now go.*"

Dawn's attention returned to Tim, still lying on the wheel on the other side of the carousel. The audience had been so captivated by the mammoth fight that no one had even noticed Raze and the gimps enter the arena and approach Tim's location.

She started towards them, briefly looking back to Gus who was now withstanding blow after blow of Denney's fist to his gut as he continued to work the chainsaw with maximum effort.

She wondered how long he could continue like that. She hoped for as long as it would take.

"*Ms. Churchill, what do you think you're doing?*" Charlie asked, annoyance in his voice. "*You're going the wrong way.*"

"Not now, Charlie. I'm busy." She clicked the button on the earpiece and silenced him.

"Raze!" she called out as she grew nearer to the Wheel.

Her younger companion looked up at her with disappointed eyes and Dawn's heart sunk.

She slowed to a jog and finally to a stop beside The Wheel. Tim looked up at her, groggy, his nose missing and blood covering most of his face. The wheel around him was also covered in blood from where his leg had been torn off. He'd already been through the shit that night; missing half a hand, shot in the arm, stabbed through the kidney, mental and physical exhaustion... and now *this*. Dawn glanced up at his dead grandmother, there was that, too. Dawn couldn't wrap her head around how Tim was still alive, but she admired him for it. He was the epitome of resilience.

"Tim," she choked out, tears in her eyes. "I'm here now, we're getting you out of this mess."

Tim clutched her hand and managed that sweet smile of his that Dawn had grown so fond of in such a short period of time.

"I knew it when I first saw you." He said, his voice barely audible above the roar of the crowd egging on the fight behind them.

"Knew what?" Dawn furrowed her brow.

"You were a winner."

Dawn shook her head.

"I'm not a winner, Tim. *We're* winners." She looked up at Raze. "We all are. We're gonna beat this thing, and we're gonna make them pay."

"Dawn, please." Tim sobbed. "Please, kill me."

She gazed down at him and felt lost. She'd wanted nothing but to save him this whole time and here he was suffering before her, ready to die. She'd been too late.

The crowd went wild, snapping her from her thoughts and her grief. She whirled around and saw Gus triumphantly holding Denney's massive arm above his head, egging on the crowd. Putrid blood spurted from the clown's shoulder and he let out a roar, not in pain, but in fury. He swung out with his remaining arm, connecting his fist with Gus's head, knocking him off balance. The severed arm flew from his hand, but Big Gus didn't falter; clearly his massive opponent had been weakened.

Denney swung again and this time Gus ducked, coming back up and tackling the clown, sending them both to the arena floor. Gus rolled over quickly, and snatched up his chainsaw as he jumped to his feet. Denney attempted to get up, but he was dazed from the fall, his size betraying him. Dawn recalled an old saying, *"the bigger they are..."*

Gus brought the chainsaw down into the center of the mutant clown's rock-solid torso, meeting resistance the first time, but he continued his assault, blow after blow, until finally blood decorated the front of his clothing and Denney let out his first roar of pain.

Dawn, Raze, Tim, and even the gimps, watched in awe as Gus finally silenced his weapon and removed it from the gory hole he'd created in Denney's midsection. He raised the chainsaw above his head, the proud victor, and placed his foot on the clown's motionless chest.

The crowd went wild.

Dawn smiled, proud of Gus, and thankful he'd been there to save her life, which then reminded her of Tim, and the smile soon disappeared from her face. She felt him squeeze her hand and she looked back down at him.

"I'm so sorry, Tim. I tried to get here in time. I tried to save you."

She wiped a solitary tear from her cheek and was surprised to see Tim smile again.

"You *are* saving me, Dawn."

She squeezed his hand in hers and nodded.

He was right. She understood now.

"Goodbye, Tim."

She placed her shotgun under his chin, and he closed his eyes, that special smile still on his face right up to the moment that Dawn pulled the trigger and his entire face disappeared in a gory mist.

She felt his hand go limp and she finally let go.

"You did good, Dawny." Raze said, patting her hand.

"Thanks." Dawn sniffled, and wiped Tim's blood from her face, turning back toward Gus.

He walked toward them, oafish as ever, but there was a new pep in his step. Maybe Charlie had been right. Maybe the fight had been just what Big Gus needed. Dawn was about to ask the group if they were ready to take the next step in the plan when Raze let out an ear-piercing shriek.

"Gus! No!"

Dawn's hand flew to her mouth as the jagged end of a pole appeared through a fresh hole in Gus's chest.

Gus dropped to his knees from the sheer weight of the merry-go-round's seahorse that now impaled him, pressing on his back and lungs. He looked down at the pole and back up at the shocked women in front of him. It looked like he was trying to say something. His chainsaw dropped from his hand, and he finally fell forward, the pole sticking into the ground diagonally, Gus's lifeless frame slumped over.

Denney, overcoming his mortal wounds either from his mutant anatomy or sheer stubbornness, worked with all his might to break another piece free from the carousel. Before Dawn even had the chance to process what had just happened, she saw a flash of movement and realized Raze was no longer beside her.

A blur of teeth and nails zapped across the arena. A churlish laughing filled Dawn's ears.

"Well, would you look at that, folks," Mark's voice filled the stadium, "It looks like the little lady is taking a shot at Denney the Clown. How do you think *that's* going to work out for her?"

The crowd dutifully burst into laughter. Denney stood his ground and with barely a flick of his wrist snapped Raze out of her death charge and sent her flying, skidding on her back across the floor of the arena, halfway propelled by her own momentum. It looked like she was out for the count.

Denney took a few steps back towards the carousel and

Dawn watched with a careful eye, expecting him to grab one of the steeds to use as a weapon. Instead, he went around to the far end and pressed his shoulder in to the side of the construct. Dawn wondered for a moment what he was doing until, with a lurch and a shake, the carousel began to lift a few inches off the ground.

"Take a look at this, folks," Mark said, "It's not often that Denney the Clown demonstrates his true strength, but we might be getting a demonstration tonight!"

"No," Dawn muttered under her breath, "it's impossible."

Denney strained, without grunting, and began rocking back and forth as the merry-go-round lifted up off the ground and at a forty-five-degree angle. Dawn turned to look at Raze's prone body. The angle Denney was pushing at, if he flipped the thing entirely over, it would fall directly on her.

Dawn broke into a sprint just as Denney had pushed the carousel all the way up into a position perpendicular to the ground. A shadow now fell over her and Raze, a huge, circular shadow. She practically slid into the smaller girl like she was stealing a base.

"Come on! Come on!"

Dawn tried not to let herself sympathize with Denney, who was also missing an arm. She grabbed Raze's scruff with her good arm, and started dragging her out of the way of the merry-go-round, which was now starting to topple towards them. She felt like she was pulling her friend incredibly slowly.

"Help! Help!" she shouted at the gimps, who were still over by The Wheel of Dismemberment.

The two came running, one on all fours, and picked up Raze between them. It was not an instant too soon, either, as the entire merry-go-round came crashing down on what would have been all of them had it not been for the loyal gimps. They managed to make it out from under the deadly shadow just by the skin of their teeth.

Implacable, Denney turned his attention back toward Dawn. A dozen normal men would have been unable to move after such an exertion. Denney the Clown wasn't even breathing heavily.

"Go, go!" Dawn shouted, ordering the gimps to do their worst.

Denney didn't take a step as the first gimp, dressed in a leather dog mask, pounded across the arena on all fours. Denney simply raised his fist like a hammer, and with a lumberjack's swing brought it down, snapping the gimp's back and squishing him into the ground so hard that blood and entrails spurted out from under him like a breaking piñata.

That brought the second gimp, still on two legs, up short. He turned to look back at Dawn. She wanted to tell him to go on, but that seemed like a death sentence. She had hoped the two killers would make short work of the wounded champ, but it seemed even a dying lion could strike terrible blows with his paws.

In his moment of hesitation, the second gimp was lost. He didn't realize it until a colossal shadow fell over him, and he looked up to see that Denney the Clown, with twice the reach of a normal man, was already within arm's length.

Denney clapped his hand down on the second gimp's head, easily encompassing it in his massive palm. He lifted the man, chains and buckles dangling, so that the soles of his shoes were two feet off the ground. The gimp punched and kicked at the colossal killer, who seemed to take no more notice than he would have at the buzzing of a fly.

With a scream, Raze, who Dawn had already counted as out, came roaring back towards Denney. She leapt on his back and began slashing away, taking out her fury at the loss of her dearest friend, Big Gus.

Denney straightened his posture to ramrod straight, and Dawn had been right to guess that without slouching he was far taller than any unmutated human. Raze was so busy hacking and slashing away at the monster's spinal column that she didn't even realize what was happening until he began falling backwards. She leapt away from him just in the nick of time, avoiding being crushed under the mountain of man meat.

The gimp in Denney's hand, which he had still not released, was bucking furiously. All that could be heard from the man was muted grunts and groans, though, Dawn reflected, that was probably true most of the time. Denney sat up like Frankenstein's monster on the slab and turned to look at Raze, who was hunched, breathing hard, just outside of his reach. Without standing up, he held the gimp out towards her.

Denney's fist tightened slowly, excruciatingly slowly. Once as a child Dawn had seen the "magic" trick of being asked to crush an egg by holding it in your palm and applying even pressure, usually with the magician clasping his hands around yours. With even pressure the egg was immensely hard to break. Dawn was reminded of that now, though with the gaps between his fingers, Denney's hand looked more like a squid grasping its prey than a hand crushing a perfect egg.

The gimp began shivering and shuddering as the vise-like pressure closed. Dawn looked for some change in Denney's expression, expecting him to grimace or grind his teeth or something, but he remained an implacable mask behind the grease-painted face of some unknown victim. Somehow, his inscrutability made the gruesome murder taking place even more horrifying.

Blood began to trickle out of the holes in the gimp's mask. His shaking and pitching became less controlled and more spastic, like a dead frog being jolted with electricity. With a sickening squish, both of his eyeballs popped out and went flying across the floor, surprisingly agile for such small things. Then the muffled grunts of pain turned to high-pitched shrieks of volume that seemed impossible to penetrate through the dual layers of his own mask and the giant's encompassing fist.

Finally, a noise like a tree branch cracking replaced the gimp's torturous shrieks. Brains, lips, and chunks of bone oozed out from between Denney's fingers. The gimp's body slumped away from his gelatinized head and Denney wiped his remaining hand off on his onesie before pushing himself back up to his feet. His attention was focused like a laser on Raze now. Dawn fired a shot into the back of his head, but he didn't flinch or even turn to look at her.

Raze stood up, dusted off her sleeves, and cracked her neck.

"Okay, pretty boy," she said. "Looks like it's just you and me now."

"Ha ha!" Mark's voice echoed through the arena, "It looks like you can't keep a good slasher down. Let's see how quickly Denney puts her out of her misery."

Raze flew at Denney, this time dodging the swing he took at her, and sliding through his legs, throwing her hands up to slash at his crotch. Finally behind him, she turned and dug her teeth deep into his right Achilles tendon. She came away with a mouthful of flesh and muscle, which shocked Dawn who had grown used to the idea of Denney being nigh invincible. But, of course, Raze had razor-sharp, metal teeth.

Denney grunted and swatted at the little woman. She ducked the blow and dug deep into his heel with her fingers, slashing and digging, slashing and digging. Angered, Denney lifted his foot and swiveled to bring it away from her, bringing his wounded right foot down hard on the arena floor. A loud crunch echoed through the stadium.

The air was suddenly still and silent. Even the audience's side conversations and the catcalls of the food vendors had silenced. A snap sounded and Denney's foot separated from his body, finally broken off at the heel from the force of his own body weight. His remaining arm whirled through the air like he was a guitarist revving up to strike a power chord. Then he toppled over, falling on his right-hand side, then flipping over onto his back.

Raze jumped on the man's head and began slashing over and over at his eyes, making shambles of his human face mask. Denney groaned and tried to grab her off, but she ducked out of the way just in time.

Blind and reduced to half his limbs, Denney flailed on the ground, but, strangely, still didn't utter a word. After a moment he stopped and seemed to regain his bearing. Dawn realized with a start that she had been simply watching, fixated, like one of the audience members she loathed so much, instead of helping her friend. It was so easy to fall into that trap. Startled out of inaction, Dawn rushed towards the scene.

There was still a jagged hole where Big Gus had managed to hack off Denney's arm. His skin might have been as hard as stone and capable of taking a frightful amount of damage, but she was willing to wager that a blast of lead pellets directly into his body wasn't going to do him any good. She jammed her shotgun arm into the hole and fired.

Denney fell still. Dawn dared to hope for a second that he had finally taken his deathblow, but it seemed he had only been shocked into a moment of submission. He rolled over onto his side, pressing the wound to the ground so she would have no further access. She walked around to his feet and fired another shell into the gaping wound where his foot had been. A second time Denney fell still, and a second time he recovered a moment later, though this time noticeably slower. Perhaps he was not immortal after all.

Both chambers discharged, she now reloaded. She could think of one or two remaining open orifices for the giant. She called out to Raze, lifting her shotgun and pointing at Denney's mouth, but Raze shook her head.

Now that the giant was on his side, Raze nimbly went to his back, slashed a hole in the trouser seat of his onesie, and shoved her arm deep into his asshole, slashing at his small and large intestines with equal ferocity. The clown-faced killer finally opened his mouth, a silent roar of pain still not quite escaping his lips, but Dawn was now able to shove her shotgun straight in. With one last blast Denney fell still, and this time he stayed that way.

CHAPTER 33

The crowd was in a state of pure rapture and Mark's jaw nearly dropped to the floor.

"Holy shit!" he said without thinking. He knew he wasn't supposed to use foul language on the air, but after witnessing the giant fall, he was too shocked to remember.

"In an unprecedented set of events we are witnessing history in the making *once again* tonight, folks."

Mark wasn't even sure how he was able to continue addressing the crowd, he felt as if someone else entirely had climbed inside of his head and taken over. Things were hazy, the lights weren't as bright as they'd seemed to be all night, and the deafening roar of the crowd was fading.

Am I about to pass out? he wondered, and snuck a quick glance at The Producers behind him.

Bits of food fell from Jacob's open mouth as he shouted inaudible obscenities while Amy's hands covered the bottom half of her shocked face. Derron looked a little worse for wear. His usually dark skin seemed a bit too pale and his eyes weren't really fixed on anything in particular.

I feel ya, buddy. Mark managed to nod, empathizing with the queen's husband.

The queen.

She stood while the others sat, with perfect posture, her hands on her hips. Her glare was fixed on Mark, and as he stared back at her, he realized her mouth was moving but he couldn't hear what she was saying. It wasn't until she had crossed the catwalk and was practically on top of him, both hands gripping his collar and shaking him violently, that the world came back to life around him.

The screaming audience, in all their fanatical splendor, was suddenly invading his ears, and the lights were once again so bright that he almost had to close his eyes. He felt a hard slap across the cheek and snapped to full attention.

"What the fuck's the matter with you!" Marisol was screaming at him.

Mark brought a hand up to his cheek and gently caressed.

"We're, uh, we're fucked," he said to her, and without realizing it, began to laugh.

"Stop laughing, Markus," she ordered, but he continued. She hissed into her earpiece, "Cut to commercial, now! And keep the sponsors rolling until I say otherwise."

As Mark's hysterics continued, he imagined that if Marisol Martinez had been a cartoon, the top of her head might have already burst into flames and hot steam would have been shooting from her nostrils by now.

She gave him another vicious slap across the face and this time he shut up.

"I'm so glad that this absolute disaster of an evening is amusing you in such a way." She folded her arms over her chest.

Mark said nothing, ashamed by his inability to control his own actions. Sure, he'd had quite a bit to drink over the course of the evening, but he didn't think he'd ever really lost his composure on the set like this before. Derron rose from his seat and approached them, his face grim.

"It's over, Marisol," he said, placing a hand on his wife's delicate shoulder. "It's nearly four in the morning. Get the little slasher back in her cell and let the contestant go."

"Let her go?" Marisol's voice boomed.

She whirled on her heels, prepared to deliver a blow to her husband's face but he was already cowering, both hands up, shielding himself from her fury. Her hand stopped mid-strike and she chuckled.

"Pathetic." She shoved him out of her way and marched toward the two remaining Producers still in their seats.

"And what about you two? Huh? You think I should just let her go?"

Amy said nothing, choosing to stay neutral.

"It was bound to happen one day, Martinez." Jacob said, wiping his dirty hands on his trousers. "It's one show, no big deal."

"No big deal?" Marisol stared at him, her eyes wide and full of fire. "I'm sorry, did you just tell me that it's no big deal?"

Jacob shrugged.

Marisol seethed in silence, the crowd beginning to chant behind her, further fueling her rage. They were growing tired of the extended commercial break. They were hungry for blood, and so was she.

"Amy, are you still in contact with that young man from the French territories?" She asked, not taking her eyes off Jacob. "You know, the wealthy one that purchased half your arsenal last spring?"

Jacob began to sweat.

"You know it." Amy smiled, crossing one leg over the other and leaning back in her chair.

"Good," Marisol grinned. "It seems we have a position to fill."

Jacob sprinted from his seat and ran for the elevator car.

"Not so fast, fat man." Amy said.

Faster than Jacob could ever hope to be, she'd taken him down and now had him in quite the leg lock. He struggled against her, but Amy was not only skilled with her weapons, she was skilled with her body.

"Put him to sleep," Marisol ordered, and Amy nodded.

The queen turned to Mark, who once again had his mouth hanging open like a dead fish.

She gently nudged the bottom of his jaw, closing his mouth for him.

"Do be a dear and get your shit together. We have a new act, *Señor* Winters." She touched the earpiece in her ear and smiled. "Jimmy, put us back on in five and get in touch with the Barn."

"Who are we bringing out next?"

"Everyone."

CHAPTER 34

Dawn dropped down to her knees, using Denney's body as a firewall. She scanned the horizon. At any minute the Barn could open up and disgorge another killer. None left were more dangerous than Denney the Clown, so all she had to do was avoid getting sloppy.

"Well, that was a hell of a thing," Raze muttered beside her, breathing heavily, and leaning against Denney's massive back.

"Where'd you get your proctology degree?" Dawn asked.

"Brown," Raze giggled. "So where do we go from here?"

"You got me."

"Well, what's the professor saying?"

Dawn blushed. Somehow, in the fracas, she'd forgotten all about Charlie. She reached up and pressed the button on her earpiece.

"You there, Whitmore?"

"Oh, look who's decided to rejoin us," Charlie's voice flickered in her ear, dripping with disdain, *"Just checking in and out whenever you feel like, Ms. Churchill?"*

"Give me a break, Charlie. We've been fighting for our lives out here. What are you two even doing?"

"All in due time, my dear. All in due time."

"What does that mean?"

There was a pregnant pause on the line.

"Do you know the old saying 'keep your friends close and your enemies closer?'"

"Yeah…" Dawn admitted.

"Well, to follow that advice you'd need to do some real soul-searching about who your enemies are. And for that matter, who your friends are."

She glanced over at the broken Wheel of Dismemberment, with Tim's now faceless corpse still hanging from it. Her eyes lighted on Raze, who was tugging on her pigtails, pretending like she was piloting a bicycle and making fish noises with her lips.

"I know who my friends are," she stated flatly.

"And do I count among them?"

She paused, pursing her lips.

"I don't know."

Charming Charlie's chilling laugh filled her head, and she almost ripped the earpiece off.

"Not so easy to identify your enemies after all, is it?"

Like a laser-guided missile, Dawn's gaze locked onto the Producers' box. Marisol Martinez was standing up in it, looking right back at her.

"No, I know who my enemies are."

"Perhaps. Perhaps not. In any case, incoming…on your right."

The sound that accompanied the green room door opening blared, and Dawn jumped up into a crouch in surprise. Jacob Graves, the improbably obese man in the land of the starving was the lone occupant of the green room. Graves was scratching and clawing at the door back into the control room.

"Jimmy! Jimmy! Please! I pay your salary! I can give you anything you want. Marisol! Please don't do this Marisol! Talk to her, Jimmy, let me talk to her! Tell her it doesn't have to be this way! I'll do anything, give you anything. I can be useful. I can still be useful!"

The heat level in the green room was rising by the second, and Dawn was struck full in the face by the smell of sizzling hair. Sweat was pouring down Graves's face. She turned, expecting to share her look of awe with Raze, but the tiny slasher was still making burbling fish sounds, clearly bored with her surroundings.

"What do we do with this asshole?" Dawn asked incredulously.

Raze smiled, snapping out of her stupor and baring her jagged teeth. "The same thing we did with the last asshole."

She slapped at Denney's corpse, sending his butt cheeks

jiggling even as rigor mortis was setting in. She flashed her claws through the air and grinned wickedly. But before Raze could attack, a thumping noise sounded over the loudspeaker. All eyes turned to the Producers' box.

Marisol stood there, her flunky Mark Winters at her side, holding a microphone which she was tapping for attention.

"I want to congratulate you on a well-fought night *Señora* Churchill. You have defied every expectation and made this a *Try Not to Die* that will *never* be forgotten."

"Yeah, well, now that Denney's dead, I guess I've run the gauntlet. Time to let me go, right? There's no greater slasher in your arsenal."

Marisol clucked her tongue and shook her head.

"This is true. You have clawed your way to the top through cleverness and making some rather surprising allies, but I have decided to grant you your wish."

The buzzing stopped sounding and Dawn glanced back in the direction of the green room to see that Graves had finally decided to step out of the baking oven. He was lying in the sand of the arena, breathing heavily and covered with sweat, his pale white skin turned bright red by the heat.

"You're letting me go?" Dawn asked suspiciously.

"Oh, how soon we forget. Was it even an hour ago that you made such a bold demand of me? You asked for a new mini-game. What was it called again, Markus?"

Winters swallowed a lump in his throat. He had the look of a chastised schoolboy, his hands behind his back. He leaned in to Marisol's microphone.

"Get…"

"Speak up, Markus."

"It was called Get in the Barn, Your Majesty."

Marisol snapped the microphone back to her own chin.

"Get in the Barn, yes, that was it. Where one of the Producers comes down from our ivory tower and faces the contestants in the ring. Well, our good friend Jacob Graves has volunteered to make your dream come true."

Dawn glanced over at Graves, lying face down in the dirt and resembling nothing quite so much as a beached whale.

"Him? I'd love a shot at you people, but killing him in this state would be like taking candy from a baby."

"I love taking candy from babies," Raze whispered, a devilish grin on her face.

"Well, you're right, of course, *Señora* Churchill, and let's not forget the odds are a bit stacked against him. You have backup, after all. So, we've decided to give Mr. Graves some backup as well."

"Who's left?" Raze muttered, "With Charlie on our side and Denney gone, they'd have to send out…"

"…Everyone left in the Barn," Dawn completed the thought for her.

"Ah man, that means The Goat." Raze swallowed hard.

Marisol's spine-tingling cackle echoed through the arena. Despite speaking low and amongst themselves, there was no such thing as a private conversation with microphones set up all over the arena floor. Dawn and Raze looked back up at the platform and saw Marisol with an arm around Mark's neck, whispering something to him.

"That's right, ladies." Marisol said finally. "You're being treated like royalty tonight. I mean, not only are you about to meet the whole *Try Not to Die* family, but you're now competing alongside one of our own esteemed Producers, and he's a pretty big deal…" she paused and addressed the audience directly, "if you know what I mean."

The audience hooted and fell into hysterics, another Jacob Graves fat joke hitting it out of the park.

Dawn narrowed her eyes as she watched Mark disappear from view. Marisol might have been the one running the show from the shadows this whole time, but she was making it perfectly clear that she was now taking over, and the audience, if possible, was proving to be more enthusiastic than ever before. The people loved her.

Dawn clenched her fist. She couldn't wait to get her shotgun in that woman's mouth.

Someone else I should have killed when I had the chance, Dawn thought, cursing herself.

She thought back to when she was in that small, dirty room

at the beginning of the evening, when it was just the two of them, before the nightmare had begun, when she still had two working hands. She imagined herself leaping onto Marisol Martinez's back, bringing her down to the floor, wrapping her hands around the woman's throat...and just when the life was starting to leave the queen's eyes, she'd ease up a bit, let her think everything was going to be okay, but just for the briefest of moments...before squeezing again, cutting off her air supply. Dawn imagined doing this over and over again, until she finally grew tired of the little game, and then she'd grab that dinner tray, the one with the greasy meat and gravy, and she'd smash it into Marisol's pretty face until it resembled the food they'd served her.

"Dawny," Raze said, wrapping her small hand around Dawn's wrist. "Are you okay?"

"Huh?" Dawn snapped out of her murderous reverie and looked down with a grimace. She'd been squeezing her fist so tightly that her hand had gone numb.

"Oh," she raised her hand up, shaking it out, wishing the pins and needles away.

The violent thoughts invading her brain all night...they were new, they were scary, but they were her own. She looked at Raze, concern in the young woman's face, and then looked down at her shotgun arm.

"One of us," she whispered.

"Girls!" a breathy voice interrupted, a shadow cast over them.

Dawn and Raze both reacted quickly, readying themselves for a fight, but they realized it was Jacob Graves standing over them, hands on his knees, still trying to catch his breath.

"Oh boy, do I have a proposition for you both."

Raze hissed and lashed out at him with one of her claws like a cat, breaking the skin on Jacob's right arm. The obese man recoiled, gripping his arm. He stumbled backward, almost falling to the floor.

"Easy, easy now. Hear me out, girls." He put his hands up in surrender. "We're fucked if we don't get out of here."

"Maybe you are," Dawn said, hopping to her feet, her

Slashvivor! *171*

shotgun trained on his pudgy face.

"Oh, come on, honey. I've got more money than God, I've got more crops on my land than the whole continent. You girls are gonna be famous, rich and famous. I'll take you home with me, you can have whatever you want. You'll live like queens."

"I don't want to be a queen!" Dawn shouted, striking Jacob in the head with her fist.

The large man winced and cowered.

"I want my life back!"

"Okay, okay. Easy! You can have that then. I'll make sure you get home safe and sound."

Marisol cackled above them.

"Bargaining already, Jacob?" She said. "Ladies, I would be careful with this one. You'll go from slasher to sex slave in no time."

Dawn gritted her teeth. *Slasher.*

"Don't listen to her." Jacob pleaded. "I just want to get out of here, and I know you do too. I promise you, I can get you whatever you want."

Dawn smirked. "I want her." She pointed up at the platform. "I want *her* down *here*. Can you give me that, fat man? Can you?"

Jacob nodded furiously, resembling a bobble head doll.

A loud buzzer sounded, signaling that the next nightmarish round was about to begin.

"Oh God, come on. You've gotta help me." He begged Dawn and Raze.

Above them, on the platform, Marisol began a charming speech, addressing the audience and discussing the importance of this final round.

Dawn looked to Raze who did not seem pleased, but she gave Dawn a nod.

Jacob breathed heavily, his face full of relief.

"First things first, destroy every mic you see."

Dawn pointed her shotgun at the ground-mounted microphone nearest them and fired without looking, filling the air with short yet ear-piercing feedback.

"That was great!" Jacob clapped his hands together. "Now she can't hear us here. Remember, every mic that you see. We have to keep that bitch in the dark. The elevator up to the platform is our only route."

Dawn nodded as the lights began to change color and the audience's engagement intensified. Spotlights appeared on the holding area and the crowd started their mind-numbing chanting again.

"Well then, let's get to the elevator."

"It's not gonna be that simple, they keep that thing locked down."

Raze reared back, prepared to attack. "So then why are we even talking to you, Mr. Pudge?"

The fat Producer waved his hands about, desperation painting his face. "Please! You want the queen? I'll give you the queen. We just gotta get to Jimmy in the control room. And trust me, he can get you up there."

"Trust." Dawn laughed and thought back to her conversation with Charlie about friends and enemies. "Trust is by no means a factor in this equation. Remember, you need us more than we need you."

Dawn wasn't sure she even believed that, but she needed to remind the fallen Producer who was in charge.

"Maybe," he said with a wicked grin, "Maybe not. But there's a way out of here."

He pointed across the arena, and much to Dawn's surprise, once it was pointed out to her she could see a small hatch, practically hidden in the detritus of the faux-neighborhood.

"What's that for?" Raze asked.

The fat man barely had to reach for a human liver to come to hand. He held it up.

"Maintenance staff. Somebody's got to clean up after you people. And I'm in charge of that."

"Well, thanks for the tip, fat man," Raze said, raising her claws and preparing to slash his throat.

"Not so fast," he said, waggling his index finger like a metronome, "The janitorial staff uses keycards. Which you don't have. And there's also a master passcode. Which you don't know. There's a lot of things you don't know, but I can help you with that."

Raze scowled and folded her arms. Dawn grabbed her shoulder.

"We'll keep him alive for now. After he ceases to be useful, no promises."

Graves shrugged. "I can live with that."

They broke for the maintenance shaft.

CHAPTER 35

"*Carlito, por favor*," Doctor Feelbad said as he trudged through the dark tunnel behind Charming Charlie. "What are we doing back down here?"

"Oh, ye of little faith..." Charlie said without looking back at him.

"*Cabrón.*" Doc muttered.

"You know, I don't always understand what you say, but when I do, it's usually not particularly flattering."

"Good, that is how I like it. Now, just tell me what are we doing down here. They need us back upstairs. We are no good to them down here."

Charlie finally stopped walking and sighed, placing both hands on his hips and turning to face the doctor.

"I'm no more worried about whether or not Razortooth and your latest creation can handle themselves than I am about our own welfare. With that being said, I admire hard work, old friend, and I especially admire hard work done well. There is quite the arsenal of untapped potential down here and I plan to use that to our advantage."

He began walking again. Turning a corner, Charlie glanced up to note the poorly painted sign. It read "Remedials," as Orwellian a term as Charlie could think of. Here were the slashers who had proven to be unreliable killers in the arena, either through madness, compunction, or disability. In theory they were supposed to be "rehabilitated" into proper slashers and returned to the Barn. In practice, the staff had little time and less money for them, so they waited, forgotten in the dark.

Charlie fished a set of keys from his front pocket.

"Catch," he said, tossing them to the doctor.

The dark hallway came alive with noise. Shrieks of excitement, wails of pent-up frustration and anger, a chainsaw revving at the end of the hall.

"Ay..." the doctor chuckled. "I see now."

Charming Charlie smiled. "If the queen wants everyone participating, then who are we to deny her such desires?"

The doctor nodded and began unlocking the doors to cells on his left and right. Slowly, but surely, slasher after slasher stepped out into the hall. Though they might have been locked up in the bowels of the arena, there was little that went unnoticed; news had a habit of spreading quickly amongst the prisoners. After so long of being hidden in the dark, plucked up only when the queen had use for them, these forgotten killers were ready to sink their teeth into whatever action Charming Charlie was about to throw at them.

"Oh, look at you!"

Charlie grinned in at the large, dark figure lurking in the shadows of his cell at the end of the hall. The chainsaw idled in his hands as he stepped forward into the light.

"You bear a striking resemblance to another young man who is unfortunately no longer with us."

"Gus," the large man said.

"Yes, that's correct. Was he a friend of yours?"

"Brother." He growled.

"Ah, I should have known. Well, I'm quite sorry for your loss, but I find myself in need of your assistance."

"I help," he grunted.

Charlie stepped aside to allow the doctor some room to unlock the cell.

As the door swung open, Doctor Feelbad found himself looking up at a man even larger than the one who'd accompanied Dawn. His long hair, unlike his brother Gus's, was pulled back into a tight ponytail, revealing a serious face riddled with a myriad of scars. His hulking frame seemed to dwarf everything around him as he approached Charlie.

"Tell me, what is your name, young man?" Charlie asked.

"Jaq."

"Ah, very nice. And Jaq, tell me, have you ever heard of the man they call The Goat?" Charlie asked.

Jaq, surprising even Charlie, nodded and grinned from ear to ear.

"I kill."

Charlie clapped Jaq on the shoulder, having to reach nearly his whole arm's length upward to do so. He folded his hands behind his back and strode down the hallway, addressing a band of freaks and mutants, many of whom did not understand him, and others of whom were far too deranged to care.

"Ladies. Gentlemen. Most of you have been trapped down here for ages without any options. You eat when they tell you to eat, you shit when they tell you to shit, you kill when they tell you to kill. It's not a bad life for a dog. But for human beings..."

Charlie paused in front of an amphibian-like mutant with long, webbed fingers for choking.

"...that is to say, for rational, thinking creatures..."

He paused in front of a nude woman with long, greasy hair who was crouching on the ground, rocking back and forth, applying a pile of her own excrement to her face like makeup.

"...what I mean to say is, most of us haven't had a choice for a long time. But today I'm offering you one, and I frankly don't care which you take. It's in the nature of the beast. We are creatures of self-determination. Some of you will you choose the path of doom and destruction, even if I tell you right now that's the path you're taking. Others of you will be very proud to choose the right path, only to find that it leads to ruination anyway.

"I can't help that. I can't fix that, but I can tell you having a choice is better than having none. So that being said, right now Marisol Martinez's armed thugs are marching down from that direction, ready to open your doors one at a time and let you out into the arena. If all you want is mayhem and destruction, go with them. It takes little thought. It takes little conscience. But then some of you have little thought and little conscience, and I fault you not at all. I've been accused of the same, many times.

"For the rest of you, though, I can offer a different path. You may not survive. That's a given. None of us get out of here alive, but you might make a difference. You might strike back. You might tell the Producers, and the Queen of Texas, and all the people trying to hold you down in the dark and feed you when they want, and clothe you when they want, and generally make you their slaves, that you wanted to do something different. That you could poke a finger in their eye, no matter the cost.

"And if that's what you want, then you go this way. Now choose."

Charlie folded his arms.

CHAPTER 36

Their scramble for the maintenance access door was cut short by Marisol's voice booming through the stadium.

"Ladies and gentlemen," Marisol announced, "Join me in welcoming to the arena floor our entire remaining roster! First I introduce to you...Teddy Ruthless!"

The door to the Barn opened. A puff of chill air boiled out from below. Dawn froze, her eyes scanning over and over again, but not seeing anything.

"What the fuck?"

"There!" Raze said, pointing.

Down on the ground, less than two feet tall, a tiny figure emerged. Furry and fuzzy, it appeared to be a teddy bear. Dawn couldn't tell from this distance whether it was an automaton like The Great Eviscerator or a mutant like so many of the others. The tiny creature was cute, pink, and had great big shining button eyes. When it opened its mouth and spoke, Dawn decided it was probably a robot of some sort after all.

"I love you!" the teddy's robotic voice said.

"This is a slasher?" Dawn asked wonderingly.

Beside her, Jacob Graves snorted. "You bet your sweet ass it is."

His eyes moved from the teddy to Dawn's backside and he licked his lips. Even in the direst of circumstances the man had the capability of finding time to objectify whatever female was closest to him.

Dawn was about to go off on him, but the teddy began to laugh, and suddenly, the doll's eyes flashed red. A portion of its fuzzy skin peeled back, revealing an aggressively fanged, chomping metal face; three long blades pierced through the stump of its arm.

"Evil doll," Raze hissed at the tiny automaton.

Dawn leveled her shotgun and prepared to shoot, but the teddy bear suddenly went flying in an arc, far over their heads.

"Out of the way, pipsqueak!" a loud voice gurgled.

It belonged to a hulking linebacker of a man with a pentagram carved into his chest. He wore pants so tight that they split down the center of each massive thigh and a goat's head mask. He had easily punted the robot teddy like a football.

"You know him as The Goat, we know him as *The Greatest of All Time!*" Marisol announced with pride.

The Goat raised a chainsaw over his head, revving it wildly, hamming it up for the crowd.

"Um...*excusez-moi,*" a silky voice with a French accent came from behind him. "You are ruining my entrance! Stop vamping it up."

Grumbling, The Goat walked out of the way, leaving the corkscrew wielding, half-naked woman whom the Producers had briefly been considering sending out earlier, standing in the doorway.

"The Connoisseur!" Marisol announced, and the femme fatale took a deep bow before exiting the Barn.

"I'll fucking kill you!" a mechanical voice shrieked, and Dawn quickly glanced over to where the little fuzzball of a teddy bear had fallen.

"They're mine!" The Goat roared, pounding across the arena floor.

"Not if I get there first!" The Connoisseur challenged him, quickly sprinting ahead.

Marisol continued to announce other killers as they stepped out of the Barn one by one.

"Uh...uh..." Dawn said, looking left then right, overwhelmed by choices. "Which one do you want to..."

"I got the naked lady, I guess," Raze said, her voice shivering.

Her shotgun arm shaking, Dawn turned to face the goat-headed maniac pounding down on her. She decided to aim for the chainsaw, not knowing what sorts of random mutations he had that would make her life miserable. As The Goat raised his weapon high above his head, preparing to bring it down on her face in a lumberjack's swing, his blow was suddenly arrested, and the sound of two chainsaws grinding against each other filled the arena.

Dawn looked up in shock and saw someone who appeared to be Big Gus, only he had a ponytail fixed tightly on the back of his head and a face far more scarred and menacing than her dead friend's. Whoever he was, she was thankful for him as he had blocked the deadly blow from decapitating her. She glanced over to the hole where Denney the Clown's carousel had emerged, before he had tipped it over in an attempt to crush Raze. Her mouth dropped open as figures began emerging from the hole. In the center of that chaos she spotted Charming Charlie Whitmore, smiling a shit-eating grin at her.

Gimps, slashers, and mutants alike were pouring out into the arena; some beginning to scale the latticework dome with varying degrees of success before being shocked off, while others were engaging the slashers who were still pouring out of the Barn.

The Goat attacked with gusto, but every deadly swing of his chainsaw was expertly blocked by Gus's twin.

Raze squealed with excitement. "Jaq!"

"Hello, Raze," the giant man said, nodding at her briefly before returning his attention to the fight.

"You know him?" Dawn asked.

"Boy, do I!" Raze clapped her hands together in excitement. "I thought he was dead for a long time, but as you can see, The Goat isn't the scariest tool left in the shed anymore!"

Dawn cocked her head, "I don't think that's how that phrase works."

Raze shrugged and then hissed when Jacob Graves's hand suddenly gripped her shoulder.

"Now's our chance, let's go!" he shouted.

Dawn nodded and the two women didn't hesitate, running alongside the Producer turned contestant, desperate to get to the control room and bring the fight to the boss. Dawn glanced back and she found herself almost wanting to stay and continue watching the epic battle behind her.

Jaq appeared as if dancing a ballet, wielding the chainsaw with grace, sidestepping and counterattacking with precision Dawn had never seen. The Goat was visibly frustrated. Every time he charged he was rejected, kicked, or repelled backward, and each time he let out a vicious roar before attacking again.

Two figures caught up to Dawn and she prepared herself for a fight before realizing it was Charming Charlie and Doctor Feelbad.

"I'm not exactly a fan of cardio." Charlie announced, out of breath. "But I'm quite looking forward to seeing an old friend."

"Who?" Dawn asked, shouting over the absolute chaos in the arena.

"Oh, Jimmy and I have quite the history. You see, before I became a resident here, Jimmy was one of my best customers."

"Customers?"

"Let's just say that his favorite meat isn't chicken."

Dawn cringed and nodded, she got the picture.

CHAPTER 37

As the group exited the arena and followed Jacob through the halls to the control room, Dawn saw a group of goons up ahead, armed to the teeth, guarding the hall, same as before when she'd come through the first time. They slowed to a stop, their backs to the wall.

"Need to get rid of them." Jacob said, sweating profusely, appearing as if he might have a heart attack at any moment.

"Doctor," Charlie said with a smirk. "Help us out, will you?"

Doctor Feelbad nodded and moved forward, placing his hands in both pockets of his lab coat. One of the goons spotted him and raised his weapon.

"Stop right there! You're not authorized—"

His words were replaced by a shriek of pain as a scalpel flew with lightning speed and hit its intended target, his crotch. He dropped his weapon and his hands flew to his groin. He made the mistake of removing the scalpel and blood began to spurt from his injured manhood, causing him to pass out. The other goons reacted, raising their firearms, but the doctor was much faster, launching scalpels like throwing stars. The hall was soon filled with cries of pain as the medical supplies punctured various body parts and Doc gave the signal for the others to move forward now that the group of goons was disarmed.

Raze launched herself up onto the wall, galloping forward, leaving a trail of penetrated cement in her wake as Dawn charged her enemies. Raze landed on the first goon and began ripping him to shreds, and the doctor pulled out his trusty bone saw, making quick work of the unlucky man trying to retrieve his weapon from the floor. The instrument met the man's cheek, painting the hall crimson, his gurgled cries soon subsided as

Doc drove the saw deeper, working with precision, quickly detaching the goon's jaw.

To Dawn's surprise, the goon directly in front of her, despite his injured hand, snatched his weapon up and prepared to fire. She dropped to her knees as the gun went off, barely inches from ending her life. She slid forward, dropping her body down flat as she grew closer to the goon. As she slid between his legs she raised her shotgun and fired, blowing off what little dignity he might have had left. The goon dropped to the floor, squealing like a pig, and the doctor silenced him, breaking his neck. Dawn whirled around, dropping two more goons with one shot as Raze finished off the last of them with her vicious claws.

Charming Charlie clapped at the other end of the hall.

"Brava! Bravissimo!"

He started toward them, but Jacob Graves didn't budge. He sat with his back to the wall, staring down at the floor.

"Fat man, let's get a move on!" Dawn shouted, cleaning blood from her face with the front of her shirt.

Charlie waved her off. "I'm afraid our fallen Producer has met an unfortunate demise. He won't be joining us."

Dawn squinted at the slumped over man, realizing now that there was a small bullet hole in his temple; the stray shot from the armed goon must have got him. It seemed a weirdly anticlimactic end for such a man.

"Good, I didn't like him." Raze announced, fixing her pigtails.

The group pressed on, finally able to access the control room. The large, steel reinforced door loomed before them.

"How the hell are we supposed to get in there?" Dawn asked with a groan.

Charlie wagged a finger at her. "Manners cost nothing, Ms. Churchill. Why not attempt to knock?"

Marisol stood on the platform, microphone in her hand, mouth open, but she couldn't find the words. In the arena below her, absolute chaos was ensuing. Slashers battled slashers while the majority of the others disabled the generators powering the electric fence that shielded the audience from the mayhem.

The fence lining the audience's perimeter, area by area, began to come down. Slashers poured into the audience in a murderous frenzy. Most audience members fought back, elated to finally be a part of the action, but others sought safety, creating a deadly stampede which crushed the skulls of patron and slasher alike as they attempted to flee the encroaching bloodbath. The portion of the arena that the panic and chaos had yet to infect was alive with noise. The morons still in their seats cheered and applauded, not yet realizing that a deadly tsunami of stampeding patrons was heading their way.

Marisol dropped the microphone, sending feedback shrieking through the arena, adding insult to injury.

"My show..." was all she managed to say as she clenched her fists.

She turned toward the remaining Producers behind her and was alarmed to see Derron running toward her at full speed. Stunned, she almost didn't know what she was doing as she caught his momentum and used it against him. Her body was almost working of its own volition, dodging his attack and giving him an extra shove to toss him over the side. The quiet man who had stood silently by her side all this time had finally betrayed her...or attempted to, in any case.

Marisol scrambled on her knees to the edge of the stage and watched with wide eyes as her husband's body tumbled through the air. The Connoisseur nimbly stepped out of the way of the falling shadow. Derron landed with a sickening crunch, his limbs splayed unnaturally, his skull caved from the impact. The slasher began examining his body with a wide grin, poking holes in his lifeless frame, shrieks of laughter leaving her lips. Marisol was left without the words to express the emotions roiling within her. She wanted to curse Derron as a coward and a traitor, but also, somewhere deep inside, she felt the pain of his loss.

She got to her feet and brushed herself off, Mark and the remaining stagehand appeared from the wings. Winters swigged vodka from the bottle, seeing no point in hiding it anymore.

"If it wasn't over before," he said, wiping his mouth, "it's sure as shit over now."

Amy Green rose from her seat and lit a cigarette. Marisol noticed Mark's eyes go wide. Tobacco was rarer in the Geiger Lands than loyalty these days. "I hate to agree with him, but we're finished." Amy said. "We have to focus on getting out of here alive. Once we make it to a safe enough distance, we blow the place to kingdom come. That's the only way to contain this shitshow."

Marisol's nostrils flared; she was now outnumbered.

"All good things come to an end, Marisol. We'll find some way to recover from this PR nightmare and entertain the masses again. In due time." Amy took a long drag from her cigarette before offering it to Mark, who gladly accepted.

Marisol walked to the edge of the box and put her hands down on the corner. To any other observer it seemed she was surveying the utter chaos that was consuming her beautiful arena. Had Derron survived, he might have guessed the truth. She was a thousand miles away...and twenty years in the past.

CHAPTER 38

Marisol's husband had always been smart enough for the most part to accede to his wife's wishes. Derron had always been delicate, tentative. But there had been a time, way way back, at the very beginning of their relationship, when he had been bolder about getting to know her, even testing her boundaries. Shortly after they had met, he had once asked her about what was so obviously a flashback, when she seemed to check out for a few seconds, even minutes at times.

"Is it very vivid?" he had asked, "like it was yesterday?"

"No, Derron," she had replied, "not like it was yesterday. It's like I'm living it right now."

1984. Just a year after the bombs fell. She'd been only twenty then. It felt like a lifetime ago. In a lot of ways, it was. Houston, Dallas, Austin all had been lit up. Texas's military bases at Killeen and El Paso. The fallout had been devastating. Very little of the population had survived the winter.

The peace accords with the Soviet Union had been signed. The United States had essentially ceased to exist, and then reports of Americans turning on each other began. Predations. Marauding. And worse: cannibalism. Sex trafficking. Crime was consuming what little was left of civilization and fallout was wiping out the rest.

On Christmas Eve, Marisol's mother had called her into the kitchen. Her mother was standing on a chair, trying to reach the back of the cabinet above the stove. She had always been an exceedingly short woman, a source of no small amount of laughter for Marisol, who, having been born in the States, had always had better nutrition and had quickly shot above her mother's height.

"*Si, mamacita?*"

"Help me with this, will you, Mari?"

Her mother clambered down from the chair, throwing up her hands in surrender. Marisol hopped up and quickly dug into the back of the cabinet. There was nothing there but a box of baking soda to keep the area fresh. It wasn't exactly an easy item to get anymore, but it was hardly a luxury. What did they need baking soda for?

"You looking for this, mama?"

She nodded, gesturing with spidering fingers for Marisol to hand her the box. Marisol's mother dug inside the little opening at the top and after wheedling around for a moment, emerged with a thin but tightly wrapped stack of paper.

She held out the money to Marisol.

"My God, mama," Marisol said, putting her hands around the cigarette-thin tube, "This is a fortune."

"It's nothing of the sort," her mother had replied darkly, "but I've been saving as much as I could for tonight."

"What's tonight?"

"It's Christmas, *niña*. You go down to the butcher's and get as much ground beef as you can with this. We can make some tamales."

There had been no Christmas the year before. Not in any meaningful way. They had huddled together, cold in their home, praying the fallout would pass them by. It had, so, in a way, they had been blessed, but the thought of having Christmas again, with the sights and sounds and smells of the season filling up the home, was almost too much to bear.

Marisol rushed out of the house and down to the edge of town, where the last remaining butcher's shop was. Charles Whitmore was a strange man. Supposedly he had been a professor at the nearby state university, though it was hard to believe because most of the people like that—academics, thinkers, the liberal effete—had died out when the bombs had dropped. Without useful skills, no one survived. Even with useful skills there was no guarantee.

But whatever Whitmore had been in his previous life—and it did seem now like the time before the bombs had fallen was a whole other life—he had swept into town and developed a surprising knack for scrounging up meat. On the rare occasions when people asked, he claimed to have been a professor of agriculture, and so had close connections with all the farmers for hundreds of miles around. The farms were still desperate for what manufactured goods they could get from the city, and the city dwellers were most assuredly desperate for any kind of food. So Whitmore had become that object of curiosity: a man who was prospering in the midst of the apocalypse.

Marisol had heard rumors, but, of course, her family hadn't been able to afford so much as a scrap of jerky or a pig's tongue all year, so this was her first time actually going to the butcher's. Had she thought about it, really thought about it, put any thought into it at all, really, rushing off at close to midnight on Christmas Eve, surely the butcher would not be open. Surely he would be busy, perhaps with his own family, but no one had ever heard of Whitmore having a family of his own. Nevertheless, the excitement of a pocket full of cash and the thought of delicious tamales filling her belly—and, even more, the thought of spending time with her mother, carefully filling each corn husk, and the two bonding as they had so rarely in the past year and a half had her brimming with such excitement that the particulars of the situation had utterly escaped her.

She rushed right up to the butcher shop and, finding it closed, cursed herself, but began banging on the door.

"Open up!" she cried out! "Please! Mr. Whitmore?"

She pounded on the door until the eyes in the surrounding windows began to make her worry. The butcher shop was on the very edge of town, and though nowhere was particularly savory in the midst of the crime wave, this place was very much out of her usual comfort zone. She quickly slouched off from the front door, deciding not to call any further attention to herself. Her hand slipped into her pocket and wrapped around the trusty paring knife which her mother thought had gone missing from the kitchen, but, in fact, Marisol had claimed as her own. So far she had only had to use it to ward off the advances of Billy Pennebaker when he had become violently aggressive with her, but she was prepared to use it in case anything more sinister occurred.

She slipped around the back of the butcher's shop. She didn't know this area very well at all, but like all the others who had made it through the dark year, and with electricity such a rare commodity, she had developed exceptional night vision. She glared around the alley in back. Nothing sprang out at her as particularly dangerous, though, being the alley behind a butcher's shop, it did stink in a manner wholly disproportionate to the rest of the city.

She tried the back door, but it was locked. She scanned the windows up above, but all the lights were out. It seemed Charlie the butcher was already asleep. And why not? A rich man like him didn't have to stay up all night suffering in the cold. He probably had an electric heater and a plush bed. She kicked a can, and as it clattered across the alley, she cursed herself for making noise again. A light turned on, shining through the individual timbers of a boarded-up window across the street. She dropped herself flat to the ground, hoping to avoid detection if it was someone less than trustworthy, which, at this time of night, it almost certainly was. After a moment, though, the light went out.

Then Marisol looked to her right. She had stumbled upon a tiny, open window. Charlie's butcher shop, it seemed, had a basement. The window wasn't designed for any sort of a person to get through, but Marisol had always been a svelte girl, and eighteen months of a near starvation diet had thinned her out even more. She suspected she would be able to slip through. And then a perverse idea came to her.

Why should she have to suffer? What had she ever done to deserve this? If she could slip in and rob Charlie the butcher, she could have the meat for mama and keep the money for herself. There was no reason mama ever had to know, and Charlie could easily afford it. The more she thought on it, the more certain she became that it was not only a good idea, not only a just and fair idea, but that it was perhaps the best idea she had ever had.

And so, wriggling like a worm, with some difficulty despite her tiny body because the window was just so damned small, she managed to find her way into the butcher's basement, one fraction of an inch at a time.

She finally slipped in and dropped down, her eyes darting around the immeasurably dark space of the butcher's basement. Even with her youthful, carefully trained eyes, she was having trouble seeing. She reached out and put her hand on something squishy and gross that had been discarded on the floor, and she instantly felt her heart fluttering a mile a minute. She forced herself to calm down, forced herself to focus on what she was doing.

She was in the basement, so all she had to do was feel along the edges of the wall until she found the staircase up into the store. Once she was in the store, she would have better light to see. She could slip a few pounds of ground beef away from the display case. The odds were Charlie would never even notice. In fact, she could probably slip a little more than that. A few sausages perhaps…maybe even a whole chicken or two? Why not simply tell mama that it had been a bonanza? That Charlie had been in a particularly festive mood, or that she had saved far more than she had realized and Marisol had decided to treat the family?

No, no, she clamped down on that idea. It was best not to get too greedy, and certainly not to tip her hand to her mother. She'd bring back a little meat for the tamales. Then, if she managed to slip away with a little more, she'd sell it herself later. Between that and the money she already had from mama, she was beginning to get a vision. She saw herself no longer suffering and starving, but turning her small nest egg into a tiny fortune, and enjoying the pleasures of it. She would be living better than Charlie Whitmore. She would be queen of the city one day.

"Just a minute, James."

Marisol paused, frantic. A light had turned on upstairs, slipping just under the crack of the door. So, Charlie did have electricity after all, it seemed. The door opened with a pronounced creak, and, as if proving the point, Charlie flipped a light switch, bathing the basement in the glow of a single naked lightbulb.

Marisol stood under the stairs, willing herself as small as possible. The top step creaked as Charlie put his weight on it, and she would have sworn it was going to break right through.

She glanced around, looking for somewhere, anywhere to hide. Then she had to literally bite her tongue to keep from gasping.

The basement of the butcher shop was a slaughterhouse, but not in the way she might have expected. It was true, along one wall a corkboard displayed a bevy of cleavers, tongs, and knives that were part of the butcher's art, but there were no pigs hanging from the roof, no chickens mid-way through being plucked. Instead, an elegant woman with alabaster skin seemed to be lounging in a porcelain bathtub, her head back and hanging out of the tub. But the woman's throat was slit, her pale complexion the result of exsanguination and not natural beauty. The tub was thick with blood.

And that was just the beginning of the nightmarescape. From the woman, who had seemingly been freshly killed, the room seemed to descend from left to right into ever deeper and deeper levels of dismemberment. A series of torsos, their heads hung as though in shame, missing only their arms, legs, and members for the men, breasts for the women, hung from meat hooks in the ceiling. Then the organized rows of bodies descended into a blur of parts, no longer identifiable as being matched; legs, arms, and genitals in a general mish-mash, some stripped of their fingers, others flayed, some already hacked into chops and steaks. Finally, there were a few skulls, picked nearly clean of all the sweet flesh of the human face and eyes, except for a few strings of ligaments that dotted the hinges.

She had to clap her hand over her mouth to keep from screaming as she recognized one of the torsos. It was Ramón Hernandez from down the block. While Ramón wasn't exactly a model citizen, being the leader of one of the newer gangs that had popped up over the last year, seeing him strung up like some wild game in the butcher's basement didn't sit well with Marisol. But she wondered if some sick part of her was actually relieved to find him hanging there. Relieved that she would no longer have to be subjected to Ramón's *special favors* in order to protect her mama.

The steps squeaked, each in turn, as Charlie came walking down, whistling a jaunty tune. Frantic, panicked, Marisol forced herself to tear her eyes away from Ramón's mangled torso. She looked for anything to hide under, inside, or behind, but spotted nothing like that under the stairs. The closest thing was an army surplus wool blanket. She pulled it over herself and huddled under the top three steps, hoping she would be as invisible as the untouched junk in her own basement.

Enveloped now in blackness, Marisol had only her sense of hearing to rely on to follow Charlie's actions. Luckily, he was still whistling, making it fairly easy for her to guess where he was. She heard a sound like the scrape of metal on metal, and braced herself. The wool was itchy, so damn itchy, how could anyone tolerate to be near this damn blanket, let alone sleep under it?

A moment later she heard hacking, hacking, hacking, and something wet struck the outside of the blanket. Blood, no doubt. Charlie had switched over from whistling to humming, and he continued to hack away at one of the bodies, preparing it in some manner for his customer upstairs. She tried to slow her breathing, retain what fleeting bit of calm remained to her. As long as she was quiet and silent and still, as long as she didn't let the terrible itchiness of the blanket or the terror that was making her stomach quake inside her make her do something stupid, all she had to do was wait through a few minutes of blindness and bone-chilling terror, then she could just slip back out the way she came, and never come near this place or speak of it again.

"I say, James, my lad."

"Yes?" a new voice called down from upstairs.

"How thick of a cut do you want?"

"Not too thin. Something that won't brown right through as soon as I throw it on the grill."

"Ah," Charlie said, not loudly enough for the man upstairs to hear, "A man after my own heart."

The concrete floor was like ice. The blanket was just like an enveloping sheet of irritating fleas, all begging her to scratch, or, better yet, toss them off. Her breath was warm against the blanket, and she was having trouble getting much oxygen. All she wanted to do was stick her head out, take one clean gulp of air, and then go back into her safe little cocoon. Every second that she didn't felt like an eternity, but she knew she couldn't. She'd have to sit there and bear it: the cold, the itch, the labored breathing, the rising sense of panic.

But she wouldn't give in. She was made of iron. She could do anything.

Finally, after what seemed like forever, she heard the same clink of metal on metal that had inaugurated her time under the blanket, apparently Charlie snatching a cleaver or other instrument from its home, and now returning it. His humming turned back into a whistle as he stepped up the stairwell. She listened for each squeaky step, and could barely believe the sense of relief she felt when the light went out and the door swung shut.

She threw the itchy wool blanket off herself like it was a boa constrictor trying to strangle her.

"Good evening."

Marisol shot up, smashing her head into the bottom of the step she had been hiding under, and then coming back down to a crouch, rubbing her now throbbing dome. Charles Whitmore's head was hanging over the stairwell, staring at her, his eyes shining in the darkness like a cat's.

"All right, James," he called, "You can turn the light back on."

The naked bulb buzzed back to life and Charlie's face was now visible, a smile right across it.

"Everything all right, Charlie?" James called down from upstairs.

"Yes. It seems a thieving street cur's gotten in somehow. Will you give me just a moment to take care of it? Then I'll be right up with your order."

James laughed. "As long as you don't start trying to sell me dog meat."

"Oh, no. Never you, James."

The door swung shut again, and when it closed it sounded to Marisol like nothing so much as the lid of her own coffin closing. Charlie clattered quickly down the stairs, as if making a point that the squeak-squeak-squeak he had been doing before had been purely for her benefit.

"If I'm being honest, it was hilarious watching you hide.

Did you really think if you tossed a blanket over your head I wouldn't notice you? Now…what to use on someone your size?"

He walked up to the corkboard of butchering implements. He tapped out a tattoo with his fingers on the board and looked back and forth between Marisol and the implements. He reached out and put his hands on a long, curved knife.

"I think for you…the cimeter."

He also snagged a long metal sharpening file and began to run the cimeter across it repeatedly, eliciting a long, metallic scrape. He turned to approach Marisol.

"That's peculiar."

Her lips barely seemed to be working, but she managed to ask, "What?"

"Normally by now they're blubbering, begging for their life. It's one of the most enjoyable parts of my job. I was going to have to move quickly anyway because I've got a customer upstairs, but now it has to be quick and you're not begging. It hardly seems fair."

"Lots of shit's not fair."

He started cackling, and back in the arena, Marisol shuddered at the memory, the first time she had ever heard Charming Charlie's laugh. It still chilled her to the bone, much as she felt like she had finally boxed up her trauma and locked it away.

"You are correct in that regard. All right. I'll be quick… unfortunately."

He made a face like he was going to have to miss the first half of a play. He put his arm around her shoulders and with the other, held the cimeter to her neck. He cocked his head. She knew she was hyperventilating, but that wasn't the look he was giving her.

"Not going to try to run, either? We have a little time. You could at least try to make it to the tiny window and get stuck."

"Not going to try to run," she whispered.

He shrugged.

"All right. No skin off my nose."

Charlie leaned in to make the final slice of her life when suddenly he paused and his eyes seemed to bug out. He looked down to see Marisol's paring knife deep in his crotch. He looked back to her eyes, and saw the amusement there. Yes, she had been playing along. Yes, she had been letting him get too close. And now she was way up inside of him, fucking his taint with a knife.

She wrenched upward with a grunt. Then again. Then a third time, making the final cut. She reached down and put her hand on his dick, and plucked it out of his scrotum just like a flower. She held it up, the stub still dripping blood. Charlie groaned in pain and slumped to the floor, the cimeter clattering out of his hands.

The door to the cellar opened up and a tentative, tiny man in glasses emerged. He looked down at her in horror.

"You must be Jimmy," she said, rising from her crouched position.

She must have been quite a sight, coated in Charlie's blood. She reached up and wiped some from her nose. Weird, she liked the smell of it. She could get used to this.

"J-James," the man stuttered.

"No, I think I'll call you Jimmy. I recognize you from some-where..." she narrowed her eyes and tried to place him. "Oh yeah, I remember now."

"You do?" He asked, wringing his hands, visibly nervous.

She laughed. "Yeah, how are things down at the park these days? Is that how you make your money to afford such delicacies?"

She shook the severed cock at him, giggling, before throw-ing Charlie's manhood carelessly to the ground. Jimmy averted her gaze, his head hung in shame.

"You don't seem much surprised by all this."

She gestured at the horror show that was all around her.

"No," he admitted, "I never believed there were any farms. But...but...I wasn't involved. I swear it. Are you...are you going to turn me in to the militia?"

Planting her hands on her hips she looked around. Things were really a mess in Charlie's basement. Not the least of which that needed cleaning up was him.

"Prostitution, cannibalism...I mean, there's probably waaay more than that on your list of offenses. Come to think of it, there's probably a hefty bounty in it for me..." she smirked. "But no, I'm not going to turn you in."

He glanced at Charlie, who had already passed out from blood loss, or possibly shock, and breathed a sigh of relief.

"He...he wasn't a bad man, you know," James dared to defend the unconscious cannibal at Marisol's feet. "He had a moral code—"

Marisol interrupted him with a snort, stifling a laugh. She looked down at Charlie herself, then at the beautiful woman in the tub, and the torsos, including Ramón's. Charlie had really enjoyed chopping people up. Whatever the reason, she didn't care, and regardless of whatever *code* Jimmy was referring to, Charles Whitmore took pleasure from it. And, if she was being honest with herself, she had enjoyed besting him and chopping him up, too. People liked that sort of thing, that sort of violence. Not much was really broadcast on TV anymore, but sometimes people still gathered downtown to watch the fights. They had long since gone beyond the old world norms of boxing or even karate matches. Sometimes men even died in the ring.

Never before had she seen her future with such clarity. It was as though she had been struck by a lightning bolt.

"No, I'm not going to kill him. I have an idea...and I want him alive for it."

Jimmy nodded and clattered down the stairs.

"Okay," he said. "I can help you with that."

Obviously eager to make himself useful, Jimmy started gathering up some sheets and packing Charlie's gaping crotch wound. She liked this, the way the man was sniveling for her good graces.

"I could use some help running this place from now on. Want a job?"

Jimmy looked up at her from the prone man, and over at all the butchering that had to be done, and all the cleaning, too. The butcher shop was a gold mine and clearly he saw the windfall that had come his way from Charlie being put out of commission. But the butcher shop was just going to be a tiny start for her to rule Texas, the way she had thought of that tiny wad of bills mama had given her as a tiny start to ruling the town. She wanted it all.

She bent over and put her hand on Jimmy's shoulder, the paring knife still in it, dripping Charlie's coagulating blood on his shirt.

"Good. I could use someone like you. Just so long as we're in agreement. I'm the one in charge."

Jimmy opened his mouth for just a second, as though he had something to say, but one more look at the blood-covered young woman seemed to silence that.

"Yeah," he agreed, bobbing his head, "You're in charge now, uh…"

"Marisol," she said.

"Marisol?"

Amy Green broke the Queen from her flashback.

She wiped her eye discreetly before turning to face the concerned woman. It wasn't often that she allowed herself to show such weakness.

"Blow it up. Blow it all to hell."

She strode across the catwalk and beelined for the exit door, her red cape billowing behind her.

"Jimmy," she said, her finger to her ear.

A moment passed, far too long for her liking, before she called for him again, yet he still didn't answer.

She placed her head in her hand and took a deep breath in, she was a split second away from completely losing it. It was taking every ounce of energy she had left not to grab one of Amy's weapons and just start sniping people from the platform.

Might help to blow off some steam though, she thought, exhaling and then pushing the murderous daydream from her mind.

"Jimmy, I'm not one to be kept waiting. You have five seconds to respond or we're going to have a much bigger problem on our hands."

She began to count down from five, feeling as though she had suddenly taken on the role of the patient parent. She was *the* queen. Jimmy would still be fellating strangers for food on the streets of the old barrio if it weren't for her. She'd have his head for this, tonight of all unfortunate nights was not the one to begin trying her.

"*Hello, my dear Marisol.*"

The seductive yet sinister tone of Charming Charlie's voice sent a shiver down her spine.

"*Would you mind sharing with me what you think could be worse than what's already unfolding in your precious arena?*" he asked. "*It seems to me that you've got enough on your hands without worrying about our mutual friend here in the control room.*"

"Where's Jimmy?" She asked, failing to mask the anger in her voice.

Charlie laughed.

"Answer me!"

"*Oh, my apologies, Jimmy can't come to the phone right now. You see, my mother always taught me not to talk with my mouth full, so I ensure that the company I keep exhibit the same manners as Yours Truly. It's been quite a while since I last saw Jimmy. What would you say? Twenty years? Perhaps more? I just can't keep track anymore.*"

There was a pause as if he were actually trying to remember.

"*Doesn't matter I suppose. What does matter, is even after all this time, I can still remember Jimmy's favorite* cut of meat." He laughed again.

Marisol turned, her face flushed with rage, her heart thumping in her chest.

"Amy!" she shouted. "Gather what you need to. We're leaving immediately. Alert the others."

Amy nodded and marched off to find Mark Winters, the dancers, and the remaining stagehand.

"You're a dead man, Charles. You and that merry band of degenerates…dead."

She marched through the door and entered the waiting room, the security guards all jumped from their seats, saluting the queen.

"We're leaving," she announced, and punched the elevator's 'call' button.

She looked up at the lights above the door, waiting for them to turn from red to green, signaling that the car was on its way up.

"Try Not to Die is finished," she barked into her com. "None of you aberrations serve a purpose anymore. I'll have you all executed as soon as I—"

"No," Charlie said flatly. *"You won't."*

She tried to fire back at him, but before Marisol could even form the words, he cut her off once more.

"I'm a man of my word, Ms. Martinez…"

She could hear the smile on his face. She punched the elevator call button again. The car should have already been on its way up by now.

"I can't wait to see you…"

She slapped at it once more but nothing was happening.

"To feel your warm flesh in my hands…"

Frantic, she ripped open the door to the emergency exit box on the wall beside her and pressed the big red button.

"To taste you in my mouth…"

The light above the door didn't change from red to green, it simply went out.

"All while you watch from across the dinner table."

Charlie chuckled once more before cutting the connection and Marisol screamed, finally letting her anger out.

She ripped the earpiece out and threw it to the floor, smashing it with her foot over and over until it was quite unrecognizable as anything at all. She kept screaming and stomping her foot, replaying Charlie's words in her head repeatedly until she was numb to them, until she had no feelings at all toward the man aside from pure loathing. Who did he think he was? She punched and kicked at the elevator door, still screaming. He could control the damn elevator car all he wanted. She'd wait for him, wait for them all.

"Um…Marisol?" Mark dared to speak.

She froze and turned around, suddenly realizing that she must have appeared completely mad to Mark and Amy and all the others who now stood watching her.

She looked up at Mark, her hair a wild mess, her mascara running down her face.

"Is, uh…is everything okay?"

She took a deep breath in, smoothing out her long locks.

"Everything's fine, Markus. A simple change of plans. Amy, arm everyone here. And keep weapons on that door." She glared at the guards and pointed with her thumb behind her. "And you," she addressed the stagehand.

He shot up straight and nodded. "Yes, Your Majesty, how can I help?"

"Fix my makeup."

She strolled past him and snapped her fingers, exiting the room.

CHAPTER 39

Jimmy jumped up from his wall of monitors and electronics and rushed to the steel door, grumbling.

"I've got a plate full of shit being served to me and you assholes have the nerve to interrupt? Now, of all times?"

He shouted at the door as he walked, flailing his arms about. He checked the screen to the right of the door and saw the dumb-shit goon who'd been incessantly knocking for the last thirty seconds. The goon stared straight ahead, a strange look on his face; perhaps he looked so uncomfortable because he knew he shouldn't be interrupting the control room while they were on the air. Jimmy took note of the name on his jacket, he'd let Marisol know and she'd make sure he was dealt with accordingly.

Jimmy grunted as he pulled down on the heavy lock and heard a satisfying click. He opened the door and began to scold the goon but was caught off-guard by a sucker punch to the nose. He cried out, his hands flying to his face, his broken nose gushing blood.

"What the fuck!" he shouted, but soon realized it wasn't the goon who'd punched him.

No, the goon was already dead, motionless on the ground from where Doctor Feelbad had discarded him, no longer needing to hold him in front of the camera. Dawn Churchill stood in front of Jimmy with a raised fist, prepared to strike him again if need be.

"What the fuck..." he said again, but this time he'd changed his tune.

"Good evening, old friend." Charming Charlie practically sang his words.

"Oh shit. No! Shit, shit, shit, shit!"

Jimmy ran from the door, back toward his seat, desperate to grab the handgun he kept stored under it.

Jimmy shrieked as a scalpel suddenly sprouted from his shoulder. He looked back to see Feelbad, still in mid-pose after throwing it. Spinning in a circle, he attempted to grab hold of the instrument, but was unable to. Feelbad had struck him in a bad spot, a nerve, maybe, that made him unable to pull the blade out.

"Surgical precision," Charlie said, patting his friend on the shoulder. He strolled into the room and settled into Jimmy's seat. "Now, now, settle down. There's no need for all the theatrics."

Charlie felt around underneath the desk and found the gun. He turned it over in his hand, frowning at it before tossing it to Dawn.

"Never did like firearms."

He shrugged and crossed one leg over the other.

"What do you want?" Jimmy asked, backing away until there was no more space left in the tiny room.

Dawn pointed both the handgun and her shotgun arm at him.

"We want to get up on the platform."

Jimmy pressed his back harder against the wall as if he could move it.

"No. No way in Hell. I'd rather die than deal with those consequences." He swallowed hard. "Nothing you could do to me is worse than what she'll do."

Jimmy motioned toward one of the screens and everyone turned toward it. Marisol's troubled face could be seen as she looked out over the arena, soaking up the chaos.

"And here I always thought she had the best seat in the house," Charlie said with a smile, "But it seems you really have the best view of things, James."

Charlie's hands ran across the control panel like a pianist's.

"Can you unlock the elevator car?" Dawn asked him.

"I'm afraid, Ms. Churchill, I've reached the limits of even my considerable knowledge."

Charlie pressed a few buttons on a keyboard and a short

buzzer sounded followed by the words *Access Denied* appearing on the monitor in front of him.

"Care to give us the code, James?"

Jimmy shook his head. Charlie raised an eyebrow.

"Loyal through and through, after all these years. And who would have guessed it? Not me, that's for sure."

Charlie gave Razortooth a signal and she pounced on Jimmy, bringing him down to the ground and holding him still, the threat of a slashed throat ever present as her steel fingertips nearly broke the skin on his neck.

Jimmy began to hyperventilate and Charlie rolled his eyes.

"Ease up on him a bit."

Razortooth groaned and loosened her grip.

"We'll ask you again. What's the code?"

"Fuck you, Charlie."

"*Idiota*," Doctor Feelbad shook his head as he and Razortooth flipped Jimmy onto his back.

Dawn took a few steps closer and crouched down, placing the handgun to his temple and the shotgun to his gut.

"Don't make us ask you again," she warned.

He spat at her and Razortooth responded with a quick slice to his forehead, splitting it open. He shrieked in pain again and squeezed his eyes shut as his own blood began to blind him.

Charlie chuckled and got down on his knees, spreading Jimmy's legs.

"What are you doing? Get away from me!" Jimmy protested.

"It doesn't have to be this way," Dawn said. "Just give us the code."

Charlie undid Jimmy's trousers and began to slide them off. Jimmy flopped around like a fish despite being held down.

"Do you remember the first time we met, James?" Charlie asked, pulling Jimmy's underwear down around his knees.

Jimmy didn't respond. He continued to whimper, but had finally stopped moving now that his manhood was exposed and vulnerable.

"You were prostituting yourself on the streets of Old Town if I recall. But, who could blame you? There was little in the way of living in those days, and, if I'm being frank, nowadays either. But I wouldn't know, you see, I've been living like a rat all these years…"

Jimmy felt a slight tug on his scrotum and he cried out in alarm.

"Thanks to you."

Charlie's grip tightened and Jimmy began to weep.

"I-I'm sorry, Charlie. I'm so sorry."

"I'm afraid it's too late for all that, however, you can still make it up to me. Tell me…what is the code?"

Jimmy continued to weep while Charlie waited, still clutching his balls in a vice grip.

"I-I can't, Charlie. I can't."

"Do you remember the first time you ever had a real meal in my home? All those years ago?" Charlie asked. "I fed and clothed you, gave you shelter, and when I found out that you kept returning to the streets, I realized we had similar interests, you and I. The desire for flesh was strong within us, albeit in different ways…but you soon learned…you soon became my best customer, you went on to become like family even."

Charlie let go of Jimmy's balls to retrieve a scalpel from Feelbad's outstretched hand.

"Do you know, after all this time, I still remember your favorite dish?"

Charlie grabbed hold of Jimmy's flaccid cock and pulled it toward him, pressing the scalpel firmly against the sensitive flesh, causing Jimmy to scream in protest and once again begin to flail on the ground.

"*Basta ya,*" the doctor warned. "I wouldn't move too much if I were you."

"Cut him, oh, cut him, please." Razortooth begged, squeezing her tiny hands around his throat.

"I agree with Raze," Dawn said, "I'm getting tired of the games. I've had a whole night of them."

She glared at Charlie, waiting for his response.

"You hear that, Jimmy? You don't have many friends in this room, so if I were you, I'd give up the code."

Charlie yanked once more and finally Jimmy surrendered.

"Zero, one, one, eight!" He screamed. "Now please, let me go! Please!"

Dawn jumped up and ran to the keyboard, punching in the four-digit code. Jimmy shuddered as he heard the tell-tale chime of access being granted.

"We're in," she called over her shoulder.

"Thank you, James." Charlie said, loosening his grip on the poor man's penis.

"Please, Charlie, please just let me go," Jimmy pleaded with him.

Charlie stared down at the pathetic, bumbling mess and deeply considered his words for a moment. He could, in fact, let Jimmy go, just be done with him and let bygones be bygones. It had been years, and truth be told, Charlie had deeply matured over time. A smile began to spread across Charlie's lips.

"Of course I'll let you go, James. But not until you've had dinner."

With a graceful flick of his wrist, Charlie removed Jimmy's penis before the man had even realized what had happened to him.

"You like it best raw, correct?" Charlie asked with a laugh before shoving the shriveled cock into Jimmy's screaming mouth.

Blood spurted from his crotch and Raze clapped her hands together while Doc tended to the wound; Charlie requested specifically that Doc ensure the control manager's survival.

"Razortooth, be a dear and tape up our friend's mouth for me. Let's make sure he swallows like a good boy."

Raze giggled as she grabbed a roll of tape from the desk and brought it back to Jimmy. He'd already spit his severed member out and was screaming again. She frowned, plucking it from the ground.

"Ewwwww," she said, dragging the word out, shoving it back into Jimmy's mouth and began wrapping his head in scotch tape.

Charlie took a seat beside Dawn and they both sat staring

up at the monitor, watching as Marisol approached the elevator doors.

"Not so fast, bitch." Dawn said, denying the elevator request.

"*Jimmy,*" the queen's voice crackled through a speaker.

Dawn and Charlie exchanged glances.

"*Jimmy, I'm not one to be kept waiting. You have five seconds to respond or we're going to have a much bigger problem on our hands.*"

"Do you want to handle this one?" Dawn asked.

Charlie smirked. "It would be my pleasure."

CHAPTER 40

Marisol sat in Mark's hair and makeup chair, sipping one of his special coffees while the stagehand, to her surprise, did a fine job of fixing her long hair back in a fashionable up-do and reapplying makeup where need be.

"Thank you," Marisol said, a strange kindness in her voice.

The stagehand, never a fan of hers, like most of the *Try Not to Die* crew, forced a smile. It didn't matter if you didn't like her, The Queen of Texas was not someone you challenged.

Mark Winters, however, had known the woman for quite some time. He knew when she was at her wit's end. It had been many moons since embarrassment had reared its ugly head in Marisol's life. He always knew the years of being in such a position of unprotested power were numbered, he just never imagined her reign would come to an end at the hands of a contestant rather than one of her rival warlords.

"Leave us," Marisol ordered the stagehand.

He nodded and scurried toward the door.

"That means you, too." She scowled at the dancers hanging on Mark for comfort.

The women hurried from the room, exchanging glances with Mark who gave them a reassuring nod.

"They love you," Marisol laughed, rising from the chair.

She approached him with a sway in her step, clearly feeling the beginning buzz of her spiked coffee.

"I used to love you." She placed her hands gently on his face, tracing his lips with her fingertips.

Mark rolled his eyes and grabbed her by the shoulders, moving her out of his way.

"No."

"You have the nerve to deny me?" She spun and faced him. "Oh, Markus, you have grown brave these last few hours, haven't you?"

"Brave?" He chuckled, removing the cap from the bottle of vodka. "No, not brave. I'm scared shitless, trust me. But tired…" he took a long swig. "Yeah, I'm tired. Tired of this show, tired of the theatrics, tired of mass murder…but most of all, I'm tired of you."

Marisol's mouth was a tight line.

"What did you think, Mari? Tell me, what did you think would happen?"

Her nostrils flared. He was mingling work and pleasure, using his bedroom name for her. It threw her off. Outside of their dalliances no one had called her that in years.

"Oh, the great and unkillable Derron James is dead. Killed himself, by the way, hilarious! Famous for all he'd survived and then what…he offs himself when things get too tough? What a fucking joke!"

A fierce crease formed in her brow, her face growing red. Mark took another long drink from his bottle of liquid courage.

"You killed him while he was trying to kill you. Thought nobody noticed? Thought nobody was paying attention? You're not the only one with eyes. And now what's this? Did you think that you'd seduce me into one last fuck? For old time's sake? Before we're all tortured and maimed in our own arena at the hands of the people you held prisoner for years? It's funny, isn't it? One precious prisoner killing another. Who have you enjoyed locking up more, me? Or Charlie?"

She finally looked away from him.

"You should have put me down there with them."

The room was silent now. Mark staring at Marisol, Marisol staring off at nothing. He wondered if she was remembering how things used to be, before she turned into a monster. She begged him to rise to power with her, but when he'd expressed his disapproval and told her he was leaving she'd called him a traitor, had him detained, eventually forcing him to rise to power with her anyway. Though it wasn't alongside her, no, Derron had taken on that role. It was as her puppet, with her iron fist shoved up his ass.

"I've been waiting for this day. It's over."

"Nothing is over, until I say it is," she spat.

Mark began to laugh. He laughed even harder as the queen's face turned an even brighter shade of red, and then had to wipe tears from his eyes, his face aching from the wide smile plastered on it. He took a look at himself in the mirror before heading for the door.

"Where do you think you're going?"

"We're still on the air," he said, in his classic Mark Winters voice that the people knew and loved, and marched out of the room.

Amy Green and the others looked at him with a new peculiarity as he retrieved his microphone and brought it up to his mouth.

"Geiger Lands!" he sang into the mic, drawing out the second word with vibrato.

The chaos below seemed to settle down as all eyes suddenly looked up to the platform.

"I'd like to take this moment to thank you all for your participation. Boy, you've all had the time of your lives tonight, haven't you? What a show!"

Mark laughed along with the audience members. Even the psychos seemed amused. The Connoisseur cackled to herself, eyes flicking from the screaming man she was riddling with holes and up to the large screen with Mark's face and back again.

"But I've got some news for you. Do you want to know what it is?"

There was some, but not much of, a positive response. One audience member even yawned.

Mark frowned. "Aww, shucks. Well I was really excited to share with you all, but I guess we'll just have to call it a night and you'll never know what it is. Oh well!"

He waved to the audience and pretended to start retracting the stage but people began shouting.

"Tell us!"

"We wanna know!"

Mark put a hand on his hip and another one up to his ear,

cupping it, encouraging more shouts and the audience began to chant.

"*Mark! Mark! Mark! Mark!*"

"That's the spirit!" He raised his arms and the people cheered.

"What the hell is he doing?" Amy asked, making a face.

"I don't... I have no idea," the stagehand answered, scratching his head. "I think he's finally lost it."

Amy peered down into the arena and the mess the chaotic night had made of it. Most of the audience were corpses, and the few remaining were killers, barely clinging to their last shred of sanity. Yet Mark was carrying on as if he had a captive house hanging on his every word. "He's like a trained animal," she said, watching as psychos and audience members alike battled to the death.

Some of the patrons really ought to have been part of the production, Amy thought.

One of the audience members had the killer teddy in his hands, attacking an old lady with it. Another one was on the back of one of the gimps, riding it like a horse, swinging a large metal pole around while a young woman joined a slasher in dismembering an overweight man near the overturned carousel.

Mark, oblivious to reality, carried on.

"There's good news and bad news, folks, which would you like to hear first?"

Amy watched in awe as he nodded in response to voices that weren't there.

"Well, the bad news is that this is, sadly, the final round of the evening." He frowned. "Oh, I know, I know. Goodbyes are never easy, but hey! There's still good news!" He grinned and raised his arms again before continuing.

"The good news is, much like the rest of tonight's show of firsts, we're bringing the action out of the arena and straight up to the stage! That's right, ladies and gents! Our special contestant who's made it to the final round gets to meet the great minds behind the curtain!"

His imaginary audience erupted with applause and

excitement. He began to dance to music that wasn't playing and held out a hand to one of his dancers. She nervously looked to the other dancer who gave her a push, straight into Mark's embrace.

She looked around, clearly uncomfortable.

"What's wrong with you?" Mark asked loudly, still dancing.

"Oh, um...sorry."

The dancer gave him a frightened smile and then played along, falling into one of their many practiced numbers.

Mark spun her in several circles before tossing her off to the side with such unexpected forced that she nearly toppled over the edge of the platform. The other dancer looked over to her with a desperate look in her eye as the stagehand gestured for them to hurriedly climb up off the stage. They quickly scrambled up to him, arms linked, and the trio disappeared into the makeup room.

"And would you look at that!" Mark shouted, his enthusiasm at an all-time high, "There they are now!"

Dawn Churchill marched through the arena with Charming Charlie, Doctor Feelbad, and Razortooth at her side. Jaq, noticing that they'd reentered, ceased dismembering The Goat who lay lifeless below him, and trotted over, joining them. They walked with a sense of purpose. Amy wondered briefly where they were headed, until Jaq and Feelbad began helping the others up over the lip of the ruined cage and into the stadium seating. They were headed for the elevator to the skybox.

"Goddammit," Amy said, pulling a heavy bag from under her seat and slinging it over her shoulder as she marched across the catwalk. "Marisol! You're gonna want to get out here. Now!

What a good-looking bunch, eh folks?" Mark smiled and waved down at Dawn's group.

Amy tossed the bag to her feet when Marisol sauntered out of the makeup room, hands on hips. It landed with a thud and she unzipped it, revealing an arsenal of weaponry.

"Take what you can handle. *No one* goes unarmed." Amy ordered the stagehand and the dancers peeking out at her. "And will somebody please snap Mark out of his fucking imagination? We need him."

She headed back to the Producers' Box and pulled out another bag, this one with a hefty set of tools. She marched them out into the waiting room and pried open the electrical panel beside the elevator.

"What on earth are you doing?" Marisol asked, following behind her and taking the rifle the stagehand held out to her.

"Trying to save our asses," Amy replied with a grunt, her arm elbow-deep in wires.

"And how exactly are you doing that?"

"They can't take the elevator if the car locks in place," she replied, her tongue poking out the side of her mouth as she plucked several wires and attached them to others.

Marisol clapped her hands.

"Brilliant, Amy, brilliant!"

"Well, I know you don't keep me around for my good looks," Amy grunted again and then laughed. She removed some tools and began to work quickly, sweat forming on her brow. The killers had boarded the car. She tried not to panic, knowing that would only cause her to make mistakes, which would slow her down. The car was rising. Floor two, three, four, and still coming.

"How's it going?" Marisol asked after a tense few moments.

Amy shrugged, and then, as if on cue, the light above floor seven turned red. The car was locked in place. Amy sighed. "We're safe for now."

Marisol grinned and patted Amy on the head. Amy turned to her and smiled, a childlike mischief in her eyes. She pointed at a pair of wires.

"But I'll do you one better. All I have to do is connect those and it'll go into freefall. I'm going to take them by surprise and crush every bone in their bodies."

Marisol turned to Mark and folded her arms across her chest. He finally seemed to be returning to reality, a grim expression etched on his face.

"See Markus? It's not over until I say it's over."

CHAPTER 41

The elevator door opened. A boy of no more than seventeen stood inside, in a perfect red monkey suit and bellboy hat. His mouth opened, moving, as he gawked at the blood-spattered band before him.

"Uh...going up?"

Raze reached out and snapped the flat-topped cap off of his head by the chin strap, affixing it on her own head at a jaunty angle.

"Why don't you catch the next one, cutie?" she asked, loudly chewing and popping what Dawn hoped was a piece of gum.

Nodding and bowing, the elevator operator beat feet away from them as fast as he could.

The motley crew clambered on board the elevator. As Jaq stepped on, it clunked down, straining at his weight.

Giggling, Raze turned the old-fashioned lever and the elevator began to ascend. She announced in a poor English accent, "Next stop: the penthouse! Women's lingerie! Sporting goods! Motherfuckers who need killing!"

Suddenly the elevator ground to a halt, and the lights went out. For a moment, they were shrouded in darkness, then the red emergency lights came on.

"Raze...what did you do?" Dawn asked, narrowing her eyes.

"I didn't do anything! I was just pushing the lever. See?"

Raze flipped the lever clockwise and counter. Nothing happened. But suddenly, an unfamiliar voice filled the elevator. The entire rear wall, which Dawn had taken for a mirror, suddenly lit up. It was a screen, and the face it displayed was Amy Green's.

"Hey, kids," she said, a devilish grin on her face, "if Mark were here, I'm sure he'd have something clever to say. And

Marisol would probably go on and on about being large and in charge. But I'm just the tech girl, and you all just stepped aboard the wrong piece of technology. Been a good fight, but now, goodbye...thanks for *dropping in!*"

Green winked and then her face abruptly disappeared as Charlie roared in pent up frustration.

"Years of planning!" he shouted, "Months of work! And this is how it ends? We don't even get a fight? Crushed to death in an elevator?"

"Eh, just remember next time to take the stairs," Raze said.

Charlie reached out, no doubt intending to choke the young cue ball, who hissed and bared her fangs in response, but the two never had the chance to settle their quibble. The elevator creaked, two loud pops sounded, and Dawn guessed that meant the car had just been detached.

With a sickening lurch, she would have sworn the entire world had just collapsed out from under her. The car began to fall at a nauseating speed, and in response, Dawn found herself weightless for just a few seconds. It was an experience like no other, and even amid the rising horror and the sudden realization of her own demise, she found herself reveling in the amazing freedom of being in zero gravity.

Jaq smashed his fist through the glass of the emergency box. He snatched the fire ax out and thrust it into the rear wall where Amy Green's visage had appeared. Dawn slammed into the floor as the elevator's uncontrolled descent was suddenly arrested, and the car screeched to a halt, held in placed by the strength of an axe head. Even as the car settled into one spot, a loud metallic creak made it clear that their situation was tenuous.

"Good work, Jaq," Dawn said, patting the giant on the shoulder. "That won't hold for long, though. We'd better get out of here."

Jaq reached up and pulled the hatch in the roof open. Raze climbed his body and hopped through with ease. Jaq threw Dawn up through the hole as if she weighed no more than a feather, and the women immediately began climbing the emergency ladder. Charlie escaped next, with a spritely hop, and reached back down to help Doctor Feelbad out. Charlie patted himself down and glanced down through the roof hole.

"Well, this is rather sad. I don't think our large friend is going to be able to join us. Solidarity, Jaq! And safe travels. Hope to see you in Hell, old boy."

Charlie held up the fist of solidarity.

"What? No!" Raze shrieked, "First Gus dies for your big plan, and now his brother, too?"

With a whirr and a buzz, Jaq's chainsaw blared to life. Charlie jumped out of the way as it sliced up into the roof of the elevator car, creating a great circular hole for Jaq to climb out of. No sooner had he done so than the axe gave way and the car went plummeting to the ground below. Its descent uncontrolled, it smashed upon the concrete below and crumpled like a tin can. Dawn winced, picturing how close they had all come to being turned to bloody gelatin by the impact.

"You're all heart, Charlie," Dawn muttered.

"I said, '*Solidarity.*' Besides, he's just fine." He gestured to Jaq and flashed her a smile. "Now, shall we continue?"

He gracefully climbed the ladder, leaving her to dangle alone.

Dawn was having a hell of a time keeping her grip with her missing arm. She kept trying to throw herself up, but it was exhausting, and she was holding up the whole procession. Jaq shot Charlie a glare and plucked Dawn off the ladder, throwing her onto his back as though she were a koala bear.

"Thanks, buddy," she said, patting his chest.

"Do they know we got out?" Raze called down from above. She was already at least a floor ahead of the others, hopping from rung to rung with ease like a little monkey.

"There's no telling," Charlie said, "Marisol has half the place bugged. But then again, they're also all fuller of hubris than Oedipus himself."

"What the fuck are you talking about, Charlie?" Dawn called out to him.

"Philistines," the former professor grunted.

"*Cabron,*" Feelbad muttered.

Dawn and Jaq exchanged glances and the big man shook his head.

"I hope he fall."

Dawn stifled a laugh and patted him on the chest.

"Ssh, behave."

The group continued to climb and it seemed to take forever. Even though all she had to do was worry about not falling from Jaq's broad shoulders, she still found herself exhausted by the time they had made it all the way to the top of the emergency ladder.

"Well, here we are," Raze said, digging her claws into the seam between the elevator doors. When she had wiggled the doors apart a few centimeters, Jaq reached in and started to pry them apart and open.

"Care to make your big entrance, Charlie?" Dawn asked, glancing at him.

"Ladies first."

Dawn grunted, unsurprised. She stepped through the elevator doors into the waiting room and was met by a chorus of interlocking clicks and clacks. An army of Marisol's security goons, all clad in black bulletproof armor, visored helmets, and carrying heavy shotguns and assault rifles were all poised, guns pointed at the doorway. At her, in other words.

Dawn raised her good arm and pointed her shotgun arm towards the ceiling.

"What is it?" Charlie's voiced wafted in from the elevator shaft.

"The last line of defense," Dawn replied.

"Ah, Marisol Martinez's Praetorian Guard. Best not to wait for them, Ms. Churchill. Start shooting. They won't hesitate to do the same to you."

"Now, hang on!" She glanced around the room, wishing she could see a pair of human eyes to attempt to gauge, but all she saw were unfeeling visors. Perhaps that was why they wore them: to create a buffer between them and their target. "All right, now listen. I know you're all paid well. And that's not nothing. God knows I grew up in the GL, scraping by for a living. Anything I could do to better my station, well I did it. I'm sure you're all the same way.

"But that gravy train is sailing. Or, I guess trains don't

sail…" Her eyes darted from goon to goon, hoping she wasn't losing them. "That ship has sailed…or, going back to the train metaphor, the gravy train is out of the station."

"Move on!" a chorus of frustrated voices called in from the elevator shaft.

"Shut up!" she hollered back at her companions. "I'm giving the big speech!"

She turned back to the goons who seemed to be growing impatient and she flashed an innocent smile.

"Now, look. Marisol Martinez's days are numbered. If it's not us today, it'll be the Russians tomorrow. Or maybe one of you in a palace coup. I don't know. I've seen the way she treats her employees. Hell, I've seen the way she treats her so-called friends and loved ones. You think her husband took a swan dive into oblivion because she was somebody worth following? No. So the question you have to ask yourself is: do you want to be the last defenders of a dead regime or the first proponents of the new regime? Which side of history do you want to be on? The side that clings to the past with all the pain and suffering that involves? Or the side that looks to the future, to the struggle, and embraces it?"

The head goon took a few steps forward. He reached up and raised his visor. He was a middle-aged man, his face thoughtful and stoic. He had seen dark things in his time. Of course he had. He had been through the war and the bombs and the dark years since. His face looked like that of a grizzled veteran who had lost many of his best friends, perhaps all in his own arms. But his eyes were full of faith and hope. This was no pessimist. This was a disappointed optimist. His lips were quivering, and Dawn leaned forward, ready to hear the words she so longed for.

"Fuck the future!"

"Ah, shit," Dawn muttered, and threw herself to the floor.

The bullets started flying fast and heavy. She fired back, first ripping through one man's thighs and sending him spilling to the floor, then with her second round blowing the head, still perfectly ensconced in his visored helmet, flying backwards off of another.

With a roar, Jaq came rushing out of the elevator shaft. He got drilled a few times, but unlike the mostly impervious Denney the Clown, she saw where the bullets made their marks. Jaq just didn't seem to care much. A moment later, Raze was underfoot, slashing through body armor and sending up tufts of bloodied padding as though they were in the middle of an absurd pillow fight rather than a gunfight.

Charlie and Doc were the last on the scene, but no less vicious for that. One of the goons attempted to jab a bayonet in the doctor's side. In response, he grabbed him and tossed him bodily down the elevator shaft, screaming all the way before he finally impacted with the collapsed car at the bottom. Charlie had a way of slipping knives into the narrow area between the men's visors and body armor, the unprotected neck area. By the time Dawn had fired off a third round, the room was a mess of bodies, smoke still drifting casually from bullet holes in the walls.

She caught her breath on the floor for a moment and Doc held out a hand, helping her to her feet.

"Well, that didn't go as planned."

She looked around, the body count of the evening undoubtedly record-setting.

"Easy peasy." Raze brushed her hands off and looked to the others. "What now?"

"Care for the final honor, Ms. Churchill?" Charlie asked, gesturing at the door to the stage.

She raised an eyebrow at him and quickly glanced at his crotch and then back up to his unamused gaze.

"Ladies first," she grunted in reply, and stepped out of the way.

CHAPTER 42

"That was a whole lot of gun fire," the stagehand whispered, cowering in the makeup room with the others. A sobbing dancer was holding on to each of his arms for dear life.

Amy Green stood with her fists balled up and an ear to the door. She could hear hacking and banging beyond the exit door in the waiting room.

"They weren't supposed to even make it up here," she said with a scowl. "How the hell did they get out of the death trap I set for them?"

"When Charles has his mind set on something," Marisol said, pausing to finish off the remainder of the vodka, "he sees it through to the end."

She sat beside Mark on the couch, one leg crossed over the other. Mark kept talking to himself and every so often Marisol would have to give him a hard slap to silence him. On the outside, Marisol showed no emotion. She appeared neither concerned nor troubled by the fact that this was it: her beasts had bested her at her own game and her time as queen had come to an end.

She glanced around the room at those who would undoubtedly face a similar fate to her own. Markus, lost inside his own mind, driven mad by the years finally catching up to him, he was the luckiest among them. He probably wouldn't even realize what was going on until it was too late. Amy, she was resourceful and tough, but she wouldn't last long, not pitted against what was obviously the best of Marisol's arsenal of psychopaths.

The poor stagehand and the dancers, caught up in all of this, Marisol raised an eyebrow at them, were they actually praying? What God did anyone think was left to listen in a war-torn world such as their own?

The last reinforced door separating those in the makeup room from the band of slashers could be heard busting from its frame. There was only the shabby, wooden door to the makeup room now. Amy jumped as she heard voices floating from beyond the door that her ear was still pressed against. She backed away slowly and grabbed two pistols from the vanity behind her.

"Everyone, get ready," she ordered, motioning to the fire-arms she'd assigned them all.

But no one moved an inch.

"Seriously?" Amy shot Marisol an exasperated look. "I can understand them, but you? You're not even going to put up a fight?"

Marisol smirked.

"How can you just sit there like that?"

Marisol folded her arms across her chest, glancing down at a dainty wristwatch.

"What, you got a hot date or something?" Amy scoffed, knuckles white around the pistol grips.

The voices beyond the makeup room grew louder. The group of slashers would be upon them at any moment.

"I may no longer have anything to reign over, I may no longer have a show, but…truth be told, Miss Green, it was never my show to begin with."

Amy made a face. "What the hell are you talking about? This whole production, everything, this thing has been your baby since day one."

Marisol stood and approached her last remaining Producer.

"You know the old phrase, *'great minds think alike,'* well that was proven to be quite true to me many years ago."

"I don't understand." Amy shook her head.

"Of course not, but that's not your fault. Look, we only see what *they* want us to see since the bombs dropped. *Try Not to Die* didn't start with me." Marisol laughed. "This is just the North American version, silly. And who do you think has been watching this whole time? Sure, they let me call myself queen, let me do things the way I wanted to do them, but only if I played by their rules. Well, the rules all went to shit tonight! Of course, I'll face some form of consequences, but all in all I think I've got my escape plan worked out. What about you, dear Amy?"

Amy's jaw dropped. She knew Marisol had been in bed with the Russians for quite some time, but not to this extent.

"You fuckin' commie." Amy spat, raising one of her weapons, pointing it straight at Marisol.

The wooden door was kicked open and it flew clear across the room, the dancers shrieked, burying their faces in the stagehand's chest, and he sobbed along with them, clutching the women tightly.

Charming Charlie stepped through the broken doorway, followed by Dawn and the others. Jaq ducked and turned sideways in order to fit through.

Charlie opened his mouth to speak, but Marisol beat him to it.

"Hello, Charles."

She grinned, placing her fingers in her ears as an explosion tore through the back end of the arena, rocking the suspended platform on which they all stood.

"What the fuck!" Dawn screamed, knocked off her feet, her ears ringing.

A helicopter could suddenly be heard from somewhere over the arena and a cacophony of gunfire rose up from the already chaotic scene below.

Dawn looked around and spotted Raze crouched in the corner of the room, terrified, hissing, as the enormous crane that the Producers had so distastefully used at the beginning of the show came to life. Dawn could see its open jaws headed straight for them and out of instinct, wished the door still clung to its shabby frame so she could slam it shut in a pitiful attempt to block the outside world from getting in.

What was happening? She thought it was over, they all did. The final showdown with the great Marisol Martinez, and yet, here they were, facing some unexpected new madness. She looked to Charlie. Even he stood with bewilderment painted on his otherwise perpetually smug face.

The ceiling above them, though weak and poorly crafted, seemed to crumble away into nothing as the crane burst through.

Dawn looked over in time to see Marisol stepping out of harm's way and checking the watch on her wrist; she swore through all the turmoil she'd heard the woman say *"right on time."*

Amy began firing at the crane, a futile act, but still, it wasn't in her not to put up a fight. The crane didn't falter for even a moment and came barreling toward her, its hefty steel frame met her body and sent her crashing into the wall, crushed on impact; her brief, shrill scream piercing everyone's ears.

The outer wall collapsed and Amy's body, or rather, what was left of it, disappeared out of sight as it fell to the arena floor fifty feet beneath them. Part of the platform floor gave way on that side of the room and Dawn screamed, scrambling across the floor, her good arm outstretched. Raze, just at the last moment, leapt forward and latched onto Dawn's arm. Dawn winced as her friend's steel fingertips pierced her skin, but the petite woman pulled backward with all her might, and they both went flying in the opposite direction of the disappearing floor.

"You might want to hold onto something." Marisol said, too calm for comfort, and sat back down beside Mark on the couch.

Without further pause, the jaws on the end of the crane opened wider than ever and came down over the makeup room, clamping down tightly, shaking the entire platform.

Charlie, Doctor Feelbad, and Jaq sprinted for the center of the room as the crane began to ascend, the entire room in its clutches. The stagehand and dancers either weren't quick enough or they didn't care, and Dawn watched as the floor broke free and the half of the platform that wasn't attached to the crane began to fall, taking them with it.

There was a great crash and an eerie silence that followed. A few random gunshots could be heard, finishing off whatever living souls remained in the arena below. The crane began its descent down and Dawn could see clearly now what awaited them below.

Dozens upon dozens of Russian soldiers stood armed amid the mountainous pile of bodies around the arena. A great, gaping hole had been blown clear out of one side and she could see through the smoke and rubble that more soldiers were pouring in with every passing second. In the center of all this new and foreign chaos, Dawn spotted a well-dressed man shouting into a radio.

"Dawny," Raze whispered, her hand on her shoulder. "What's going on?"

Dawn shook her head, unable to answer.

"I don't know about me, but all of you are taking a little trip." Marisol said, not even rising from her seat. She stroked Mark's cheek and he laughed to himself, completely oblivious to anything occurring. "Don't worry Markus, you're coming with me."

Charlie was scowling.

"Always the forward thinker, eh, Marisol?"

Her eyes met his, a mixture of pity and arrogance in her stare.

"You *almost* won, didn't you?"

Charlie looked away, sucking his teeth.

The platform finally met the ground and anyone standing was once again knocked off their feet from the impact. The soldiers advanced, weapons trained on the survivors, but to Marisol's dismay, this included her.

"Hey!" she shouted at the man in the suit who was barking orders in Russian.

He pointed at her and gave another order. She couldn't understand what he was saying, but she knew the moment the soldiers began pulling gas masks down over their faces that whatever he'd just told them meant nothing good for her.

Canisters were launched at the group and an odorless gas began to hiss from them.

"No!" she screamed. "No! This wasn't the deal!"

The man in the suit gave her a smile before putting his own mask on.

Marisol coughed, her howls of betrayal stifled. She tried holding her breath but the gas was too thick. She slumped over, beginning to fade. The last thing she saw before passing out was Raze clutching Dawn's hand. The two killers went to sleep side by side.

CHAPTER 43

Dawn woke with a roar in her head, groaning as she struggled to sit up. Her entire body ached. The past twenty-four hours had not been kind to her. She glanced down at her arm. Someone had removed her prosthesis while she was passed out. The base that held it was still intact, Doctor Feelbad's work apparently being too good for them to easily pry off. Though, judging by how the area ached, it had not been for lack of trying.

How long have I been asleep? she wondered, gripping her forehead with her hand. The headache was unbearable.

She looked around the room. It was clean, almost too immaculate to be considered a holding cell. She knew she must have been taken prisoner, but to be held in a room such as this? She realized the cot she sat on was actually a rather comfortable mattress and the room was decorated quite nicely. There were two doors, one with no knob or handle, which she assumed was the exit, and another slightly ajar on the opposite side of the room. Beside it stood a wardrobe. She cocked her head, curiosity beginning to nibble. As she was about to stand up and make her way toward the wooden door across from her, she froze.

Her nostrils flared, filling with the scent of something so delicious, so savory…

She turned her attention to a large oak desk in the corner of the room and her eyes went wide. She nearly tripped over her own feet as she sprung from the bed toward the desk. A wide tray of food sat waiting for her and before she even knew it, she was chewing on the sweetest, warmest bread she'd ever tasted in her life. Her hand worked quickly, ripping chunks off the loaf of bread and dipping them into a stew beside it. Her eyes rolled into the back of her head. She was in Heaven.

She took a deep breath and decided against overeating. Besides, she wasn't even sure what was in the stew or if she should have been eating it. She felt the headache beginning to subside and took a few cautious steps toward the door, opening it the rest of the way with her foot and jumping back, ready to fight whatever, or whoever, might have been hiding behind it.

She laughed out loud when she saw that hidden behind the door was a small room containing a toilet and a shower stall. Her bladder suddenly ached and she could now smell herself.

"Oh, the power of suggestion," Dawn said with a smirk and began undressing.

She was confused, unsure of why she would be treated to a shower or food, or anything really. The Russians obviously had taken her from the arena. Her and her friends. She thought of Raze, Jaq, Doc, even Charlie...where were they? Were they just waking up as well? Enjoying their own meals and showers? As she turned the handle, the faucet sprang to life, raining hot water down onto her. She moaned in bliss, resolving to worry about the others later.

Dawn must have washed her body—as best she could with one arm—about twenty times. She washed until all the blood and filth and agony from the arena circled the drain no more and the water at her feet was clean. She dried off and wrapped herself in a plush, stark-white towel. She still couldn't get over how clean this place was.

She laughed again when she opened the wardrobe and her eyes fell upon at least a dozen different items of clothing, all in her correct size. She decided on something basic and easy to move in, just in case she found herself in an unfavorable situation in the near future. She struggled with getting dressed. It was a little more difficult to slip on a pair of leggings and a tank top than it had been getting her other clothes off before the shower. Eventually she did it, albeit with a thin film of sweat on her clean brow, but she stood triumphant, clad in all black, and shoved her feet into a snug-fitting pair of matching boots.

Dawn stood awkwardly in the center of the room, wondering what she was supposed to do next. She glanced over at the food and shrugged, figuring now was as good a time as any to finish it off, but a sudden click at the knobless door and the slide of a bolt told her otherwise. She backed away, toward the desk, and gripped the bowl of hot stew in her hand. She had no weapons, so she'd have to improvise.

A short, stout woman with dark hair and a fierce unibrow entered the room wearing a modest pantsuit. Dawn raised the bowl, prepared to smash it into her face. The woman gave Dawn a dirty look and said something she couldn't understand.

"English?" Dawn asked, her hand hurting from gripping the hot bowl.

The woman sighed and waved a hand at her. "No fight, I am harmless."

Dawn made a face and looked at the bowl.

The woman rolled her eyes and said something in her foreign tongue again, clearly frustrated with Dawn, and put her hands on her hips.

"Um…okay, sorry." Dawn gave a weak smile and placed the bowl back onto the desk.

"Good." The woman said.

She approached Dawn and instantly Dawn tensed up.

"You come with me now." The woman motioned for Dawn to come toward her, and, begrudgingly, Dawn obliged.

The woman gently took her by the arm and led her out of the room. The hall was empty, but just as immaculate and bright as the room Dawn had been kept in. There were several secure doors that matched her own on both sides of the hall and Dawn finally asked the questions that were burning holes in the back of her mind.

"Where am I? Where are the others? Why did you take us from the arena? Is Raze okay? What about the doctor?"

The questions left her mouth in an uncontrollable flood and the short woman began to chuckle.

"Your friends, they sleep now. You do not worry about these things."

"Don't worry? How am I supposed—"

The woman hushed her with a glare and a sharp word she didn't understand. Suddenly Dawn felt like a small child and she blushed, looking down at the floor as she continued to walk.

They finally approached what looked like an office door with a frosted window and some characters inscribed in the middle. The woman knocked twice and someone hollered from inside.

"You go in here now." The woman opened the door and the smell of cheap, hand rolled peasant tobacco wafted into the hall.

"No, wait a second! I don't—"

"Goodbye." The woman shoved her into the office and closed the door, quickly locking it.

"Hey!" Dawn shouted, pulling on the knob and pounding on the door to no avail. "Come back here!"

There was a deep laugh behind her that sent a slight chill down her spine. She turned around slowly and was surprised to see the well-dressed man from the arena standing at a window.

They stared at one another for a moment and finally the man smiled.

"Welcome to the motherland."

CHAPTER 44

There was an awkward silence and thick tension in the room. Dawn sat rigidly in an oversized chair while the man from the arena looked through some paperwork on his desk, a cigarette in his teeth.

She had never expected to visit Russia before. Technically, from what she could tell by the large map on the wall, she was in what was called the Tajik SSR. She'd given little thought to what she expected a minor Soviet bureaucrat's office to look like, but upon reflecting on the matter, she decided it was exactly like this.

There were no personal effects, no pictures of a family or children. Only a black and white portrait of Premier Yanayev hung on a wall opposite the map, and that seemed to be as standard issue as all of the weirdly cheap looking staplers, paperclips, and pencils on the man's desk.

He hadn't volunteered his name, and though it was written on a nameplate on his desk, she couldn't read the Cyrillic letters, and she wasn't sure she would have been able to pronounce even if she'd been able to read it.

He himself was short and balding, with dark skin and bushy eyebrows. What little hair remained on his head was, at least, jet black. The only thing about him that betrayed her stereotypes of Soviet apparatchiks was that he wore a bespoke suit she would have found more at home in Milan or London.

He cleared his throat and closed the file he had been flipping through, apparently signaling that he was ready to begin discussing things.

"Cigarette?" he asked, his English surprisingly unaccented.

"No," she replied, involuntarily trying to hold back a cough before hastily tacking on a "Thank you."

He nodded and took another puff.

"You are an impressive young woman."

"Uh...thanks?"

The man waved a hand at her and then put out his cigarette, immediately lighting another.

"Tell me, Dawn, have you enjoyed your morning so far?"

She shrugged. "Yeah, I guess. The shower was great, and the food was good. So, um, thanks for all that."

"So, you think you have been treated well then?"

She nodded.

"Then please, relax. You're too nervous and it's making me uncomfortable."

Dawn bit back a laugh. *"You're* the uncomfortable one?"

The man put out his cigarette and sat back in his leather chair, folding his hands in his lap and raising an eyebrow at her.

She got the hint and sat back, allowing herself to sink into the big, comfy seat, crossing one leg over the other.

"Much better. Now, what questions do you have for me? I heard you speaking with Ara, so I know you have a lot on your mind."

"How did you hear us? We weren't anywhere near your office."

The man smiled and stood, walking to a large cabinet and opening the doors, revealing several security monitors as well as a sound system. Displayed on the monitors were empty hallways. The man pressed a button and the pictures changed, now displaying rooms almost identical to the one she'd been in, but with occupants. Dawn couldn't control it, her smile spread from ear to ear.

Raze slept soundly, curled up in a tiny ball in a corner of her mattress.

Jaq did pushups in the center of his room.

Doctor Feelbad was buttoning up a pressed, white shirt, his hair wet from a shower, and though she leaned in to try to sneak a peek, to her disappointment, she saw that his face was still covered by a surgical mask.

Charlie sat at an oak desk, reading aloud to himself,

apparently practicing his elocution with a speech from some ancient Roman orator.

Dawn narrowed her eyes as her gaze fell upon the peculiar scene displayed on the final monitor.

"What's Mark Winters doing here?"

Mark sat on the floor, hugging his knees to his chest, rocking slightly back and forth.

The man shut the sound system off and Charlie's voice was abruptly cut off. He closed the cabinets and returned to his desk, lighting up a cigarette.

"I believe, with time, and with your help, Markus will be a wonderful addition to our team."

A crease formed in Dawn's brow. "Team? What team? I don't get it."

The man chuckled.

"As I said earlier, you are an impressive young woman. I don't know how things were for you back in North America, but here in the Soviet Union we value such skilled workers. We want you to be as happy as possible, and I would like to make you a very desirable offer."

Dawn's facial expression was frozen on something that looked like it fell in between dumbfounded and bewilderment.

"I need someone to handle the day to day now that Marisol Martinez no longer has a handle on things. You would report directly to me, of course, and I would be able to get you whatever you wanted or needed…within reason. Maybe a dacha and a personal driver."

Dawn's mouth hung open and she was sure she looked like an idiot, but she didn't care. The words coming out of the man's mouth were ridiculous.

"What the fuck?" was all she could say at first.

The man just stared at her. She assumed he was allowing her to process what he'd just said.

"Where is Marisol?"

"She's been detained. We don't take kindly to disappointment."

Dawn swallowed hard.

"Okay…so…what? You want *me* to be a Producer?"

The man chuckled, almost choking on his cigarette.

"Ah, North Americans and your silly names for things. You can be called this, yes, if you'd like. You can even call yourself queen." He laughed hard again, coughing and clutching his stomach.

"But I'm supposed to stay here? Why can't I go home? You want to make me a communist?"

The man smiled and held back another guffaw. "Dawn, you are impressive but quite young and naïve. Everyone is a communist now, and North America is a wasteland. We have decided to cease all efforts of restoration and reclamation there. It is simply a chunk of land still grasping at straws that belonged to a world that has ceased to exist. It will be a dead continent soon."

Dawn looked down at the floor and felt a wave of nausea wash over her, the sad realization that she would not be returning to the GL sinking in. But the wave soon passed as she told herself to suck it up and put her big girl panties on. She had a very strange decision to make.

"What happens to my friends?" she asked.

"They will be treated with the utmost respect. They will have access to the entire facility. We have some of the best coaches and personal trainers in the world. They will learn discipline, they will hone their craft, and we will foster each individual's talents."

"I'm sorry, what? Coaches?"

"Yes, absolutely."

"So, you have murder coaches…"

The balding man smiled, it was a bit unsettling.

"You may have been too young to recall the Olympics. Do you know what that is…or rather, was?"

She sighed. "Yes, I remember the Olympics."

"Good. Where the prestige of the Soviet Union is at stake, the people come together to provide the very best. During the Olympics, the Soviet teams were always the pride of both the winter and summer games. Now, your competition, uh…what do you call it?"

"Try Not to Die."

He smiled at her again. "Yes, that's it. You see, we call it

'*Zbezhat' Neizbezhnosti Smerti, Dazhe V Techeniye Korotkogo Promezhutka Vremeni!*'" He exclaimed the name with pronounced enthusiasm.

"Catchy," she said.

"Thank you," he replied with a grin. "I came up with it myself. In any case, these competitions, game shows, whatever the respective countries wish to call them, they are the new Olympics."

"So, you're telling me the whole world does this?"

"Precisely."

"And you want me to be the new Marisol Martinez?"

"Well, no, obviously she wasn't exactly what we were looking for. But you, you are what she calls a slasher. We call you athletes! You are an Olympian! And who better to join the ranks of the elite than an Olympian herself?"

Dawn, still in awe, let everything sink in. She seriously considered his offer, but every time she rolled the idea over in her head, she thought of the others.

"So, my friends, they're not prisoners here?"

"No, of course not! They will be joining the motherland's most revered athletes. Some of the finest in the world!"

With each word, the man grew more and more excited.

Dawn smiled, Raze's voice echoing in her head. *One of us.*

"Good. I won't be joining you, I'll be joining them instead."

The man stood and walked to the window, his dramatic gaze fixed on something outside.

"That is an acceptable answer. We have prepared for this as well."

He walked to the door and unlocked it with a key attached to his wrist. He spoke in a low voice in either Russian or Tajik, she had trouble telling them apart, they all just fell in the category of foreign for her. The woman from earlier, Ara, brought him a long, large box, and atop that box sat her shotgun. He returned to his desk with the items and Dawn's eyes were wide, fixed on the weapon that had literally been a part of her only hours before.

"The main difficulty we ran into was how we would get ammunition for this, uh, shall I call it an arm?"

"Well, yeah, it's my arm alright."

The man nodded. "Yes, I'm afraid we don't have archaic weaponry quite like this."

Dawn took offense.

"It would be far too expensive to procure ammunition for something such as this." He tossed the shotgun from hand to hand. "Were you very much attached to this? No pun intended."

She made a face at him. "I mean, I kind of need it."

He carelessly tossed it onto the desk and removed the lid from the long box sitting before him.

"I hope you'll be pleased with this new *arm*."

He removed a shiny, sleek piece of expensive Soviet tech from the box and held it out to her. Dawn's mouth dropped and she nearly drooled.

"It's...wow." She couldn't find the words as she reached out and ran her fingertips over the smooth surface of the weapon. She grabbed hold of it and was surprised by how light it was.

"It's one of the finest fully automatic weapons the Soviet Union can provide."

"And it's mine?" She asked, feeling once more like a child, blushing at how the mere thought of attaching such a striking weapon to her body could fill her with such excitement.

"It's all yours. Your doctor friend, he will be the one fitting you for the new equipment. I'm quite pleased to have such a skilled surgeon on the team, by the way."

She smiled, and it was truly genuine.

"You may join your friends in the cafeteria now." He motioned toward the door. "Linguistics and customs training for the new team members begin in three hours."

She stood and started for the door, but paused and turned back to the man in the suit.

"Marisol...what will happen to her?"

"My colleagues and I are meeting this afternoon to discuss this matter. Why do you ask? Do you have a fondness for her?" The man narrowed his eyes.

"No, not at all. I just have a...special request."

ONE MONTH LATER

The bear of a man—no pun intended—wrapped his huge, hairy knuckles around Marisol's neck. She'd not picked up nearly enough Russian in her time here to pick out his name from Mark's ongoing ramble, but she judged it to be Medved or something like that.

She kicked and slapped at Medved, occasionally attempting to claw his eyes out, though since she had taken to gnawing her fingernails down to nubs in captivity, this was less effective than when she had been able to have regular manicures.

The slasher had decidedly less pizzazz than almost anyone else in the Russian Barn. He didn't seem to have a back story or a favored weapon, or anything particularly interesting about him. He was just a hulking, stinky Siberian wrapped in a bearskin. The bear's upper jaw he wore like a hat, forming a creepy second head above his own, but otherwise the pelt just dangled over his back. His penis, tumescent now that he was in the midst of strangling someone, flopped from side to side, uncovered like the rest of his front.

He whispered something in his fishy breath into her face. She wasn't sure whether it was supposed to be seductive or threatening. Sighing, she slammed her fists into his chest and used it as a brace to push the entire rest of her body back, away from him. He cocked his head quizzically, even the bear head over his own scalp seemingly confused. Black cigarette burns were starting to fill her field of vision, a symptom of the lack of oxygen. She was already feeling weak in the muscles, so guessed she'd have only one shot at this.

She glanced down to line up her shot, and Medved did the same, realizing belatedly that his own steady grip was about to be the cause of one of the worst pains he would ever feel. Satisfied with the math in her own head, Marisol simply let herself go limp, and her legs came arcing down, slamming full force into the naked bear-man's balls. Groaning in agony, he dropped her, and grabbed at his own crotch, dropping to his knees in the process.

She gulped air, delicious, delicious air, but didn't let herself be distracted by the glory of having her windpipe free at last. She grabbed at the bear's head and drove one of each of the bear's long, curved fangs into Medved's eyes. The Russian slasher shrieked in pain, and she continued shoving until he convulsed, the fangs slipping into his brainpan and finally he fell over, dead.

She looked up at the pulpit where Mark Winters stood. His clothes were a little less flashy, more in the style of Soviet announcers. Drab, even. And his two dancing girls had been replaced by two appropriately attractive, but not distractingly so, peasants and workers of the glorious revolution in boring, unrevealing clothing. He had also taken to the Soviet style of announcing like a fish to water, picking up Russian like he had been born into it and bringing his own particular style to a decidedly out of place material.

"That's what you throw against me, Markus? Me? This show's a joke compared to what I used to put on. A poor, carbon copy. A light purple mimeograph. A..."

Her parting shots were smothered as a rag covered her mouth and a sickly-sweet smell like cleaning solution filled her nose. She bucked back against the figure holding her tightly around the waist, pressing the chloroform-soaked rag to her mouth, but he held fast.

"Shh shh," he whispered, "I've been so looking forward to this."

She didn't need it to recognize the voice, but the marquee behind Mark had changed to the leering face and killing stats of Charming Charlie Whitmore.

Dawn was doing curls one handed. She'd never much been into gyms and exercise regimens, having found life in the Geiger

Lands perfectly exhausting enough. Bored, she let the barbell drop to the padded floor and pulled out the blood-spattered Rubik's cube she had managed to escape from the GL with. She'd found it exceptionally challenging to do one-handed. So far she had managed to put together an entire side of white, except for the speckles of blood.

"Hey, sis! Spot me!"

She glanced over at Raze, who was lying down at the bench press station. Raze had taken to calling her "sis" lately, and she hadn't yet found it necessary to object. She found it kind of endearing, in fact.

"You know I'm not really good at this," she said, approaching the little fireplug of a girl and holding her good arm over the weight.

"Bah," Raze said, brushing off her concerns as though they were an annoying horsefly. "All that disability stuff is for the tourists. I know how strong you really are."

Dawn couldn't stop the grin from crossing her lips. It was true. She wasn't quite up to Jaq or Doc's seemingly preternatural strength yet, but she could lift more with her one arm than most people could with two.

"Don't overstrain yourself, girls," Feelbad said, lifting a medicine ball and tossing it.

Raze rolled her eyes. "Doctors, they always find something wrong with ya, don't they?"

As Raze settled into her rhythm, Dawn glanced up at the live broadcast on the gym television system. Charlie seemed to have set up an entire kitchen in the middle of the arena, and was doing awful, horrible, no good things with a bell-shaped cheese grater to what was left of Marisol Martinez.

"I am surprised," Doc said, suddenly right by her ear.

A few weeks ago, she would've jumped out of her skin, shocked by the silent approach of the beast of a man. Now she was just used to it. It was Doc's way.

"Yeah, me too," Raze said, straining to push her weight up in the air.

"What? That I let Charlie have her?"

Doc nodded.

"Well, you know, Charlie's an artist. I would've just slapped some paint on that canvas. I uh...I just wanted her to suffer more."

"Bull," Raze said, stretching out the syllable for almost ten seconds before finally completing the word, "Shit."

"*Si*, I don't think it's that, either." Doc nodded.

Jaq, doing pull-ups with ease in the far corner of the room, mumbled his agreement.

Dawn glanced at the faces of her unlikely friends. She also couldn't help but glance at the face of her absent friend. A picture of her and Tim in the arena together hung on the wall. They were propping each other up and smiling in a brief moment of levity. It had been captured from the last *Try Not to Die* broadcast, and was kind of grainy, but it was still her favorite picture. Remembering Tim's honesty and earnestness, she knew she couldn't lie to her tribe.

"All right," she admitted, "maybe it's because Charlie's family. Like, a really fucked up uncle who would cut off your arm and eat it, but, still...family. We're all a family."

"Does that make this home?" Raze asked with a smile.

"*Una casa jodida*," Doc muttered, wandering off towards the shower.

"What he said," Dawn agreed.

Her weight in its cradle, Raze reached out a hand. Dawn had seen that hand rip out throats, tear through sheet metal, and even, in one particularly memorable instance, rip the bowels out of a clown's anus. But right now she didn't see a killing implement, or a killer. She saw a young woman looking for comfort. She took her hand.

"I guess it's not what I expected," Dawn said. "Not where I expected or who I expected to be with, but I like this place and everybody in it. And a long time ago someone I loved once told me that, 'Whatever strange place you find yourself in, make that your home.'"

Raze sat up and leaned in to nuzzle her chest. She would've wrapped her other arm around her if she had one. On the screen, Charlie's blood-spattered and maniacally laughing face lit up as he gleefully disemboweled Marisol Martinez.

STINGER

Rudy grunted behind the gas mask which had become an unfortunate necessity for survival in recent weeks. His belly grumbled. Nothing ever seemed to be going right anymore. Somehow the Geiger Lands seemed even more desolate and desperate than they had ever been. And now they weren't even getting the original *Try Not to Die* anymore, just the boring new Russian version.

Charming Charlie was strapping some passed out lady to a gurney, and waking her with smelling salts. Same old song. Same old tune. Even Russia bringing in the best of the Geiger Land slashers hadn't really injected any new life into the same boring old formula. Who cared what happened to this lady?

He glanced up at the wall where the widow and hundred thousand orphans of the silverfish-like mutant he had smashed a month ago writhed, a living tapestry on the wall. In desperation, he had started trying to eat them a few weeks ago, but even to a starving man and even well-cooked and seasoned, they were utterly inedible, like charbroiled rubber. So he had simply resigned himself to accepting them as new roommates. Probably they'd eventually go crazy from hunger themselves, and devour him, but that didn't sound so bad. In the meantime, he just wished there was something worth watching that could keep his attention for five fucking minutes anymore. With its boring plotlines and nondescript killers, *Try Not to Die* had jumped the shark ages ago.

"Let's see what else is on," he grunted, his voice distorted by the gasmask's internal filters.

He flipped the channel.

AUTHORS' NOTE

Thank you for reading SLASHVIVOR! Whether you liked it or not we hope you'll take a moment to leave a review on Amazon or your favorite book review site. Reviews are vitally important to us as authors both to help us market our book and to improve our writing in the future. Thank you!

- Stevie Kopas and Stephen Kozeniewski

ACKNOWLEDGMENTS

Our gratitude goes out to Matt Worthington, Tristan Thorne, and the entire team at Sinister Grin Press for taking a chance on this wacky book. We'd also like to thank Christine Morgan for the (sort of) sanity check. And, of course, David Niall Wilson and the Crossroad Team for bringing it staggering back from the dead.

Stephen would like to thank Stevie for being so easily tricked into…er, being willing to collaborate on this novel. And Stevie would like to thank Stephen for donating all proceeds of the book to her.

ABOUT THE AUTHORS

Stephen Kozeniewski (pronounced "causin' ooze key") is a two-time winner of the World Horror Grossout Contest. His published work includes the Splatterpunk Award-nominated THE HEMATOPHAGES and its Indie Horror Book Award-nominated prequel SKINWRAPPER. He lives in Pennsylvania, the birthplace of the modern zombie, with his girlfriend and their two cats.

Bibliography

Billy and the Cloneasaurus
Braineater Jones
Every Kingdom Divided
Hunter of the Dead
Skinwrapper
Slashvivor!
The Ghoul Archipelago
The Hematophages

Stevie Kopas was born and raised in New Jersey. She will never turn down a good cup of coffee and might even be a bit of a caffeine addict.

Her work includes bestselling dystopian series The Breadwinner Trilogy (*The Breadwinner, Haven, All Good Things*), *Madness Burns, Never Say Die: Stories of The Zombie Apocalypse*, and *Slashvivor*. She also has several short stories featured in anthologies like the At Hell's Gates series, *Man Behind The Mask*, and the acclaimed Women in Horror series from Kandisha Press.

She currently resides in East Tennessee with her son, husband, and stinky old dog.

Curious about other Crossroad Press books?
Stop by our site:
http://store.crossroadpress.com
We offer quality writing
in digital, audio, and print formats.

Made in the USA
Las Vegas, NV
30 July 2023

75448011R00146